Something Shady at Sunshine Haven

Something Shady at Sunshine Haven

An Accidental Detective Mystery

Kris Bock

TULE
PUBLISHING

Dedication

Dedicated to all the smart, funny, supportive women who are in midlife and beyond, including my former critique group Ellen Rippel, Sue Borchers, Susan Stone, and Cathy McQueen; my mystery writers chat buddies Sarah Baker, Sam Bond, Sue Bradford Edwards, and Becky Clark; wise woman Natalie Reid; "fan-girl editor" Sinclair Sawhney and the team at Tule; my mother-in-law Jackie Miller; and especially my mom, Sharon Eboch, who is learning and showing that life after 80 has a lot to offer.

Chapter One

MY CHILDHOOD HOME had faded in the harsh Arizona sun and now showed its age—rather like me. I'd never dreamed of living here again after thirty years of traveling the world.

This is temporary. You'll find a way out.

"Do you need help?" My sister's tone made it clear the correct answer was no. She'd already hinted that picking me up at the airport had been one more burden in her busy life.

"I got it." I eased out of the car and limped to the trunk to retrieve my travel backpack, still getting used to my new cane. My thigh throbbed where the doctors had dug out the shrapnel and stitched it back together with Frankenstein scars. My usual fast stride was an awkward hobble up the walkway. My luggage might have been "light," considering it held everything I owned, but it still nudged the airline's weight limit.

The front door opened, and I forced a smile. Jen disappeared inside, and Dad and I stood face-to-face.

Our smiles faltered. I dropped the backpack and stumbled into his arms. Tension drained out of my body. I blinked back tears and felt his frailty, the tremor in his hands. He smelled like Dad with a hint of a newer scent, something that only seemed to come from old men.

"Welcome home," he whispered.

"It's good to be home." I needed to rest and heal, and where better to do that than in my parents' house? In a few weeks—I promised myself weeks, not months, and definitely not years—I would be well enough to return to journalism. "How's Mom?"

"Good. Well, you know. She's settled in. She can't wait to see you."

I didn't ask if she'd remember me. I hadn't noticed signs of Alzheimer's on my last visit, but that had been a year ago, and Jen assured me Mom had faded fast. She also made it clear that since I was home with no job, it was my turn to take care of our parents.

"Sit," Dad said. "You need to rest that leg."

Behind him, Jen sighed loudly. "Don't coddle her. She needs to stay active." You wouldn't know from the way she acted that Jen was younger by two years.

Dad winked at me. "Come and sit anyway."

Jen hustled outside. She glanced back through the open door. "Welcome home." She sped down the path without waiting for an answer.

I closed the door and looked at Dad. "I guess I caught her on a bad day."

"No, just a day. Hey, a friend of yours runs the care home. She gave me a message for you. Said it was urgent." He shuffled through the mail on the little table by the door.

I couldn't think of any friends in Arizona. I hadn't had any here since my childhood. My friends were scattered around the world, wherever news was happening. If she ran the nursing home, she might hope I'd write a story on the facility to promote it, or do some free PR work. Drat. Were people going to treat me like I had nothing better to do than give away my time?

Double drat. I did not, in fact, have anything better to do. And I wanted a nap.

Dad handed me an envelope. I leaned on the door and propped my cane against the table so I had two hands to tear open the envelope. The handwritten message inside was brief:

Kitty—Please come see me ASAP. I need your help.

—Heather Garcia

"She sounded . . ." Dad hesitated. "She asked about your journalism and begged me to bring you in as soon as possible."

Begged? This could be interesting after all. But who was Heather Garcia? Someone I knew in high school, given her use of my old nickname. Maybe I'd recognize her when I saw her. Or maybe not. *I* hadn't changed a bit, of course, but other people sure looked different after thirty years.

"We can go see your mother whenever you're ready," Dad said.

See Mom in a nursing home, literally losing her mind? I'd never be ready for that.

"No time like the present." Plus I could find out more about Heather Garcia's desperate plea for help.

The nursing home was less than twenty minutes away in low traffic. Automatic doors opened into a large lobby with clusters of cushioned chairs, like a fancy hotel lounge. A woman sitting behind a reception desk greeted Dad by name. When he paused before a waist-high gate, something buzzed, and Dad pushed open the gate. Handrails lined each side of the hallway ahead, but the pale yellow paint took away some of the hospital feel. It smelled of lemon-scented cleaning fluid. Better than medicine and sick people.

Mom's room was the third on the left, small but cheerful, with a single bed, dresser, desk, and chair. She looked like herself, although her face twisted in confusion when I entered.

Dad said, "Look who's here to see you, Mother. Our daughter Kate has come home."

Mom reached out with both hands. "Kitty!"

I hadn't gone by that nickname in decades, but it was better than being forgotten.

"You look tired," she said. "And you've cut your hair."

I was tired, but I'd worn my hair short for over a decade. Was she remembering me from some previous era? If she thought I was still twenty, then "tired" was a delicate understatement for how I'd changed.

She brushed hair off my forehead. "You should grow your hair out again. It looks so nice long, when you bother to style it."

"Thanks, Mom." Maybe she hadn't changed much after all. "How are you? Are you . . . happy here?"

"It's a hospital. Too many people die here. So much death! I'll be happy when I get to go home."

I wasn't about to explain that she would never move back home. This might be the one area where her confusion benefited her.

She seemed cheerful enough as we chatted. Still, seeing my parents fade wasn't easy. She frowned at my cane a few times, but she didn't say anything about the bombing. Had she forgotten? Had she never been told? I struggled to find safe topics of conversation. Certainly not her health or mine, or the people dying around her. We wound up mainly talking about my sister's kids, my smile stiff as I tried not to cry.

Shoes squeaked in the hall, and a loud voice passed, talking about hospice.

"Don't forget to visit Heather Garcia while we're here," Dad said.

Was he giving me an excuse to escape? I took it.

The director's office was behind the reception counter. I walked in, prepared to pretend I recognized the person. A glimmer of familiarity hit me as the woman looked up from her desk. She was my age, with brown hair to her shoulders, a strong jaw, and dark eyes framed by laugh lines. She stood and extended her hand. "Kitty! Or I guess you go by Kate now."

"Yes, I prefer Kate." Technically, my name was Katherine. I'd grown up as Kitty, but I'd started using Kate the first year of college as it sounded more like a serious journalist.

She beamed as we shook hands. "I've followed your career. You probably don't remember me."

The vague familiarity wasn't clicking into anything definite. "It was a long time ago."

"Isn't that the truth? I was two years behind you. I took

journalism my sophomore year, when you were a senior."

It was coming back. "You were on the school paper that year."

"Right. You were such a go-getter, even then."

We gazed at each other long enough for it to become awkward. I'd never attended a high school reunion and didn't follow childhood friends on social media. Heather seemed nice enough, but nostalgia for the "good old days" held no appeal. I hadn't hated high school, but people who called it the best years of their lives had peaked early, had poor memories, or were liars.

She broke our gaze and headed for the door. Was this strange reunion over already? What about her request for help?

She closed the door and returned to her desk. "Please, have a seat. I shouldn't have kept you standing, with your leg. We were all horrified when we heard."

I managed a tight smile. I wasn't surprised my injury had made the local news, or the grapevine anyway, as I was something of a hometown celebrity simply for getting my byline in the papers via the Associated Press. *I* wasn't supposed to be the news story, but at least I wouldn't have to explain the limp over and over. I sat in the chair across from her and leaned my cane against her desk.

"I have a problem," Heather said.

I tensed. "About Mom?"

"Oh, no, she's delightful, very popular with the staff and the other patients." Heather shuffled some papers on her desk. "No, this is . . . something else." She glanced at the closed door, leaned forward, and lowered her voice. "Can I tell you something in confidence?"

My journalism senses, dormant and neglected for weeks, gave a faint tingle before subsiding in exhaustion.

"It depends. I won't spread gossip. I hardly know anyone around here to tell." I smiled. "But if you confess to murdering someone, I'll have to report you."

"Ha. Nothing like that. I hope."

I stared at her. "You'd better tell me what's bothering you. If I can keep it a secret in good conscience, I will."

Her hands clenched on her desk. "I need to know that you're not here as a reporter."

I nodded and settled back into the chair with the trustworthy expression I'd mastered. Or possibly I simply looked tired. "This is off the record. I'm on leave anyway."

"Okay." She spread her fingers and pressed her hands on the desk. "Two of my patients died last week."

My stomach churned. People came to this place for the ends of their lives. My mother . . .

Shut down that thought. Snap into journalist mode.

It was more of an ooze than a snap, but I found a logical question. "Is that unusual?"

"Most of my patients are going to die here eventually, except those in the short-term care wing. Still, people can live for years with Alzheimer's and dementia, if they are otherwise healthy." Now she had the soothing, professional voice she'd no doubt perfected on hundreds of patients' families. "Our usual turnover is one every month or two."

"Two in a week could be a normal variation then." Good. I sounded calm, even if part of my mind still ran in circles screaming, "No! Not my mommy!" I cleared my throat and asked, "Was something suspicious about these deaths?"

She sighed. "Not exactly. I mean, they were old, but both women were in reasonable health and died suddenly. That happens sometimes. Some sick people will survive for days or weeks, even after they can no longer talk or eat. Others seem fine one day and the next morning they're gone."

She gazed into the distance, perhaps replaying some of those scenes.

Her focus snapped back. "These two were like that. One complained of stomach pains and vomited a few times. The other seemed unusually weak and confused, according to the nurse who gave her medicine that evening. With Alzheimer's patients, it can be hard to identify a separate illness from the normal disease progression." Her voice wavered. "They were both dead by morning."

"The vomiting could be food poisoning. That can kill a person in poor health."

"These two incidents were a week apart, and no one else got sick either time. With food poisoning, you'd expect a wider outbreak."

I frowned. "What was the cause of death?"

"Officially, heart failure. We file death certificates, but unless the death is clearly questionable, no one would order an autopsy." She clenched her hands together. "One more thing. Two weeks ago, another woman got very ill, yet she recovered. Now she's fine. No one else in the unit got sick at the same time and we don't know what she had."

"Food poisoning seems unlikely with three patients sick

that far apart. Could a virus spread that slowly?"

"With the first woman, the nurse tested for bacterial infections, and for antibodies, which should show up if the immune system is fighting a viral infection. The tests didn't show any sign of either. The other two died so quickly we didn't have time to test. One of these cases alone wouldn't worry me, but the three of them together . . ."

Alarm bells clamored in my mind. Was I reacting as a reporter or as a daughter? I dragged in slow, deep breaths to force back the nausea and become the logical, skeptical correspondent. I'd covered stories where hundreds or even thousands of people had died in natural disasters or acts of war. Two old women dying in a nursing home wasn't much of a story.

Except that my mother was now an old woman living in a nursing home. "What exactly do you suspect?"

"I'm probably being paranoid. But once in a while, you hear stories about a nurse or aide who decides the people in their care would be better off if they didn't have to suffer any more." She looked away and whispered, "How could I forgive myself if more people died because I wasn't willing to ask questions?"

"Have you talked to the police?"

"Definitely not." Her eyes pleaded with me. "It would be disastrous for the home. People would want to remove their parents and spouses. Even if these deaths were perfectly natural, the rumors would destroy us. I can't do nothing, but I also can't put the entire operation at risk over a vague possibility."

I couldn't argue with that. The press would love a story

about a murdering caregiver, and a false rumor could taint a business for years. I suspected I knew the answer, but I asked, "What exactly do you want from me?"

"I'd like you to investigate. You're a journalist, you know how to find out things, and I trust you more than some random private detective. I want you to learn what happened, which hopefully will put my mind to rest. Am I being paranoid, or is someone killing my patients?"

Chapter Two

HEATHER KEPT QUIET while I pondered the situation. Part of me knew if there was any chance my mother was in danger, I had to investigate. A larger part of me wanted to be back in Syria, Iraq, or Afghanistan, covering important world events, not checking on the slim possibility that some twisted mind might be killing people who were already old and ill. I would have attacked a story like this as a young reporter trying to make my name, but it was, at most, local news.

And part of me still wanted to go home and sleep.

I'd never in my life passed up a story for a *nap*.

Fear shot through me, not for my mother or the other patients, but for myself. I'd been afraid often enough, afraid for my life. This was different—I was afraid of losing myself.

"I'll help." It came out too fast, too loud.

Heather sighed. "Thank you. What's the first step?"

Stop taking prescription painkillers and hope that cleared my brain fog. She didn't need to know that, though. I thought a moment. "I assume you do thorough background checks on employees before hiring them?"

She nodded. "No one with a criminal record can work here. Of course, that doesn't mean they've never committed a crime."

"Understood. I'll investigate everyone. Things that don't make it into criminal records may still appear in a news story."

Heather pulled a paper from the stack on her desk. "I printed a list of employees for you. Legally, I can't give you personal information, but this is public."

I folded the paper. "I'd better investigate the patients in question as well and interview their families."

She pursed her lips. "That might be tricky. Maybe I can arrange to hire you as a temporary outside consultant. We can say you're doing a follow-up on behalf of the home, to check satisfaction, or something vague."

My leg twitched, bumping my cane leaning against her desk. I grabbed the cane before it could fall and pressed my foot to the floor to steady my leg. "There's always the possibility someone will recognize me as a reporter, so I'll say I'm working on an article."

"On what exactly?"

I needed something to encourage people to talk. Emotions would be fragile so soon after a loved one's death.

"People tend to have strong opinions about what the government should be funding. We can say I'm looking into the financial strain it puts on families when someone has a long-term illness." I surreptitiously squeezed my thigh where the muscles were knotting and threatening to spasm again. "That gives me an excuse to ask about money."

Heather frowned. "Most patients here have little money of their own. They sign over assets to us in order to get the promise of continued care."

My sister had complained about the nightmare of dividing Mom's and Dad's finances, so Mom could get the long-term care she needed without bankrupting Dad. Some couples wound up divorcing after decades of marriage so they wouldn't both lose everything.

"Then no one leaves an inheritance?"

"I wouldn't go that far. We don't take literally every penny. Sometimes, the patient signs over a house, and that's enough to offset the cost of care. Most people have a small bank account, usually administered by a family member, so they can buy special items for the patient. Clothes, flowers. Take the patient to lunch. Get their hair done. Depending on the individual's situation, they might leave a few thousand dollars. But we cater to the middle class, so anyone really rich wouldn't be here."

"People have killed for a few thousand dollars."

Heather's nose wrinkled. "I suppose that's true. Do you think an employee could be coercing patients into changing their wills? Surely, I'd hear about any unusual bequests. It's only been a few days since the last death, so maybe not yet."

I shrugged. "A more direct way would be to steal bank cards and empty the accounts."

"And kill the patient . . . why? To hope no one notices in the confusion and grief after death?" She pushed back in her chair, her hands gripping the edge of the desk. "Somehow, that's more horrible than the thought of killing someone out of the misguided idea that you're ending their suffering."

"We live in a horrible world."

"I guess you'd know that, the things you've seen. I've spent my life trying to help people." Her eyes widened. "I didn't mean—that is, what you do is important too. I wasn't criticizing."

"I understand." I hauled myself to my feet. My leg cramped and I had to grab the desk for support. I tried to keep my face calm as I commanded the pain to go away. It didn't obey.

Heather rose as well. "Honestly, I admire you. I didn't have the nerve to pursue journalism. I could never do all the things you've done."

I resisted the urge to say, "Yeah, but you can walk." She probably assumed I'd stood with a grimace because I was upset. I was worse than upset, I wanted to scream and smash things and then curl up sobbing. But that had nothing to do with what Heather had said. "We each do what we can." I hoped that was appropriate. I'd already half forgotten her comment.

Heather looked down. I couldn't tell if she'd noticed my suffering and was trying to give me privacy, or if she was wrapped in her own thoughts.

I dragged my focus back to the practical questions. "The point is, we shouldn't assume anything. If you have an 'angel of mercy,' that first patient might have been a trial run or a failed attempt. Then why didn't the killer try again with the same target? Maybe the victim passed some kind of test by surviving. Or maybe the two deaths and the illness aren't even related. You're suspicious because of the timing, but maybe that part is a coincidence. Maybe one death was natural and one was murder."

She winced.

I fumbled for my cane and shifted my weight onto it. I

needed to get out of there, get home, take a painkiller, lie down . . .

Damn it. Getting off those things would be hard.

I put the list of employees in my shoulder bag. "I'll start on this and let you know what else I need. We probably shouldn't do anything by e-mail, in case your system isn't secure. I'm at my parents' house. You have the address."

I headed for the door.

"I have an idea," she said.

I closed my eyes and held back a sigh.

"There are physical therapists working next door. Massage therapists too. They see our patients, but they also take other clients."

I turned to face her. My smile felt stiff enough to crack and fall off. I didn't need yet another person telling me what I should do to "get over" my injury.

She leaned close and lowered her voice. "If you start going there, you'll meet more of the staff and patients. People chat a lot during their therapy, so you can get gossip. Between that and your mother being here, you'll have every excuse to visit anytime and go almost anywhere."

I'd seen enough of doctors to last me the rest of my life. Still, I would need ongoing physical therapy, and Heather's plan saved me the trouble of finding another clinic.

"I'll do that," I said.

"I have to admit, as much as I hope you don't find anything wrong, this is sort of exciting. Being part of an investigation again."

My smile came more easily. "Like our exposé about how much filler was in the cafeteria hamburgers?"

She chuckled. "Or our breaking story about the basketball team getting suspended for drinking in the hotel after an away game. We were really changing the world."

I shrugged. "It was the world we knew. A small, simple world in retrospect, but we cared about it."

Her humor faded. "Yeah. Things aren't so simple anymore." She locked her gaze to mine. "Maybe my world is still small compared to yours, but I care about it."

I put my free hand on her arm. "I understand. We'll find the truth."

She nodded and opened the door. I felt her watching as I limped down the hall. I must have looked more like one of her patients than a source for answers.

Stop it. It's not all about you.

Most of the people in this building had it worse than I did. Unfortunately, I didn't take comfort in knowing other people were suffering too.

Still, I could help Heather, and the patients, by uncovering the truth. If Heather's suspicions were right, I might even save a life or two, if only to give them a few more months of dying slowly.

What a heroic job I had.

By the time I found my mother's room, the worst of the cramping had eased, but if I sat down again, I might not be able to get up. Then I really would have trouble convincing people I wasn't a patient.

My parents held hands as Dad said goodbye. I'd rarely seen them so openly affectionate. Her illness was drawing them closer together, or at least encouraging them to express their feelings more. But would a point come when she no longer recognized him?

I bent to kiss Mom's cheek. I should haul her out of there. If someone was killing patients, how could I leave my mother in danger? But I couldn't remove Mom without making a stink and having to explain everything to Dad and Jen. That could jeopardize the nursing home and my investigation. Heather's fear of rumors was well-founded, and she had trusted me with this secret.

Maybe we could take Mom home for a "visit" for a few days, while I checked into things. On the other hand, Mom was here because she needed more care than Dad could give. I could hardly take care of myself, so pretending I could handle Mom's needs was ridiculous. No, I'd simply have to find out quickly whether the danger was real.

Quickly. Hah. Dad had to slow down for me as we left the building. It was hard to imagine doing anything quickly. Hopefully, this inquiry wouldn't require too much legwork.

I glanced at the clinic next door as we headed to the car. I could start this investigation right now by stopping to ask about physical therapy. But my leg hurt and my heart hurt, and I felt like a toddler about to throw a tantrum because "I don't wanna!" I'd call later.

Back at the house, I settled into my childhood bedroom. I tried to content myself with a double dose of ibuprofen and some pain relief cream I could rub directly onto my leg. The wound had closed without infection, although I'd have some dramatic scars. I'd never worried about whether my legs were "ready for swimsuit season" or such nonsense. I was concerned about function, not form. At least that's what I told myself as I massaged my leg and tried not to hate the scars.

The doctors had been irritatingly vague with their prognosis, promising only that with time, physical therapy, and most of all, patience, I might return to a "normal" life. But "normal" for me wasn't the same as normal for most people. I might always need the cane, and I couldn't imagine dodging bullets and crouching in bombed-out buildings with it.

I put the cane on the floor out of my line of sight and studied the list of employees Heather had given me. The words seemed to blur together. I had work to do, calls to make. But my eyelids felt heavy, and either the over-the-counter painkillers hadn't kicked in yet, or they simply weren't strong enough. I leaned back on my bed with two pillows behind my shoulders and one under my knees. So tired. So uncomfortable. I wanted to sleep until the pain went away, but that wouldn't happen, and the pain made it hard to sleep.

For the first time in my life, at forty-nine, I felt old. My body had never let me down in the past, the occasional injury barely interfering with my work. I traveled the world, often to the most rugged and dangerous places, sleeping on the ground or in bombed-out shells of buildings. Bizarre food, even half-spoiled, had never upset my iron stomach. Now everything ached, my leg threatened to collapse under its own weight, and the good painkillers made me queasy.

Could I do this? Did I still have what it took to be a journalist, even for such a safe, local story?

I thought of Marie Colvin, the journalist who'd lost an eye in Sri Lanka after a grenade attack. She'd worn an eye patch for over a decade, until a rocket in Syria killed her.

Our paths had crossed several times over the years. She hadn't let a missing eye slow her down.

I wouldn't let a mere injured leg stop me. In the field, you don't have time to give in to fear. If your emotions paralyze you, you can't do your job. You focus and put aside the emotions for later. I had to do that now.

One call. I could start with one call, and I'd make it count. I fumbled for my phone on the bedside stand and opened my contacts. I found Sierra, a young research assistant at the news agency, and waited while the phone rang.

"Kate! How are you? It's good to hear from you."

"I'm okay. Home in Arizona." I snuggled back into my pillows. "I need a favor."

"Anything." She was always enthusiastic, but she sounded genuinely excited. "Does this mean you're coming back to us?"

"Not yet. Hard to say when, but probably not for a few months. This is a private project, strictly off the record for now. I can pay you a little for after-hours work—"

She laughed. "Oh, Kate, you know what our hours are like here. There's no 'after.' I'll fit in your project. No charge for you."

"You're an angel. I'll send you a list of names. Um, maybe I'll take a picture with my phone and e-mail that. I don't have a computer set up here."

"No problem. Standard background checks?"

"Start with standard and we'll follow up on anything suspicious. These people shouldn't have any active criminal records, but find out about juvenile records, or charges that didn't go anywhere."

"Am I looking for something in particular?"

"Anything suspicious, really." I pondered what kind of early signs you might see in someone who later decided to kill elderly patients "for their own good." Was there a specific mental illness associated with that attitude? I didn't want to tell Sierra what I was investigating. I trusted her, as far as I trusted anyone in journalism to keep a secret, but word had a way of spreading in a busy office. "I'd like to know about criminal behavior, anything suspicious financially, but also anything . . . deviant, I guess you'd say. Animal cruelty, that kind of thing."

"It sounds like you've stumbled on something interesting."

"Maybe, maybe not. Hard to say at this point." I didn't want her to get too curious, so I didn't entirely muffle my yawn. "So how are you? How are the kitties? Any new boyfriends?"

"Overworked, rambunctious as usual, and maybe." She chuckled. "I have a date Friday with someone I met online. He claims to be a cat lover, so we'll see."

"If it goes well, send me his picture. If it goes poorly, send me a picture of the cats." I yawned again.

"Will do." Voices rose in the background. She muffled the phone for a moment to answer someone and then was back. "Send me those names and I'll get started. It might be a week or two."

Ugh. Of course she was busy. Anyone involved with a newspaper was always busy. But someone might be killing patients at the nursing home, and my own mother could be the next victim. Probably not, but still . . . "I don't want to wait weeks."

"So you did find something good!"

"Not really." Definitely not good from the perspective of a patient's daughter anyway. But I'd promised Heather to keep things quiet for now and, as much as I liked Sierra, I wouldn't trust any aspiring reporter to pass up the chance on a story that might help her career. "Just doing a favor for an old friend. It's probably nothing . . . but I'd like to be sure. Keep me posted on your progress, and I'll do some research myself."

"I'll start at the top of the list and you can begin at the bottom. Gotta go."

"Thanks."

She'd already hung up. I took a couple of close-up pictures of the list of names and attached them to an e-mail. Sierra was smart and ambitious, and she still saw me as a useful ally. But *secret* and *newspaper* were a tough combo. I was largely on my own.

I lay back and closed my eyes, thinking of all the things I needed to do, trying to ignore the constant throbbing in my leg.

I had to set up physical therapy appointments, and find a local doctor in case I needed a referral for the therapy. I didn't know if the prescriptions from Germany would transfer here. I'd have to keep close track of the paperwork to make sure I didn't get stuck with thousands of dollars in medical bills. At least I worked full-time for one news agency and had health insurance and short-term medical leave. Most correspondents were freelancers.

Such a glamorous life.

The tablet I'd used in the field had been lost or destroyed in the attack that had injured me. Dad had a computer I could borrow, but I wanted a laptop I could use while reclining in bed with my leg propped up. So I needed to buy a computer and get it online. Nothing too fancy, as I had a tight budget. The news agency wouldn't pay for a new tablet until I headed back into the field.

Then I needed to investigate the three patients in question, and their families, as well as the employees. I should also keep in touch with my boss so she didn't forget me. And I had my family to worry about as well—Mom's health and safety, Dad's state of mind, Jen's resentment.

So much to do. For once, I had plenty of time.

But getting my body and mind up to those tasks was another issue.

I reached for the duffel bag leaning against my bed. I hadn't unpacked it yet, and maybe part of me didn't want to, as if putting my clothes in the dresser would be a statement of permanence. I pulled out the embroidered leather pouch I'd gotten in Afghanistan and spilled its treasures onto my lap.

One by one, I set them on the bedside stand. The blue glass "evil eye" charm from Turkey for protection against bad luck. The hamsa charm, a hand-shaped pendant with an eye on the palm, also for protection against the evil eye. A tiny, smiling stone Buddha. A scarab charm of turquoise faience. Worry beads, a rosary, and three polished pebbles. A white jade pendant with a carving of a phoenix. A piece of shrapnel the doctors had removed from my leg, a reminder of my brush with death and my determination to rise from the ashes, like the phoenix.

I traveled so much that I didn't bother keeping an apartment anywhere, so nearly everything I owned went into my duffel bag. That meant both bulk and weight were concerns, and I'd hunted down the tiniest, lightest versions of everything I needed. Still, I saved room for this little horde of treasures amassed over the last thirty years. I didn't value the charms for their supposed luck and protection. They hadn't protected me anyway—or maybe they had saved me from worse injury or death. Who could tell? Regardless, I valued them because each one carried a memory. Places I'd been, stories I'd written, things I had done for people in need. Now, these pieces would serve as a reminder of what I could accomplish. A reminder that my work mattered, that I had mattered, and that I would matter again someday.

I held the phoenix pendant and vowed to make a difference again. I'd start with protecting my mother.

Chapter Three

I FELT BETTER after twelve hours in bed. Not twelve hours actually asleep, because even after I gave in and took a prescription painkiller, I didn't sleep that well. I felt guilty taking another narcotic so soon after swearing I'd quit, but more than anything, my body needed rest. If I saved the serious drugs for nighttime, maybe my brain would have time to clear during the day.

In the morning, I took the maximum prescription dose of ibuprofen before trying to move. I then spent twenty minutes doing the reclining exercises the doctors in Germany had prescribed before getting out of bed. Loosening my muscles that way allowed me to put some weight on my leg without screaming, but I still crashed into the wall twice on my way down the hall.

I'd gotten a long lecture from a heavily accented orthopedic surgeon on the importance of goals during the recovery process. I set the ambitious goal of only crashing into the wall once next time.

I leaned against the bathroom doorway and stared at the bathtub. I really needed a shower, but did I have the strength to handle one? Plus, I'd forgotten my toiletries in my bedroom. I'd been too tired to even brush my teeth last night.

The stairs creaked and Dad emerged into the hallway. "Everything all right up here? I heard some thuds."

"Just practicing my breakdancing. Seemed easier than attempting the shower."

His eyes widened behind his glasses. "Oh, I should have thought. Let me get the chair."

"What chair?"

He continued past me down the hallway. "After your mother fell last year, we put a plastic chair in the bathtub, and Gary changed the showerhead for one on a long hose. You can sit while you shower."

That sounded delightful. I'd have to thank Jen's husband, though no doubt my sister took credit for making it happen. It felt weird to let my father wait on me, but I shuffled out of the way and rested my butt on the edge of the counter while he dragged in the chair. I even asked him to get my toiletries bag.

I hated being dependent on someone. I hated being weak and slow.

It was only temporary.

The therapist who taught me to walk with a cane had said, "You're a fighter, and that's good. But you need to pace yourself. Sometimes, you'll need to let people take care of you."

Who knew that would be harder to accept than the pain?

I made a face and glanced in the mirror.

My mother looked back at me.

I shook my head to dispel the illusion. We didn't look that much alike. At my age, Mom had still been coloring her hair and wearing it down to her shoulders, carefully styled.

My hair was going gray, turning a lovely shade of silver, in
my opinion, and I wore it in a cropped pixie cut. But we had
the same bone structure, and my face was showing my age.
The wrinkles were mostly laugh lines, except for the grooves
between my eyebrows. I tried to rub out those furrows with
my finger even as I lectured myself that looking one's age
should not be an insult.

Dad came back with my toiletries.

I grinned. "My kingdom for a toothbrush."

His gentle look told me he saw right through my attempt
to appear cheerful. "Anything else you need?"

"Not right now. Thanks, Dad."

"I'll start breakfast."

"Give me twenty minutes." Normally, I could be show-
ered and dressed in eight, but now, twenty would be a
struggle. Was everything going to take twice as long, or
more? If it did, and I wore out quickly, I'd never get through
the investigation. But I needed to get far enough to see if
Mom was in danger.

Maybe having that goal would help me focus and stay
motivated. I'd been pretty depressed for the last month. Now
I could prove I was still a journalist. I was still *me*.

The shower felt wonderful, and I was famished by the
time I sat for Dad's pancakes. He even gave me one in the
shape of a cat, complete with ears and tail, like he used to do
when Jen and I were kids. He and I chatted and laughed over
breakfast, catching up without touching on any of the
serious issues. Maybe he needed a break as much as I did.

Finally, Dad rose and cleared the dishes. "I'd better get
moving if I'm going to meet the fellows for coffee. Do you

want to come?"

I glanced at the clock. Nine forty-five a.m. already. "No thanks. You have fun."

He met some of his retired buddies at a nearby coffee shop several times a week. On another day, I might have enjoyed hanging out with them, but I had too much to do and too little energy to waste a drop of it.

"Can I use your computer while you're gone?"

"Of course. Will you need the car today?"

Ugh, I hadn't even considered transportation yet. Fortunately, my injury was to my left leg, so I could still drive. But my parents had never replaced their second car after an accident a few years back. How many investigative reporters-slash-amateur detectives had to worry about sharing a car with their father? Even teenage Nancy Drew had her own wheels.

"Maybe this afternoon. I need to make some calls first."

Driving was another reason to get off the narcotic pain-killers ASAP.

"All right. I'll be back a little after eleven." He rested his hand on my shoulder for a long moment before he left.

I felt pretty good after the hot shower and breakfast, but I didn't know how long the stamina would last. Should I do as much as possible while I could do anything, or should I conserve my energy?

When you don't know what to do, get organized. I set up on the couch with a heating pad wrapped around my thigh, a cup of coffee steaming by my elbow, and a notebook in my lap. My own little kingdom, almost as good as a blanket fort. My parents' black and white cat, Harlequin, jumped up beside me and nestled down next to my bad leg. He started purring. I'd heard of the healing power of a cat's purr, and stories of pets knowing when their people needed comfort. I suspected Harlequin was more interested in the warmth of the heating pad. The early November temps were still hitting eighty degrees, but it hadn't warmed up that much yet, and my parents didn't turn on the heat until December, if then. Cats always acted as if only a fleeting sunbeam stood between them and death on the frozen tundra.

Half an hour later, I had a two-page to-do list. Fifteen minutes after that, I'd broken the list into categories: the clinic investigation, my leg, and "other," which mostly had to do with reorganizing my life around being in Arizona for an indeterminate amount of time. Some things could wait, while an asterisk marked more urgent items.

A distressing number of items had an asterisk.

I'd have to subcontract whenever possible, as I'd done by asking Sierra to start background checks. But as much as I might want to outsource my physical therapy, I'd have to handle many things myself. I'd tackle any in-person interviews, both because I'd promised to keep the investigation secret, and because I didn't trust anyone else to know what questions to ask and how to interpret answers.

I also couldn't afford to spend much money on assistance. I'd keep drawing a salary for a while—and once again, I thanked the universe that I was one of the few journalists who wasn't a freelancer—but print journalism didn't pay well, and I had extra expenses. Besides the medical co-pays, I needed a computer, and if Dad and I wanted the car at the same time, I'd have to use taxis or ridesharing. Sierra would work in exchange for future favors, but I'd have to watch my cash outlay elsewhere. In theory, Mom was worth any amount of money. In the real world, one had to have money to spend it.

Calls first. I reached for my phone.

It rang as I touched it. I jerked my hand away, stared at it a moment, shook myself, and checked the number, which showed only as Private. I answered anyway.

"Kate Tessler?" The man's voice came through a little too loud.

I held the phone farther from my ear. "Yes?"

"I'm one of the board members at Sunshine Haven. I understand you've taken an interest in us."

Curious. "Well, my mother is in your care."

"Yes, of course. And we will take excellent care of her, as we do all our patients. But that's not what I meant. You spent a long time yesterday closeted with Heather Garcia, our director."

Had Heather told him about our meeting? His wording didn't make that clear. But she'd said this was confidential. "Heather and I went to high school together. We had a short chat."

"You're saying you only talked about old times?"

"I don't see what business it is of yours, Mister . . . ?"

He cleared his throat. "I simply want to make sure Ms. Garcia isn't putting us in an unpleasant position. I know you're a reporter. Any story you want to write must be cleared in advance."

"I'm not sure you know how journalism works. I don't

have to get permission from the subject to tell a news story."

More throat clearing. Finally, he said, "You signed certain papers when your mother entered the facility. I'm sure you wouldn't want us to remove her."

"First of all, I was out of the country and didn't sign any papers. Second, I highly doubt that it's legal for you to evict a patient because a relative is a reporter, doing her job. If you think otherwise, we can have our lawyers discuss it." I was bluffing, but I suspected he was as well.

"So you are investigating us."

"I didn't say that. But there's one thing you should know, Mister—what is your name?"

He mumbled at first, and I could almost hear his teeth gritting when I made him repeat it. Henry Wilson had something to hide.

"Mr. Wilson, I had no plans to write a story on Sunshine Haven. But when you threaten a journalist, it makes us suspect there is a story, and a good one. Not necessarily good for you, though."

A long silence.

"Miss Tessler, we've gotten off on the wrong foot." His voice had a gentler tone. "I apologize. It's entirely my fault."

I didn't argue.

"I'm afraid I might have given you the wrong impression. It's merely that some reporters—not you, of course—like to fling mud. They word things in a misleading way, or skirt libel laws by asking questions that give the wrong impression. I've had to deal with that kind of thing in the past, and I don't want it to happen again."

"I'm not interested in making anyone look bad, unless

they've actually done something wrong. Since my mother is in your care, I hope you run an honest, safe, and exemplary facility."

"Of course, of course. I'm glad you understand. I overreacted."

He certainly had, but to what? He hadn't mentioned patient deaths, and it didn't sound like Heather had told him about our meeting. Had someone else described our closed-door conversation? Was that enough to get this kind of panicked reaction?

I asked, "Did you call me on behalf of the board, or yourself?"

He hesitated. "I'm calling you in my capacity as a board member."

In other words, the rest of the board might not know what he was doing. And they probably wouldn't approve of the way he had handled this. "How did you get my number?"

"It was in your mother's files."

So he had access to Sunshine Haven's patient records. Would a board member? I debated between poking him more, to see what reaction I could get, and letting him think he'd won. I decided on something in between. "Mr. Wilson, I'm going to be around Sunshine Haven a lot, since my mother is there. Perhaps we could meet sometime."

"Oh, er, certainly. Only I don't actually have an office there. The board position is separate from my main job, you understand. Perhaps we could have lunch sometime. Set it up with my secretary."

"What's the number?"

"Um . . . one moment. Let me give you the office number." It took more like thirty seconds for him to track it down.

"It's been interesting chatting with you, Mr. Wilson." I emphasized the name he'd tried to hide from me.

He mumbled something and ended the call.

The board members hadn't even been on my radar. Now, Henry Wilson had moved to the top of my list of people to investigate.

"Bad move, Wilson." I snuggled back against my pillow with a grin. I was such a good reporter that suspects practically threw themselves at me!

I could think of three possibilities for his nervousness. He knew something about the deaths and wanted to hide it. He had an entirely different secret, something serious enough that he panicked at the thought of a reporter on the premises. Or he really had overreacted because of past unpleasant and unfair experiences with reporters.

Of the three options, I doubted the last one. Something was wrong at Sunshine Haven. I had to find out what it was.

I looked down at Harlequin, dozing beside me. "Watson, the game's afoot."

Chapter Four

HAD I, AGAINST all odds, stumbled onto a real story in the middle of my convalescence? I wanted to ask Heather about Henry Wilson, but I'd have to watch how I contacted her. Had someone spied on us? Surely her office couldn't be bugged or her phone tapped, but better to not take chances. We'd have to pretend we were merely old friends, closer than we'd actually been, reigniting our friendship.

First up, I called the therapy office next to the nursing home. They couldn't get me a new patient appointment until Monday. I didn't want to wait four days to check out the place, so I insisted on stopping by that afternoon to fill out paperwork. The receptionist said someone could give me a tour at 3:30 p.m. Then I could visit Mom, and if I caught Heather alone, I'd warn her about a possible spy.

After lunch, I did another set of exercises for my leg and had a medically recommended recuperation session—I was determined not to call it a nap. Then I prepared to face the outside world again. Dad said he'd go with me.

"Are you sure you don't want to take a day off?" I asked.

The last few months must have been hard on him. He'd wanted to come to Europe when I was in the hospital, but he couldn't leave Mom so soon after she'd moved into Sunshine Haven.

His smile was wistful. "I don't know how much time I have left with your mother. I don't want to miss a day, not while there's still a chance she'll know me."

I nodded and turned away, my chest and throat tight. We spent the short drive to the nursing home in silence.

With more than twenty minutes before my appointment, we headed to Mom's room. When Dad paused to talk to one of the nurses in the hallway, I entered the room alone. Mom wore a pink sweatsuit and sat in a chair knitting and watching TV. She looked so normal, although the sweatsuit wasn't up to her previous fashion standards. When she glanced up at me, her expression crumpled into confusion.

Dad had introduced me the day before, giving her a clue to my identity. It felt too weird to say, "I'm your daughter, Kate, formerly called Kitty," so I found a smile and said, "Hi, Mom! Dad will be here in a minute."

I sat on the edge of the bed, resting my hands on top of the cane propped between my knees.

Mom squinted at it. "Is that for me? I can still walk, you know."

"No, this is mine."

Mom must have known what happened. My memories of those first weeks were fuzzy, but we'd spoken on the phone. Later, Jen had insisted that I avoid "worrying" Mom, so I'd downplayed the unpleasant stuff and chatted about other things.

I said, "I had a little accident, and I'm still getting better."

"Oh." She frowned. "You should take better care of yourself. You take too many chances."

"I'll be more careful." I glanced around the room, searching for inspiration. How could I have nothing to say to my mother, whom I hadn't seen in a year? So much had happened in that year. Too much. Most of it I didn't want to discuss.

Dad came in with a nurse, who asked a few questions and left.

Mom said, "Such a nice girl."

The "girl" was probably forty, but Mom had always referred to my friends as girls.

Mom had been a good judge of character. Had that survived her fading faculties?

"How do you like the staff here?" I asked.

"Oh, they take good care of me. It's like being at a resort." She leaned forward and lowered her voice. "Except the fat one. She's rough."

I had never heard Mom call anyone fat before. She would have considered the word itself rude, and she only made personal comments about Jen and me.

"I . . . uh . . ." I tried to focus on the second part of her statement. "What do you mean? She's rough? Does she hurt you?"

"Big hands. Like a . . . like a . . . she has big hands." Mom leaned back and stared into space.

I looked at Dad.

"I know the nurse she means," he said. "She's a hefty gal. Good at lifting the patients who have trouble getting from the bed to a wheelchair and so forth."

That didn't seem particularly suspicious, but I asked, "Do you know her name?"

Dad shrugged. "Gail, maybe?"

Mom was focused on her knitting again.

"It's not one of her best days," Dad said softly.

I nodded. "I should go to my appointment."

I still had fifteen minutes to get to the building next door, but I wanted out of there. I felt guilty about it, but that didn't change my desire to flee.

"We'll be here," he said.

The door to Heather's office was behind the front counter, where the staff greeted visitors. If anyone had reported our closed-door meeting, it was probably the person working there. Today, the receptionist was African American, about thirty, well-groomed, and pleasant-looking. I was pretty sure the receptionist the day before had not been Black. Hispanic or Asian, maybe? How could I not remember for sure? Noticing people was part of my job. One more thing to blame on the painkillers—I hoped. I made a note of her nametag: Carla.

"Is Heather in?" I asked.

She gave a professional smile that didn't reach her eyes. "I'll find out if the director is available. Your name, please?"

I preferred to avoid any official record of my visit. I shifted so I could see through the office doorway and caught a glimpse of someone seated at the desk. "I see her. I'll just say hi."

I ignored the receptionist's open mouth and hurried around the counter, giving her the choice between tackling me and letting me go. People almost always went with the second option.

Heather glanced up from some paperwork. "Hi Kit—Kate. Everything all right with your mother?"

"She's fine. I was wondering . . ." I could feel the receptionist hovering behind me as I scrambled for an excuse. "Are you still in touch with Elizabeth . . . um, what was her last name?"

Heather looked past me and raised a hand. "It's all right, Carla. We went to high school together." She turned her attention back to me. "Elizabeth Farrell? Or are you thinking of Liz Lui?"

A chair creaked behind me, and I resisted the urge to check that the receptionist had retreated. I found a pen and notepad on Heather's desk. Making sure my body blocked anyone's view from the doorway, I scribbled a note while I babbled. "No, tall, dark-haired girl. In the year between us, I think."

I had no idea if there was an Elizabeth in that class, let alone if she fit that description. I pushed the note toward Heather.

Her eyes widened as she read it: *Did you tell Henry Wilson about our talk?*

She shook her head. I made a "hurry up" gesture.

"I'm . . . I'm not sure. Uh, was she on the basketball team?"

"Yes, that's the one." I reached across the desk and added to the note: *You have a spy.*

"Oh dear," Heather mumbled. She glanced at the door and said in a louder voice, "Right. I can't think of her last name. I'm not in contact with her."

"No problem. I only wondered." I mouthed the words "Call me after work" as I backed toward the door. "See you."

She nodded and watched me leave, frowning. Surely she was clever enough to take precautions, such as not calling me from her work phone. These days, everyone watched CSI shows and thriller movies, so people generally had some understanding of surveillance. What they learned from those shows was ninety percent wrong, but at least they knew the technology existed.

As I left the building, I glanced back at the bright, clean reception area. Such a pleasant-looking place, like a shiny apple hiding a worm.

The PT clinic shared the same parking lot as the nursing home. The walk over was still long enough to tire me, but as the automatic doors opened, I straightened and tried to move as smoothly as possible. Silly, no doubt, to downplay my injury in front of the people who were supposed to help me overcome it, but I hated the thought that everyone might take one look at me and analyze my body. I wasn't simply an interesting problem to solve. I was still me.

I entered a small waiting room with rows of chairs on two sides and the counter ahead of me. An older woman flipped pages in a magazine, while two seats away, a little man sat with his hands on his knees, staring straight ahead. On the other side of the room, a middle-aged woman peered at her phone.

Behind the desk, a woman barely out of her teens greeted me. "Good morning. Or afternoon I guess." She giggled. "Whatever. Can I help you?"

I introduced myself. As she gathered paperwork, her

bowed head showed the dark roots of her bleached hair. "Have a seat and fill these out. I'll need your insurance card and ID."

It took almost half an hour to complete the detailed health questionnaire and the forms for insurance. During that time, a woman in scrubs took the old man into the back, for treatment I assumed. An older woman using a walker came out and left with the middle-aged woman. A couple of other people came and went. Overall, the place was quiet except for an occasional clang that sounded like weight machines in use.

With the paperwork taken care of, the receptionist said, "I'll see if a therapist can show you around. Have a seat."

She disappeared in the back, and I leaned on the counter. I'd had enough of sitting upright. My thigh throbbed. I really wanted to lie down with my leg elevated, but I didn't think that would be appropriate in the lobby. I imagined stretching out on the floor until someone stepped on me or ran over me with a wheelchair.

The girl returned, wheezing a bit as if she had asthma. See, I could notice details if I tried.

"It will be a few minutes," she said.

"What's your name?"

"Daisy."

"How long have you worked here?"

"Three years. I'm training to be a physical therapy assistant." That gave me the opening I needed to chat—she hadn't known what she wanted to do after high school, but working the desk here had ignited her interest in physical therapy. Becoming a licensed therapist would require too much school, but she could train as an assistant and work with one of the senior PTs.

After a few minutes on that, I led the conversation back to the clinic itself and learned it had four physical therapists and six assistants who could supervise people doing exercises. Two massage therapists, an acupuncturist, and a hypnotherapist rented office space after hours but weren't part of the main staff. The billing manager was "kind of grumpy," Daisy admitted in a whisper, but who wouldn't be when dealing with insurance companies all day? Everyone else was nice. I didn't learn anything relevant to my investigation, as far as I could tell. If anyone was killing patients, it was probably someone in the nursing home, not here.

A short, muscular woman in her thirties came out from the back of the clinic.

"Oh, here's Berta," Daisy said. "She can show you around, and she'll probably be your main therapist. She's tough, but if you want to improve quickly"—Daisy grinned at the woman—"and you have a high pain tolerance, she's your girl."

"I think I have a pretty good tolerance for pain," I said. "But maybe I should wait until after our first session to decide."

Berta chuckled. "The important thing is communication. I'll push you, but you have to tell me if I push you too hard."

"I can do that. I want to improve quickly."

"I'll look over your chart before our first meeting, but for now, let me show you the place. I have about ten minutes before my next client."

Berta led me through a hallway into a large room with all

kinds of exercise equipment. Several people were working out, most of them over sixty. The two younger people in the room, a man and a woman, rotated among the patients, offering advice and encouragement. Smaller rooms were used for consultations, exams, and massages. A swimming pool for water exercises was kept at a toasty ninety degrees. The place looked clean, well-organized, and friendly. Maybe being a patient wouldn't be so bad, even if I was a generation younger than most of them.

I half listened to Berta explain one of the exercise machines while I peeked down a back hallway that seemed to lead to offices. In other words, none of my attention was on the floor in front of me. My toe caught on something and I pitched forward. As I instinctively reached out with my hands, my cane knocked against a treadmill with a bang that wrenched it from my grip. I came down hard on my left foot, pain shot up my bad leg, and I yelped.

Berta had her arms around me, holding me up. She was about my height, five foot two or so, but she set me back on my feet like a mother propping up her wobbly toddler.

"Careful," she said in that annoying way people had of warning you after the fact. She led me to a bench. "Everything okay?"

I nodded and glanced down to see what had tripped to me. Nothing more than a cord that was taped flat to the floor. My own fault for not looking where I put my feet. I squeezed my thigh to try to keep the muscle from cramping.

"I'm fine. Clumsy, but fine." I could feel everyone's gaze on me, like drivers slowing to gawk at a car accident.

Berta knelt beside me. "Good. If you were hurt, we'd

have to fill out more paperwork, and I hate paperwork."

A woman sitting at a leg exercise machine said, "I bump into walls, ever since I had my hip replaced, but I've been getting a lot stronger. You'll like it here, dear."

"Thanks." I wanted to ask if she was a resident of Sunshine Haven. She seemed reasonably fit and sharp, but the nursing home had different units depending on the patient's needs. I didn't want to offend her if she wasn't in nursing care, though.

Berta gestured toward my leg. "May I take a look?"

The other people returned to their activities, so I nodded and pulled up the leg of my baggy shorts. I winced at the sight of my scars, but Berta didn't show any reaction. She ran her hands over the jagged scars gently, almost like a caress, and then kneaded my muscles. The pressure sent a jolt through me so I sat up straight and sucked in a breath. But after a minute, the muscles relaxed. Maybe physical therapy wouldn't be complete misery after all.

"There," Berta said. "I can't do anything officially until you're my patient, but what's a little massage between friends?"

"Thanks. That helped." I rose and made sure my shorts were covering the scars again.

Now what? It was one thing to question politicians and rebel leaders who had opened themselves to scrutiny by their public positions. Even victims of violence or disasters often wanted to share their experiences. Asking nosy questions while hiding the reason for my interest was more difficult. I could hardly interrogate elderly patients, and if Berta was going to be my physical therapist, I didn't want to set the tone for our relationship by asking questions that might sound like criticism. I'd have to get people gossiping, but how could I make sure they gossiped about the right things?

It was a problem, and not one I felt up to facing right then. When Berta glanced at her watch and said she had to meet her next client, I had my excuse to leave, even if I'd learned nothing.

Back in the parking lot, I eyed the long walk to the other building and headed for the car instead. I'd had enough standing and walking for one day. I called Dad to let him know where to meet me. I felt bad for not going in to see Mom again. I didn't like seeing her the way she was now. But how many more chances would I get to see her at all? She annoyed me sometimes—okay, a lot of the time—because she always had advice, and it usually wasn't what I wanted to hear. But she was there if I needed her. Now, I couldn't count on that.

I settled into the passenger seat, pushing it all the way back and reclining so I could stretch out. I'd hardly done anything physical and I was shaky with fatigue.

This was pointless. Even if someone was killing patients, how could I ever identify the killer among all the Sunshine Haven staff, patients, and visitors? I didn't know what I was doing. I was wasting time, exhausting myself for nothing. Maybe I should tell Heather to call a real private detective, or take her chances with the police.

Maybe I should give up.

The murderer was probably a figment of Heather's imagination. Who could blame me for focusing on my own recovery instead of some mythical villain? Only Heather knew I was working on this. I wouldn't have to admit to Dad and Jen that I was willing to risk Mom's life.

Except everything Heather had said, paired with Henry Wilson's overreaction, signaled a story worth pursuing. My journalistic instincts hadn't completely vanished, apparently. Sunshine Haven had a shadow, something darker and more vicious than the everyday tragedy of infirmity and aging.

But could I do this?

If not me, then who? I had investigative experience, access to inside information, and a stake in the outcome. Everything one could ask for, except for two working legs and enough energy.

Oh well. No one was perfect.

If I was going to uncover the secrets buried at Sunshine Haven Care Home, I needed a solid, efficient plan—and perhaps more assistance. I didn't like asking for help, but maybe it was time to get over that.

Dad came across the parking lot. He looked older than he had an hour ago. This was hard on him, and maybe at some point, Mom's death would feel like a blessed release from suffering, but not yet. She might not be the woman we remembered, but we weren't ready to let her go.

Was someone killing patients before their time? I had to find out. For all of us. But my first day on the job had proven it wouldn't be easy.

Chapter Five

AFTER DINNER, I reclined on the couch with my heating pad and the purring cat. Dad had the TV on. It hurt my neck to turn toward it, I didn't know any of the current shows, and the blaring commercials gave me a headache. Still, it seemed too early to retreat to my room. My leg throbbed. I tried to imagine the pain flowing down my leg and out my foot. The pain stuck its metaphorical tongue out at me and stayed right where it was.

I really needed to get a laptop or tablet so I could work while stretched out with my leg up. Sierra had sent a batch of background checks, but trying to read them on my phone seemed like a recipe for an even greater headache.

The doorbell rang. Dad and I looked at each other and shrugged. He muted the TV and rose.

I edged Harlequin off my stomach and swung my feet to the floor. I didn't want Jen to see me "being lazy." I rolled my eyes for thinking that way, but there it was.

A woman's voice came from the hallway. It didn't sound like Jen. Too friendly. Heather entered the living room. Dad hovered in the entrance and then retreated.

Heather perched on the couch next to me. Harlequin yawned, stretched, and allowed the visitor to stroke his back.

"I'm sorry to drop by without warning," Heather said, "but I thought we should talk."

"I agree. I was hoping you'd get the hint this afternoon." I described the strange phone call from Henry Wilson.

She frowned, scratching Harlequin behind the ears. "I can't believe Henry would do that. It's totally inappropriate for any board member to call you like that. He could get in a lot of trouble. He could get *us* in a lot of trouble. And Henry is one of the good ones. There are board members I . . . have mixed feelings about, but Henry isn't one of them."

Harlequin squirmed away from her and crawled into my lap. She must have started petting too hard.

"Maybe I'll go see him in person tomorrow," I said. "If he's hiding something, a direct assault might push him to do something stupid and reveal himself."

"When you say it that way, it sounds dangerous."

I shrugged. "I've interviewed warlords. I think I can handle one . . . what is he, in his regular life?"

"He owns a chain of local grocery stores."

Sure, war criminal, drug lord, grocer. All dangerous people one should avoid. "Successful?"

"Originally, quite, but in the last decade, they've had to reorganize and close some stores. As Phoenix has taken over the neighboring towns, the big chains have popped up all over. It's harder to compete, especially when you insist on supporting local growers and paying your staff a living wage with benefits."

A grocer who took care of his employees. Quite intimidating. "He sounds like a decent guy." I stretched my leg forward and propped my foot on the coffee table.

Heather's hands fidgeted in her lap. Did she realize how much she expressed her emotions through her hands?

"What I've told you so far is public knowledge," she said. "It's in the news. But I've also heard stories about Henry's kids. They're in their forties, and even his grandchildren are adults now, more or less. Some of them work in the business, but the ones who might actually want to take it over are either incompetent or unscrupulous. Henry probably would have retired by now if he had a clear line of succession."

"I'm starting to feel sorry for the guy." Maybe his inappropriate phone call was simply bad judgment brought on by stress. But the man Heather described didn't sound like the man I'd spoken to. Which one was the real Henry Wilson? "In any case, I'm not sure what any of that has to do with your business or our mystery."

Heather spread her hands. "I can't imagine either. It's not like Henry would benefit by patients dying."

I lowered my voice, although I didn't think Dad's hearing was good enough to listen in from another room. "What about his children and grandchildren? Do they have anything to do with Sunshine Haven?"

"A couple of the teenage granddaughters volunteer. Many of the kids have over the years. It's good for college applications. Right now, one girl is doing clerical work and one leads craft activities."

"They wouldn't have access to drugs."

"Certainly not. All drugs are locked up and only the licensed nursing staff and doctors have access."

"What about patient records?"

"I couldn't swear that a volunteer never had a chance to

peek at patient records, especially the girl in clerical, but I doubt they'd understand what they were reading. You don't really think one of those teenage girls is targeting patients, do you?"

I leaned back and stared at the ceiling. Teenage girls had been known to kill, but this seemed a stretch. For one thing, how would Henry Wilson have found out about it? And wouldn't he insist the girl leave her job? More likely, if Wilson was hiding something, it had nothing to do with the patient deaths. Or else the connection was so convoluted I couldn't glimpse it yet.

I sat up and smiled at Heather.

"It's probably nothing, but I'll visit Wilson to make sure we're not missing anything." I didn't tell her my suspicions that this might be a separate scandal. She seemed fond of Henry Wilson, and I didn't want to strain her loyalty. "Promise me you won't warn him."

She opened her mouth, closed it, rubbed her lips together, and finally nodded.

"In the meantime, we shouldn't talk about any of this at your office, or over an office phone line."

Her expression was bleak as her hands clenched and released, clenched and released. "Something is wrong, isn't it? I was hoping I overreacted."

"It's too early to say. For now, keep your head down and leave it to me."

Maybe I should've been more comforting. My journalism training was reasserting itself, though, dusting the cobwebs out of my mind. I couldn't afford to trust everything a source said. Criminals sometimes offered to help the police as a way of taunting authority or trying to get inside information on an investigation. Heather could have killed the patients and felt so guilty she wanted me to expose her. She could even be trying to use me for some kind of complicated power play, drawing my attention with the threat to my mother and then shifting me off on this tangent about the board to get rid of a business enemy. We weren't friends. We hadn't spoken for thirty years. I really didn't know her at all.

I sat close enough to touch her, feeling miles away and alone.

DAD MUST HAVE wondered about Heather's visit, and he probably suspected she'd come for more than old friendship, but he didn't ask. That was a relief, since my skills included reporting facts, not creating cover-ups.

Friday morning, I called Henry Wilson's office. His secretary tried to put me off until the following week, but I hinted at urgent and secret matters, and she agreed to a 10 a.m. appointment. Sierra had sent another batch of background checks that I couldn't read on my phone. Time to buckle down and buy a laptop, though then I'd have no more excuses to dodge research.

Dad sent me to a little local place owned by the grandson of one of his friends. I entered the narrow, cluttered shop and squinted in the dim light until a tall young man stood from behind a desk.

"Can I help you?"

I dodged shelves and tables piled with equipment to approach him. "I need a laptop."

He was maybe twenty-five, with large freckles scattered over his light brown skin. He wore his wiry, reddish hair buzzed close to the head. He grinned and suddenly went from rather ugly to quite attractive. "You're the journalist. Your dad called my granddad and said you were coming, and I should take good care of you. I'm Simon Washington."

"Kate Tessler." We shook hands. "How long have you had this place?"

"I've been working here since I was ten. I took it over from my grandmother when she retired last year at age eighty. She worked in computers for sixty years."

We chatted about family before turning to computers. Simon had a strong recommendation, and the remarkably reasonable price suggested I was getting a friends of family discount. I asked him to set it up with everything I'd need— the basic programs, my favorite web browser, and so forth.

"I'll have it ready in an hour, if you want to come back."

"I have an appointment, but I should be back by eleven." I didn't want to ask Sierra for too many favors, or give her too many clues to a potential story. And while I certainly wouldn't ask anyone to do anything illegal, having a young hacker on hand could be useful. "I could use a research assistant. Someone really good with computers to investigate people for a project I'm working on. Do you know anyone who works cheap?"

Simon's eyes were a remarkable sea-foam green I'd only seen once before, on an Afghani shepherd. Those eyes brightened. "I know exactly who you need. I'll call Mac."

Good name for a computer geek.

"Thanks."

I headed out to see Henry Wilson.

The office building was in a line of strip malls. I entered a lobby with hallways off each side. The decor focused on Southwest native art, with sculptures on the end tables and baskets mounted on the walls. A dark-haired receptionist greeted me and escorted me to Henry Wilson's office. I faced a stocky man with thick white hair and laugh lines on his weathered face.

He rose and offered his hand. "Ms. Tessler? My assistant said this had something to do with our conversation yesterday, but as far as I know, we've never spoken before."

His Texas drawl sounded nothing like the "Henry Wilson" on the phone.

I shook his hand as my mind scrambled. Could he have disguised his voice before? But why, if he was going to give me his name? More likely someone had pretended to be him.

He gestured to a chair. "Please sit."

I took my time lowering myself and propping my cane against the armrest. I could pretend I'd come for another reason entirely—claim I was considering an article about his company—and brush off any reference to us speaking previously. I could poke a bit to see if I could uncover any connection with the person who'd called me.

Or I could explain the truth, at least the part that related to Wilson himself.

The direct path usually got you places faster.

"Someone called me yesterday claiming to be you. Can you think of anyone who might do that?"

His bushy white eyebrows rose. "Good heavens, no. Unless you spoke to my son, Henry Jr. That would be an easy mistake. He's traveling on business right now."

"Is he on the board at Sunshine Haven?"

"No, that's me. What's this about?"

"A man called me yesterday, claiming to be on the board. He didn't want to give a name at first, but when I pressed him, he gave me yours. He'd heard I was at Sunshine Haven and warned me not to write about it. I'm a journalist, but I wasn't investigating anything. I was there because my mother is a resident. He seemed unduly paranoid."

"That's highly irregular. I don't know what to tell you. I'll look into it. That is . . . Hmm."

I nodded. "Where would you start? I doubt anyone is going to admit to pretending to be you. Can you think of any reason your son might have called me?"

"About Sunshine Haven? Absolutely not. He doesn't have anything to do with it."

"How many men are on the board?" I felt confident the voice had been a man. Whether it had actually been a board member was another matter.

"Only three, including me. Santiago Morales and Lucas Williams are the others. But I can't imagine either of them would do such a thing."

"Maybe they didn't, but someone did. Let me know if you think of anything helpful." I slid my card onto his desk.

He rose as I did and offered his hand again. I got a whiff of spicy, exotic cologne that made me lean a little closer. He had charisma, the sort that came from confidence and apparent straight-shooting.

"Thank you for coming to see me. If I may ask . . . are you writing about Sunshine Haven?"

"Not at the moment. We'll see."

He nodded, looking troubled, and remained standing as I made my way out.

I was ninety percent convinced Henry Wilson hadn't called me the day before. It could have been one of the other male board members, so I'd try calling them to see if I recognized the voice.

I sighed. I'd added two more names to the list of people to investigate, but in reality, the field was wide open. The person who'd called must have something to do with Sunshine Haven, but they could be an employee or even a patient's relative. Although, if the caller had gotten my unlisted number from Mom's records, that suggested staff.

In some ways, I'd moved further away from finding out an answer. But I had learned one thing—someone definitely had something to hide.

I headed back to the computer store. I needed that laptop and help with the research. My mind already seemed sharper now that I was only using the prescription painkillers at night, but my body kept reminding me it still needed to heal. Plus, I'd gotten so little aerobic exercise lately that crossing the parking lot left me weak. I fumbled for my keys in my shoulder bag and managed to drop them. Bending to pick them up without spilling my bag, losing my cane, or wrenching my leg took a full minute and left me growling with frustration.

As I got the keys in the door, I muttered, "You need patience. You're almost fifty. If you can't learn patience now, then when?"

Never, a little voice whispered. *You might as well give up. It's too late for that.*

At least I knew myself well enough to have realistic expectations.

When I entered the computer store, two figures behind the counter broke apart. My eyes were still adjusting to the dim light, but I thought they'd been kissing. Simon gave me a sheepish smile and ran his hand over his short hair as I came toward them. The young woman next to him was the stereotypical cheerleader type: fair, blonde, and gorgeous.

Simon put an arm around her. "This is Mackenzie. Top of her class in computer science at ASU and one of the best video gamers in the state. If she can't find something on the internet, it doesn't exist."

I held out my hand. "I'm Kate. Are you interested in doing some work for me? I should warn you, I can't pay much."

"That's all right." Her voice was low and pleasant. "I charge two hundred dollars an hour to set up networks. That pays the bills and gives me time to do what I want."

I blinked several times, trying to process the idea of two hundred dollars an hour. "I was thinking of ten dollars an hour. Why would you want to help me research when you can make so much more?"

Lovely blue eyes gazed at me. "Because you've been everywhere and done everything. I want to learn."

"About journalism?"

"About *everything*."

Well then. I wondered how many people had seen the

pretty young woman and totally missed the real Mackenzie. The ones paying her two hundred dollars an hour hadn't undervalued her anyway.

"I can find anything on the internet," she said, "but I don't always know what to look for or what to do with it. How do you know what's important? How do you judge what's true?"

"Excellent questions for a reporter. Not necessarily ones I'd expect from a computer programmer."

"I want to start my own business. I need to know how to hire people, who to trust, how to negotiate." She grimaced. "That's the hardest one. I need a mentor. Not for computers but for life. For being a woman in a man's field, like you've been. You know, *adulting*."

I'd certainly faced sexism on the job, including editors who refused to send me into areas that were "too dangerous," as if death were somehow worse for a woman than a man. But female conflict correspondents had advantages as well. People tended to underestimate us, lower their guard, and reveal more than they'd intended. Plus, we could go into places men couldn't, such as the women's quarters in Arab communities.

It was a shame Mackenzie, some thirty years younger than I, would face the same stereotypes. But they were unavoidable, so she might as well learn to make use of the advantages.

"You've got yourself a mentor. One rule, though: whatever you find out for me is absolutely confidential."

"I can keep a secret. Even from Simon." She smirked at him.

"I won't even ask." He glanced at me. "But let me know if I can help with anything. After all, you're practically family."

Not sure where he got that idea, but since I was getting a cheap computer and his girlfriend as a helper, I didn't argue.

"All right, Simon, if my laptop is ready, I'll head home." I wanted to take the weight off my throbbing leg for a while. "Mackenzie, can you come by my house in about two hours? I have some names to investigate."

"How about if Mac brings the laptop?" Simon asked. "I'll beef up the security if you're going to be secret agents."

"Sure." That would save me the awkwardness of trying to get through doors with the laptop under one arm and my cane in the other hand. I gave Mac my address and headed for the door. I managed to get out of the store without knocking over the piles of stuff, catching my cane on a table leg, or stumbling over my feet.

The closest parking spot had been across the street. No way would I walk all the way down to the corner to use the crosswalk, so I squeezed between two cars and looked both ways. Fortunately, traffic was light on this side street, and once a truck passed, I limped forward.

An engine revved to my left. I glanced over, as a silver car pulled out of a parking space thirty feet down, heading in my direction. I picked up the pace, even though I was only a step or two from the center line.

These days, I was clumsy enough that I had to watch where I put my feet, but at the edge of my vision, the silver shape quickly got larger. Safely in the next lane, I turned to scowl at the driver. A car pulling into traffic should have the patience to let someone with a cane get out of the way.

Sun glared off the windshield, blinding me and hiding the driver from view. The car swerved into my lane, horn blaring.

It barreled straight at me.

Chapter Six

I DOVE FOR the edge of the street. Slammed down on my shoulder and hip. Rolled.

The wheel of a parked car stopped me. Tires screeched on the pavement and hot air ruffled my hair as the silver car shot past.

I blinked several times. Why wouldn't the world stop moving?

Finally the buildings and vehicles stopped doing the wave. I levered myself onto my elbow. The vicious attack car was too far away to make out the license plate.

I flopped back down, cursing. Everything hurt. My cane had somehow ended up ten feet away.

A bell jingled as the computer shop door opened. Simon and Mackenzie spilled out and rushed over.

I ignored their exclamations and questions. "Help me up."

"Are you sure?" Simon asked. "You shouldn't move if you're injured. I can call an ambulance."

"I'm not going to lie here and wait for them." My leg was screaming. The black pavement was hot under my exposed arms and the back of my head. "I'm fine, but this isn't comfortable. Please, help me up."

I resented having to ask a second time, resented even needing the help. Apparently life was trying to teach me a lesson about that, and I wanted to strangle life for its efforts.

Simon hauled me to my feet and Mackenzie retrieved my cane.

As I leaned against my car and brushed myself off, Mackenzie said, "That person didn't even stop. Do you think they know they almost hit you? Maybe they were texting."

I drew in a deep breath and let it out. Again, in and out, getting my heart rate under control. "How much did you see?"

"Not much. We heard the horn and looked out." She frowned. "I guess if they honked, they saw you."

"You didn't get a good look at the car or driver?"

Simon shrugged. "Just a gray car, probably a compact, but I couldn't tell the model. I couldn't see anyone in it."

"Gray or silver?" I asked.

"Either, I guess," Simon said. "Shiny gray would basically be silver."

"I thought more of a metallic white, like the manufacturers would call pearl or something," Mackenzie said. "But the store windows aren't too clean."

Simon raised an eyebrow. "Damn it, Jim, I'm a computer doctor, not a maintenance man."

I could identify two dozen different types of military vehicles, but all I could say was that the vehicle had been a car, not a van or truck. And we couldn't even agree on the exact color. "No point in reporting it, I guess." My limbs still trembled from the adrenaline, but my stomach settled and my heart dropped back to a modest speed.

A white van approached in the lane we were partially blocking. Mackenzie stepped to my side while Simon turned toward the van as if he could protect us with his body.

The van crept forward, giving us plenty of room, and the passenger-side window rolled down. The driver called through it, "Everything okay?"

Simon held up both hands in front of his chest, palms out, clearly demonstrating his harmlessness. Oh, the life of a Black man in America. "We're fine. Helping a friend who took a spill."

The van pulled forward a couple more feet. "Kitty?"

I squinted to make out the driver in the dim interior. Before I could decide if I knew him, he said, "It is you!"

The van's emergency lights went on. A man about my age hopped out and hurried around the van, an official city vehicle.

"You don't recognize me."

His voice had a pleasant, husky rumble, lower than I would have expected from his medium height and build. His brown hair showed some gray, but when he flashed a grin, thirty years dropped away, revealing Todd Paradise. He'd been a year behind me in school, but since he was the junior class president, I'd interviewed him several times for the school paper. I wouldn't say he was part of the "popular crowd," being too caught up in causes such as the environmental club and student council. But with his good looks and a name like Paradise, the girls had swooned over how much they wanted to "visit paradise." The jokes over his name were certainly better than the meowing I'd gotten with the nickname Kitty.

"Todd, how are you?"

"I'm great, but what about you? Are you hurt?"

I shrugged. "It was nothing."

It was too late to do anything about the gravel embedded in my knees and clinging to my hair. I tried to stand straight, meet his gaze with a smile, and keep my cane half-hidden beside my leg. Why did meeting someone from the past make me feel like an awkward teenager again? Decades had passed, and I had become a competent, accomplished professional woman. But a "cute boy" showed up, and I felt myself blushing and worrying about my hair.

I cleared my throat. "What are you doing with yourself these days?"

"Well, actually, I'm the local mayor." His eyes twinkled with laughter.

I chuckled. "Still playing politics? Congratulations."

"Yep, worked my way up from the school board."

A car stopped behind his van, honked, and then pulled around the van too fast.

"If you're sure you're all right, I should get out of the way, but I'd love to catch up sometime." He pulled out a wallet and handed me a card. "Give me a call?"

"Sure." It wasn't the *least* likely thing that could happen. I waved as he drove away. The official city vehicle seal showed our little town within the greater urban area, so that's what he meant by "local" mayor. I hoped he was still passionate about doing good and hadn't gotten caught up in the dirty games and greed of politics. It was probably easier to stay true to himself and make effective changes at the local level. If he'd started on the school board, chances were he had kids, and therefore had likely married. I wondered if his wife was anyone I'd known.

I turned back to Simon and Mackenzie, who were watching me with curious expressions.

Mac's smile twitched. "Kitty?"

I sighed. "Not anymore."

I thanked them, got in my car, and drove home with extra care, checking cross traffic at each light. I'd let Simon and Mackenzie believe the close call had been an accident. Enough stupid, distracted drivers filled the roads to make that plausible.

I couldn't believe the timing was merely a coincidence. I'd keep an eye out for any suspects driving something similar, but lots of people probably drove smallish white/silver/gray cars. Even finding someone who owned one would be a long way from proving that person had tried to run me down or that they were involved with whatever was happening at Sunshine Haven.

Back home, I examined my new injuries. I had bruises on my right arm and hip, and scrapes on that hand and elbow. I cleaned them and smoothed antibiotic ointment on the scrapes and pain relief cream on the bruises. Then I changed into a long-sleeved T-shirt to hide the damage. Various body parts ached, background noise to the screaming in my left leg. I hadn't landed on that side, but I must have used the muscles when I jumped, or rather flung myself forward in a stumbling fall. At least I'd been able to do that. Yay, progress.

After a lunch of soup and sandwiches with Dad, I practiced the meditation exercises designed to help with pain and

PTSD. I'm not sure how long I managed before I fell asleep, but I'd earned the nap. Maybe the meditation was helping, because I didn't dream about either the bombing or the car racing toward me. Or maybe I was simply too exhausted to dream.

I was awake but groggy, lying on my bed and massaging my thigh, when the doorbell bonged. I tried to find the energy to sit up.

Dad hollered, "Kate, there's a young woman here to see you."

"Send her up," I yelled back.

We'd have more privacy working in my bedroom. Yeah, it had nothing to do with me not wanting to tackle the stairs.

Murmured voices came closer until Dad and Mackenzie appeared in my doorway.

"Come on in, Mac," I said. "You've met my father? Dad, Mackenzie is going to help me with some research."

I'd intended to come up with a more specific cover story, but somehow, nothing had occurred to me while I slept.

Mackenzie sat cross-legged on the bed next to me, each of us with a laptop. First, I asked her to show me her online research skills by researching her own name. I called it an exercise to see how she'd tackle a background check, but I also wanted to see what came up. She seemed nice, but I hadn't had a chance to check into her. Of course, she might have been able to avoid bringing up anything suspicious about herself, but at least enough items came up to prove that she was who she said she was, complete with scholarships and awards.

I showed her some sites for background checks and credit

checks. Most people would be amazed at what you could find online, often for free. Public records included vehicle records, civil court records, sex offender status, warrants, marriage and divorce records, adoption registries, and property records including deeds, mortgages, and liens. That didn't even include the extensive information most people shared on social media, from their hobbies to their drinking habits.

I had to balance my confidentiality promise to Heather against my need to make progress fast, which required help. I described the phone call warning me to mind my own business. I implied that the call had led me into this investigation, merely as a precaution. The caller might have been overly paranoid about negative publicity, or they might have been trying to hide illicit activity. I claimed I wasn't sure if the caller was a man or a woman, and they hadn't given their name, so we had to check everyone.

I also implied that I wouldn't let anyone tell *me* what to do (true), as if I weren't really suspicious but I didn't like to be threatened. Mackenzie struck me as someone who liked to do things people told her she couldn't or shouldn't do, so I figured she'd relate.

We went over the background checks Sierra had done, identified a few potential suspects, and Mackenzie moved to the desk with her laptop and instructions to dig deeper. Meanwhile, I lay back and thought. Things had been happening quickly and my brain wasn't working at full strength yet. I felt scattered and distracted, pulled in too many directions. I needed to stop reacting to the moment and come up with a plan.

I updated my to-do list:

- Find out about the causes of death. Could anyone have been suffocated or poisoned? What other methods of murder could be mistaken for natural death?
- Interview the families of the people who died and the woman who got sick. Had the family members noticed anything suspicious? Did anyone seem to have a reason for wanting a relative dead? The answers might help me figure out whether the two deaths and the illness were connected. Even if one was murder, the others might be natural, serving only to call attention to the suspicious death by the coincidence of the timing.
- Check into finances. Who benefited from the deaths? If the killer was an "angel of mercy," money probably wouldn't be an issue, but one should never discount greed.

Basically, while Mackenzie looked for suspicious habits or backgrounds to identify *who* might have killed patients, I pondered *why*.

Next, who was trying to stop me from investigating? Was that connected to the deaths, or had I stirred up something entirely different? If someone had tried to run me down because I was investigating the deaths, then the killer already knew I was hunting them, so I could go on the offensive. But the close call with the car might not be related.

- Confront the receptionist who'd been on duty during

my first meeting with Heather. Had she told anyone about that?

- Who had been driving the car?
- Who had called me claiming to be Henry Wilson?

I could start on that last one right away by calling the other two men on the board. It took some time and finagling to get through to them, at which point I pretended to be selling something. Mackenzie gave me a few curious glances but didn't ask questions.

Neither man sounded like the one who had called me, as far as I could tell. On the other hand, neither voice was so different that it couldn't have been the man on the phone, if he'd disguised his voice. Still, it made more sense to lie about being a board member than to lie about which board member you were, so the caller probably wasn't any of them. That was a dead end.

My stomach grumbled. Almost five o'clock. Dad and I hadn't discussed dinner, but he usually ate at six. I considered sending Mackenzie downstairs to scrounge up snacks, but if she was working for free, I should at least make sure she was learning from the experience.

"What have you found out so far?" I asked.

"Focusing on the staff who have the most contact with patients, I've identified four people who raise some questions."

She moved back to the bed so I could see her laptop screen. "Berta Lopez is a physical therapist. She mainly works at the clinic next door, but she also does in-room visits at Sunshine Haven and sometimes fills in for the care staff when someone's on vacation. Looking at her social media activity, she's spending an awful lot of money, far more than she must be earning. She bought a brand-new car last year and went on a cruise last summer. Her mother was a teacher before she died and her father works in construction, so it's probably not family money. If she has a rich sugar daddy, she doesn't talk about him."

Berta was the PT I'd met when I visited the physical therapy office. I'd liked her, but I'd also met violent warlords who were charming. The ability to be pleasant for half an hour didn't prove much.

"Okay, we need to find out where the money's coming from." Could she be stealing from patients? Could she have killed those who got suspicious?

"There's a woman from Bosnia, Ana Marija Jurić, I'm probably not pronouncing that right. Her work visa is almost expired. She's made some complaints on social media about her fear of being deported and the high cost of an immigration lawyer. She seems to blame the government here for making things so difficult." Mackenzie shrugged. "That's not necessarily suspicious, but if she's desperate . . ."

"She could be looking for ways to make extra money. She could even be lashing out in anger, trying to punish her employer or those around her for her problems. On the other hand, she might be working hard to convince Sunshine Haven to fight for her right to stay." I remembered the "hefty gal" with the "rough hands" that Mom didn't like. Dad had thought her name was Gail, but he wasn't sure. "Do you have a picture of her?"

She switched over to an internet browser and brought up

Facebook. "Her profile picture is a flower and most of her posts are text only. I could keep looking."

"Don't worry about it." I could find the woman at Sunshine Haven. She still didn't seem that suspicious, but if she was the one Mom didn't like *and* she had a grudge, she might be worth a closer look. "All right, who's next?"

Mackenzie clicked back to her notes and scrolled down the screen. "Maximilian Richards is on probation for drug charges. He's been working at the home for three years. The drug arrest was eighteen months ago. I'll bet he would've lost his job if he hadn't pleaded no contest and plea-bargained for probation. As it was, I think he was demoted. He has to clean up after patients, deal with dirty diapers, things like that. He's told some stomach-churning stories on his blog."

"He posts publicly about his job? That could make his bosses angry."

"Well, he only blogs as Nurse Max, and he calls the nursing home The Asylum, but it wasn't hard to trace the connection. And he's not critical, really, just honest about the, um, less glamorous aspects. His stories are pretty funny."

"Still, two strikes against him. It sounds like he's disgruntled about his job, and if he has a drug problem, he could be trying to steal money, drugs, or both."

She nodded. "And the last one is really interesting. Felicity Carver. One of the few registered nurses on staff, rather than nursing assistants. Nothing at all suspicious about her current activities, but she has no past. She seems to have appeared about five years ago. No address before that, no public records, no social media activity. Nothing."

"Huh. Heather, the director of Sunshine Haven, might

know about her. This woman can't have applied for a job without a history of employment and education."

"Witness protection maybe?"

"I guess. If that's the case, we'll have to be careful not to expose her."

"I try not to leave any trace of my online investigations," Mackenzie said. "You know, some people are in witness protection because they know a lot about crime. They're not always innocent victims."

A knock sounded on the door. I jumped and hoped Dad hadn't overheard any of our conversation.

"Come in," I said.

The door swung open. "I wanted to know how many for dinner," Dad said.

I looked at Mackenzie. "You're welcome to stay."

I hoped that was true. I figured Dad wouldn't have asked if he wasn't going to have enough food.

"No, thanks. I should get going, unless you want me to do something else."

"That's enough for today. Thanks, Dad. I'll be down in a few minutes."

He pulled the door closed.

I lowered my voice. "Let me think about all this and decide our next steps. What's your schedule for the rest of the week?"

"I have class tomorrow morning at ten," Mackenzie said. "I'm supposed to do some computer upgrades for a local company in the afternoon, but I can put it off if necessary."

"No, I'll try not to interfere with the work that actually pays your bills unless it's urgent. I'll call you when I have a plan."

"All right. Thanks. This was interesting." She closed her laptop and put on her shoes.

I stretched my leg a few times and got to my feet. I lurched to the doorway and grabbed the wall, graceful as a newborn giraffe. My right shoulder ached, and my hand and elbow stung. At any given time in the last two decades, I'd had a few bruises and scrapes, but the most recent ones bothered me more. Maybe because the injury seemed stupid, crossing the street in a quiet Arizona neighborhood, rather than dodging bullets or scrambling through rubble. Maybe because I'd been sitting around instead of on the go, distracted by the next course of action. Maybe it was the chilling knowledge that if it hadn't been a simple accident—if someone had targeted me—it meant I had stirred up a snake, and the place where my mother lived might be dangerous.

Or maybe I was simply getting old and tired and weak.

I pushed that thought away and took some more ibuprofen before I followed Mackenzie downstairs. I let her out and found Dad and Harlequin in the kitchen.

"Can I help?" I asked.

"Your sister left us lasagna." He opened the oven and a delicious smell of melted cheese wafted out.

I should have been grateful, but that was not the emotion rising in me. Jen had told me in no uncertain terms that it was now my turn to take care of Mom and Dad, but apparently, she didn't trust me to do it. Of course, I hadn't done anything about grocery shopping or cooking. I'd been too busy trying to make sure the nursing home wasn't putting our mother in danger. But Jen didn't know that, so she probably assumed I was being lazy.

I sighed. Being a sibling was complicated. I spotted the paper label for the lasagna on the counter, so at least she'd bought it premade. It was hard enough to compete with Jen when it came to organization and helping others. I didn't need her flaunting home cooking too.

Dad set the lasagna on the stovetop. "Do anything interesting today?"

"Um, I bought a laptop. Thanks for the tip on Simon's store."

"No problem. That's what family and friends do—share information." He wasn't facing me, but his voice sounded grumpy.

"Right . . . how about you? Anything interesting happen today?"

He turned, leaned against the counter, and crossed his arms. "Well, I found out that my daughter was almost hit by a car, and she didn't tell me."

Chapter Seven

I STARED AT him with my mouth hanging open. "How did you—oh, Simon."

He nodded. "He was worried about you. He told his grandfather, who called me."

The speed of the grapevine was both impressive and annoying, but I shouldn't have been surprised. Our city might now be part of the larger Phoenix metro area, but in some ways, it was a small town. I curled my hand to hide the scrape and resisted the urge to rub my shoulder, which suddenly throbbed as if it wanted to join the discussion. "It wasn't a big deal. I'm fine."

"You still should have told me."

I felt about thirteen again, squirming and avoiding his gaze. "I didn't want you to worry."

"I'm your father. It's my job to worry."

"You already have so much to worry about, with Mom and, well . . ."

"And you almost getting killed two months ago?" He sat diagonally from me. "I'm incredibly grateful that you came home alive, but I'm not a fool. I know Ms. Garcia wanted to talk to you about something important. I know you're working on some project, and now you have this assistant, who I hope can keep you out of trouble better than I can. But don't you think I'll worry if I don't know what's happening?"

"I didn't mean . . . it's only that I've been on my own for so long." It wouldn't comfort him to know how many times I'd had a close call or minor injury and hadn't told my parents. "You're right. I'm sorry."

I had been foolish to think I could keep things hidden from him. Moreover, I had been unfair. I could argue that he might or might not need to know about a potential killer at Sunshine Haven, balancing Mom's safety against confidentiality and keeping quiet to avoid alerting the potential killer. But Dad deserved to know, maybe needed to know, what was happening in my life. He had always been supportive, even when I knew he feared for my safety. He'd never told me I couldn't or shouldn't do something. I needed to return the favor.

He slumped back in his chair. "If we're going to be roommates for a while, maybe we should set some ground rules. I assume you don't want me to give you a curfew or warn you about boys."

I had to smile. "No."

"I don't want you to treat me like a child either. I understand, with your mother the way she is, it might be tempting. Your sister certainly seems to think she's the adult now. But I still have all my wits about me."

My heart squeezed. "Dad . . ." I placed my hand on the table between us.

He put his hand over mine. "I'd like to help. Tell me, am I too old to help?"

"Of course not." I took a deep breath. "I'll tell you everything, but you have to keep it confidential, and you can't do anything until we discuss it first." I winced at giving my father orders. How did Jen dare to boss around the people who'd raised her? But I was responsible for this investigation, and even equal peers had to divide authority sometimes.

"Fair enough." He rested his elbows on the table and leaned forward with a grin that made him look ten years younger. Maybe this distraction would be good for him. If he felt helpless over Mom's condition, protecting her from danger could be empowering.

I told him about Heather's concerns and the strange phone call. I described my meeting with Henry Wilson and gave an overview of the research Mac and I had done. Harlequin jumped on the counter when he thought we weren't looking. Dad grabbed the cat in time to save the lasagna. Harlequin paced and muttered complaints as Dad covered the lasagna and put it back in the warm oven. Throughout all this, Dad listened and asked intelligent questions.

I wound down and gave Dad a minute to process everything.

He sat and nodded a few times. "Is this what your life has been like for the past thirty years?"

"Not exactly. When I was based in the US and in Europe, I mainly did political reporting, not crime." I chuckled. "Those years in the Middle East had challenges, but it was actually pretty rare that someone tried to kill me."

Dad drew in a sharp breath.

Whoops, maybe that wasn't as funny as I'd meant it to

be. "If that's what happened today. It could be a coincidence."

He shook his head. "I doubt it."

"Still, the driver could have been trying to scare me rather than remove me from the picture. If they were trying to kill me, they did a terrible job of it. There's a reason they haven't made a movie called *Attack of the Killer Compact*."

"Maybe."

I replayed the event in my mind. "Thinking back, the car didn't even clip me, and I'm not that agile these days. It should have bumped me, caught my foot or something, if the driver was aiming straight at me."

One look at Dad's face told me he wasn't entirely comforted.

"I'll be careful," I said. "You should be too. Help me keep an eye out for anything suspicious. Make sure we lock the doors and windows. Watch out for suspicious people claiming they need to fix the phones or check for termites, that kind of thing. Don't give information to strangers, even if they claim to know me."

"It's like being in a movie!" Dad laughed, but the smile quickly faded. "You haven't told Jen any of this."

"No. I . . . I don't think that's a good idea." How could I word my complaints about her, how she'd overreact, criticize, and try to do everything her way?

"It's your call." Dad patted his lap and Harlequin jumped into it. "I wish you girls . . . well, maybe someday. What else? How can I help? It sounds like you have a lot to check, but I wouldn't know where to start with that online research."

"I have Mackenzie for that." I leaned back and thought out loud. "I'd like to know more about our suspects. Right now, it seems like anyone could be doing anything. We don't know if someone is killing patients, and if so, what that person's motive is. We don't know if the fake Henry Wilson is involved in patient deaths, or if he has a guilty conscience over something else. That means, we don't even know how many crimes we're investigating, if any."

Harlequin put his front paws on Dad's chest. "You have too many questions."

Harlequin meowed as if in answer.

"And too many suspects," I said. "But some things that look suspicious may have simple explanations. If I . . . if *we* can reduce the list of people to investigate, we can focus on the most likely culprits. That does mean more internet research but also talking to people or maybe following them."

"I can help with that. In fact, all the fellows could help. They'd like to, I'm sure."

Uh-oh, what had I started? "Dad, it has to be confidential."

"We don't have to tell them everything. We can ask them to follow specific people, find out certain things. They won't ask why if we say it's a secret. The men in my coffee group may be old retired guys, but we have a lot of life experience. And a lot of free time."

Having a whole group of helpers might save time and effort, or it might turn the investigation into a Keystone Cops comedy. "I don't want to put anyone in danger."

"I'll make sure they understand, but we've survived this

long. Most of them will think it's fun, being private detectives for a while."

I pictured a bunch of seniors in trench coats and fedoras. "Sherlock Holmes had his Baker Street Irregulars, the ragtag kids who gathered information for him. I get an old guys brigade?"

"We could call ourselves the Coffee Shop Irregulars." He chuckled. "Although at our age, we spend a lot of time trying to be 'regular'!"

Men. No matter how old they got, they still loved a poop joke.

"Let me think about it before you say anything to them. I'm not sure how we'd use that many people. Since everyone we're investigating works at Sunshine Haven, we need people who can get in there without raising suspicion."

"Joe and Marty Washington visit your mother every week."

"Simon's grandparents?" Why was I surprised to hear that Mom had friends visiting? It was nice that they hadn't forgotten her, even as she was forgetting them.

He nodded. "The four of us used to go out for dinner every Wednesday. Marty was in your mom's book club, and they played that game the ladies like, bunko."

I'd never heard of that game. My parents' secret lives. "I gather you trust them."

"With my life. Literally, Joe and I were in the service together. And Martha—well, you'll like Marty."

"Was she the one who ran the computer store until Simon took over?"

"Right. Clever woman. Ahead of her time."

"And her name is really Martha Washington?"

"Yes, and she's heard all the jokes before."

"I see why she goes by Marty." It sounded like Dad had known them for decades. He'd been in the Marines before I was born. "Why haven't I met them before?"

"We fell out of touch when we had kids. Most of our friends were your friends' parents. Joe and Marty's kids were a few years older."

Harlequin jumped down. Dad brushed his hands on his pants, which didn't do much to remove hair from either the hands or the pants.

"You were away by the time we reconnected," Dad said. "These last few years, in retirement, we started seeing each other more."

I'd missed out on a lot of my parents' lives. We talked on the phone every couple of weeks, but somehow, I'd assumed they weren't changing, even though I was. I'd have to make the most of this chance to get to know my father again.

"Okay, the Washingtons are in."

It was a good compromise. We had some extra help but not too many people, which could get confusing and hard to control. Should I include Simon as well? That way, I wouldn't be asking so much of his girlfriend and grandparents when it came to keeping secrets.

I held off on that decision. I'd already expanded my PI team from one (me) to five, with Mac, Dad, and the Washingtons. If I kept going at this rate, I might as well announce my "secret" investigation on the nightly news.

"We can use the same cover story I used with Mac. I got the suspicious phone call from the man claiming to be Henry

Wilson. Now, I want to know if something sketchy is going on. We won't mention the suspicious deaths or that Heather asked me to investigate."

"I'll ask them to come here in the morning, okay?"

"Eight a.m.? I'll see if Mac can stop by before her class and we'll have a council of war."

We smiled at each other. Who knew that being colleagues and friends could bring us closer than being father and daughter?

USING THE PRESCRIPTION painkillers only at night helped me sleep, while sticking to over-the-counter meds during the day left my mind clear, or at least clearer. If they didn't help as much with my leg, and all my other current twinges, well, I could tell myself the pain kept me alert. That sounded better than "can't truly relax for even a second."

I should have gone into marketing.

In any case, I almost felt like my old self when we gathered around the kitchen table in the morning—my father, Joe and Marty Washington, Mackenzie, me, and a box of rapidly disappearing doughnuts. After I asked three times if anyone needed more coffee without getting out of my chair, Mac took the hint and poured refills, and the chatter faded.

"Thanks for being here," I said. "Let me explain what we're doing." I described the mysterious phone call. They already knew about the car causing my fall, so I didn't mention it, but no doubt they filed that under suspicious circumstance as well. "I'm ninety percent sure the man who called me wasn't actually Henry Wilson. That means the field is wide open. And of course, if there's something suspicious at the home—embezzlement, stealing drugs, or whatever—more than one person could be involved. Mac and I have identified some employees with suspicious backgrounds."

I paused. Would anyone question our cover story?

Joe, who looked a little like Simon but with darker skin, no freckles, and white hair, said, "I always wondered how well those places did background checks. Too many ways you can hide things." Did he suspect he wasn't getting the whole story? If so, he seemed willing to play along.

Marty Washington nodded. "You want to know who's taking care of your family. Or you, if it comes to that." A plump, lovely woman, she could have been any age over fifty. Her dark hair had been straightened and smoothed into waves. She must have dyed it, if she was eighty.

"I'll let Mackenzie describe what we found," I said. "She'll be in charge of collecting and organizing your reports."

This would be good leadership practice for her.

She cleared her throat and took a sip of coffee, but her voice was steady as she passed out a list of suspects and described the puzzles revealed by online research.

- Berta Lopez, physical therapist spending more money than she earns.
- Felicity Carver, registered nurse, no past prior to five years ago.
- Ana Marija Jurić, nursing assistant, Bosnian

immigrant with a work visa about to expire.

- Maximilian (Max) Richards, nursing assistant, on probation for drug charges.

- Heather Garcia, director. We didn't have anything specific against her, but I wanted to make sure she wasn't maneuvering me for reasons of her own. I said I'd added her to the list simply because as the director, she should know what was going on at the place she ran.

In addition, I still wondered how the fake Henry Wilson had learned about my first meeting with Heather. Since the home was open to visitors seven days a week, at any time of day, it had multiple receptionists. According to the employee records, June Songpole should have been on duty at the time in question, so she seemed the likely spy. But since I wasn't telling Mac or the Washingtons about my deal with Heather, I didn't tell them my suspicions of the receptionist either. I'd tackle her on my own.

As they discussed the information, I nibbled another doughnut. A piece of frosting dropped to the floor. I leaned to pick it up and bit back a cry of pain. I surreptitiously nudged the chunk of frosting toward the wall with my foot. I'd take care of it later with a broom.

"I have home addresses for everyone," Mac said. "You know where they work, but some of them may not work a regular schedule. When you're visiting Sunshine Haven, find an excuse to chat with people. We might also arrange some 'accidental' meetings outside work. Use your imagination."

"But don't get carried away," I said. "Your safety comes

first. And keep in mind, each of these people is probably innocent. We don't want to upset or embarrass them."

We also didn't want a lawsuit or a news story because we accidentally slandered someone in the course of our investigation.

"If you find anything odd, let Mac or me know," I said. "We'll decide on the next step."

"Should we divide up suspects to follow?" Joe Washington asked.

"Honestly, a stakeout isn't nearly as much fun as it sounds. You could follow someone around for days and learn nothing. Any crime is likely to be happening behind closed doors and possibly only visible on a computer."

"How do you uncover anything then?" Marty asked.

I shrugged. "Luck. Tips. And poking sticks into dark corners to see if anything wriggles. I've already stirred up one snake." I made eye contact with each of them in turn. "I want you all to be safe. Use your charm to get people talking, but don't let them know you're investigating anything. You're my secret weapons. But someone is anxious about my presence, and I can use that. I'm going to get more aggressive with my questions. The man who called me was already jumpy. I'll see if I can get him to jump higher."

Everyone was silent for a moment. They looked worried.

"May I make a suggestion?" Joe asked.

"Of course." As long as he didn't tell me to leave the danger to the men.

"Let someone know where you'll be and what you're planning to do. And if someone sends you a note asking for a secret meeting and telling you to destroy the note, don't do it."

I laughed. "I'll keep you informed."

"Really, Kate," Dad said. "Let someone know before you go anywhere alone or meet anyone."

"That's a sensible precaution," I said. "It applies to all of us. We won't always know who we're going to talk to, since some of this will depend on running into people at Sunshine Haven. Let's make Mac the point of contact if you need to report that you're going to follow anyone or take any chances at all."

"You can call, text, or e-mail me," Mac said. "We'll meet tomorrow to see where everyone is. Any questions?"

"Do we get codenames?" Joe asked.

Mac's eyes danced, but she kept her tone serious. "I don't think that's necessary."

"You don't mind if we use them among ourselves?"

"Uh, no, have at it."

"I have some good ideas," Joe said.

His wife gave him a stern look. "No assigning codenames without approval from the person getting the name."

While they bantered about that, Mackenzie left for her class.

I snagged the last doughnut and thought about how to prod the snakes out into the light.

Chapter Eight

THE WASHINGTONS HEADED to Sunshine Haven. Dad and I followed a few minutes later. With several people visiting Mom at once, it might not seem as odd if someone wandered off and chatted with the staff.

In the parking lot, I scanned the cars. Some must belong to visitors or patients at the physical therapy offices. Even if the car that had almost hit me belonged to an employee, they might not be working this shift, or they might have more than one vehicle. Still, maybe I'd spot some bumper sticker or mark on the car that I'd only noticed subconsciously. The lot held half a dozen smallish gray or silver cars, and several more white ones. None caused me to say, "Aha!"

I could only keep an eye out and use car color as one small point of reference if we narrowed our suspect list.

As we passed the reception desk, I waved the others on while I stayed behind to talk to June Songpole. Her smooth, young face, framed by black hair, was only vaguely familiar. How had I missed her silvery-gray eyes, even when I'd been doped up on pain meds three days before? But her regular schedule would have put her at the desk during my first visit.

I leaned on the desk to take some weight off my leg and gave her my best tough reporter stare. "You were here the other day, when I spent some time with my old friend Heather."

Her eyes widened. "Yes?"

"Who did you tell about our chat?"

Her gaze darted side to side. "I didn't . . ." She sat up straighter and firmed her expression. "I'm not a gossip. Mr. Mendelson always warns us about that."

"Mr. Mendelson?"

"He's the memory care program coordinator."

"What does that mean?" We were already off topic. Curiosity is a curse.

"He trains the care staff and volunteers to ensure each patient gets the right care plan." June shuffled some things on the desk. Her long, painted fingernails had little stars on them. "Oh, and he screens new patients and explains things to the families."

"Okay." I needed to get back on track. "So he wouldn't approve of you gossiping."

She shook her head. "No, he's always talking about patient confidentiality."

"That's fine, but I'm not a patient. And you did tell someone about my meeting with Heather, didn't you?"

"Honestly, I wouldn't gossip!" June lowered her voice. "Please don't get me in trouble. I wouldn't do anything to hurt anyone here, honestly."

I didn't entirely trust anyone who felt the need to use "honestly" that often, but if she had mentioned my meeting to someone, she was too frightened to admit it. Maybe I should have tried a gentler approach. After all, she was a young American office worker, not a suspected terrorist or military commander.

Did I know any gentler approaches? None came to mind.

I eased off the desk. "All right, I'm going to talk to Ms. Garcia now, if she's available."

The girl's eyes widened.

I sighed. "I won't complain about you, but make sure you don't gossip about your boss's meetings either. She wouldn't like that."

June nodded. "I'll let her know you're here." She picked up her phone and pushed a few buttons. She gave my name, so she knew who I was. "You can go back."

I went in Heather's office and closed the door. I would've liked to know if June called anyone to report my presence, but I couldn't spy on her and keep my conversation with Heather private at the same time.

I limped toward Heather's desk. "I have some questions."

"I thought we weren't supposed to talk while I'm at work."

"That ship has sailed. I believe someone already thinks I'm investigating. And they don't like it."

She blew out a long breath. "That's not good. What am I going to do? If one of our staff has been killing patients, we'll be ruined."

I plopped into the chair across from her. "Not to mention people dying."

"Yes, of course, and we can't let it happen again." She sighed. "I sound callous, but I want this place to succeed, to be a great home for patients, and I . . . we can't afford more scandal."

"*More* scandal?"

She winced. "We reorganized some time back to improve patient care. We'd had some complaints."

That was a dodge if I'd ever heard one, but I'd likely get more from news archives than pressing her. I settled back into the chair and stretched out my legs. "There's no guarantee yet that you have a killer."

"But if someone is worried about you investigating, doesn't that mean they're guilty?"

"Probably, but guilty of what?"

She shook her head. "You've lost me."

"Someone seems to be anxious, maybe even panicked, simply because they know I'm a journalist, and you and I talked. You're focused on the deaths because that's what has you worried. But how would anyone know I was investigating *that*? Unless your office really is bugged and they heard the whole conversation."

She peered around the room. "Can you check?"

"Sorry, journalist, not spy. If anything, I'm usually the one doing the recording. But I wouldn't worry. How would they know to bug the office in advance? They'd have to be . . ." She wouldn't like the idea that someone had been spying on her long term. "Anyway, the point is, I've stirred up someone, which suggests something illicit. Could be illegal, could be legal but secret, like an extramarital affair. Could be related to the deaths, could be something else entirely. I don't want to make assumptions yet."

She placed her hands palm-down on the desk. "So I don't have to bring the police in yet?"

"I don't have anything solid, so let's wait on that. I need to know more about the patients who died, and the woman who got sick. Symptoms, who was on duty, that sort of thing. And I want to talk to the families."

"I shouldn't—but—give me an hour and I'll see what I can do." She drummed her fingers on the desk. "In the meantime, if you're here to visit your mother, you might take her to the sunroom. It's a lovely space and a lot of the families enjoy sitting there to visit. In fact, Mrs. Gregorian's family came in a little while ago, and they always take her there."

"Mrs. Gregorian?"

"Yes, you probably won't get much out of her, but you might like speaking to her family. They can tell you about her experiences here. How she was treated when she was sick, for example." She raised her eyebrows and I could practically see the thought bubble over her head yelling, *Hint, hint!*

The spirit of confidentiality might be broken, but at least Heather had avoided telling me flat out that Mrs. Gregorian was the patient who'd gotten sick but recovered.

"All right, thanks." I rose, took two steps, and turned back. "One more thing. Do you know any employees who drive a silver or gray car?"

She stared. "Probably several of them. Can you be more specific?"

"Unfortunately, no."

She shrugged. "My Taurus might fit, depending on how broad you want to go with the color. Officially, I think it's called champagne. Why?"

"Never mind." If all else failed, I'd get someone watching the parking lot, or maybe tracking down registrations. I'd followed slimmer leads before. Though not often.

Mom's room was packed. Between my parents, the Washingtons, and to my surprise, my sister, I could barely get in the door. I greeted Mom and suggested we move to the sunroom.

"We were waiting for you, so you'd know where to find us," Dad said.

Jen helped Mom stand, but then Dad edged between them, offered Mom his arm, and led her out. The Washingtons followed, while I lingered behind with Jen, who glared at me for some mysterious reason.

"I didn't expect you here today," I said.

"Mom had an appointment to get her toenails trimmed. Someone had to be here to make sure they did it right."

"I thought you wanted me to take over stuff like that." Not that I particularly wanted to, but she'd made it clear that it was *my turn*.

"Would you have done it?"

"If I'd known about it." It had never occurred to me that someone would need an appointment to get their toenails clipped, or that such a momentous event couldn't happen without our supervision.

Jen huffed out a sigh. "If I have to explain everything, it's easier to do it myself." She stomped out of the room.

I closed my eyes and took a couple of deep breaths. I really didn't have the time or patience to deal with her issues right now. On the other hand, I didn't have the tolerance to put up with them long term. Add "sort this hostility with Jen" to the to-do list. Way, way at the bottom.

She stood outside the door, hands on hips. "Do you even know where the sunroom is?"

"I suspect I could have found it. I am a journalist, you know. I do have some ability to uncover simple facts."

Jen rolled her eyes. "If you want to make sure Mom is getting good care, you can't merely stop by once in a while to chat with her. You need to be on top of everything. This place is better than most, at least now, but the only way we got Mom in at this price was because of the reputation it had two years ago. They seem to be trying hard, but for how long? They'll start cutting back on staff to save money again, and patients like Mom will suffer." She hurried down the hall. I could barely keep up with her pace and also process her words. She turned at a wide doorway and entered a large, sunny room with clusters of tables and chairs. She paused to look around.

I grabbed her arm. "What kind of problems did the place have before?"

She twitched her arm away. "Poorly trained staff and not enough of them. Patients got urinary tract infections because their diapers weren't changed, or gum infections because their dentures weren't cleaned. One woman got sores on her feet from wearing the same compression stockings for weeks."

"What?" My stomach clenched. I'd seen people suffering from hygiene-related illnesses and wounds, but I didn't expect it in America, at a nursing home supposedly run by medical staff.

Jen hugged herself tightly. "Horrible stuff. Some patients were heavily sedated and only allowed to leave their rooms with a family member. That was the staff's way of making sure no one got injured in a fall, but what an awful way to live."

"They can do that?"

She blinked moist eyes. "No, but yes. It's called medical restraint, using drugs to keep people immobile like that. It's illegal, but there's a clause about using the minimum means necessary for safety, and it was abused."

I leaned heavily on my cane to keep from collapsing under the weight of this new knowledge. "But it's not like that now?"

"Not since the lawsuit." Jen gave herself a little shake and strode across the room to join our parents.

I slumped against the wall, thinking about what she'd said. I'd heard horror stories about nursing homes before, but the topic had never been a particular interest of mine. Children dying in war was a bigger issue. But now that my mother was in this facility, the problems of caring for an aging population took on greater meaning.

Heather must have quite a job, trying to keep patients healthy, family members happy, and costs reasonable. If Sunshine Haven had received such bad press a couple of years earlier, no wonder she worried about its reputation.

How long had she been working here? Had she been part of the problem, or only part of the solution?

The answer might turn up in her background check. In the meantime, I needed to identify Mrs. Gregorian and her family. The room held two groups besides ours. Three elderly people, possibly all patients, sat at a table playing cards while a heavyset woman in a white uniform looked over a man's shoulder. They probably weren't the Gregorians, but the woman might be one of the nursing staff we wanted to investigate.

Joe Washington strolled toward me.

I said softly, "Check that woman's name tag, and if she's on our suspect list, listen in a bit."

He nodded and kept wandering the room, as if admiring the views from the windows.

The other group had a white-haired woman with a walker next to her chair, a man and a woman probably in their fifties, and a girl who might have been in high school. The women were all seated, the older two holding hands while the girl talked animatedly. The man stood behind them, glancing around and shuffling restlessly. He might welcome an interruption.

I made eye contact as I approached.

"Hi, I'm Kate Tessler, Ursula's daughter." I nodded toward my mother.

He gave Mom a split-second glance. "Quincy Russo."

"Is that your mother?"

"Mother-in-law."

So it might be Mrs. Gregorian.

We chatted about the place in general. He clearly didn't like Sunshine Haven much, but that seemed to be his discomfort at being in a nursing home, rather than specific complaints. His wife gave me puzzled looks, but Quincy seemed happy to have someone to talk to. Meanwhile, the young woman described a recent dance recital. Across the room, Joe Washington laughed with the nurse and her charges. Dad and Marty Washington visited with my mother, while Jen glared at me.

Finally, I asked Quincy, "What happens if she gets sick

or injured? Or haven't you had that problem yet?"

"Oh, she was real sick not long ago." He glanced at his mother-in-law with an odd expression. "Recovered, though."

His wife stood to join us. "You're talking about when Mom was sick?"

I nodded. "My mother is new here, and I want to make sure they'll take care of her properly."

"Of course. We were so worried about Mom. Her recovery was a miracle."

Quincy grunted.

"That sounds pretty serious," I said. "What did she have?"

"We never did find out. They called us because Mom was vomiting. We figured stomach flu or food poisoning, but the nurse insisted no one else was sick. And then Mom went unconscious."

"Not exactly," her husband said.

"Close enough."

I looked between them. "What happened?"

"They called it stupor," Quincy said. "We could wake her up, but she kept dozing off again. I mean, she's usually out of it, but this was extreme. You couldn't keep her attention for more than a few seconds."

"Sounds scary. I'm glad she got better." I gazed at the patient, trying to think of additional questions.

She was slim and I thought she'd be tall, although it was hard to tell since she was sitting with her shoulders hunched forward. She had fluffy white hair, oversized glasses, and a yellow sweatsuit. As I watched, her eyes drifted closed and her head dipped forward.

The young woman said, "Mom, I think Gran is tired."

"Let's get her back to her room."

The two women roused the patient, who seemed surprised to see them, and helped her stand at her walker. They stayed close to her as she shuffled toward the doorway. I got a glance at her nametag and confirmed that I'd found Mrs. Gregorian.

Quincy lingered behind, watching them. He said softly, perhaps to himself, "It would have been better if she'd died."

I stared at him.

Quincy quirked a half smile and shrugged. "Someday, you'll understand."

He strode after his family.

Surely, if he'd tried to kill his mother-in-law, he wouldn't have spoken like that to a stranger. Was he simply tired of visiting Sunshine Haven? Tired of the expense, the time spent, the worry? Did he think his mother-in-law's life was pointless now?

I looked at my family. Would I ever get to the point where I thought Mom would be better off dead? Where her passing would be a relief?

Alzheimer's patients could live for years. That had seemed a comfort at first. It was a horrible disease but not an immediate death sentence. Now, I imagined visiting day after day, watching Mom slip away, while we fought to give her as much comfort as possible.

I shook away those thoughts and reviewed what the Gregorians had said about the illness. Vomiting and a stupor. She'd recovered, even though they didn't know what was wrong. But it wasn't clear if Mrs. Gregorian had been treated somehow.

I hurried after the family, dodging around a man who'd entered the room in the last few minutes. I spotted Quincy heading into one of the patient rooms. When I got there, I rapped on the open door.

"Sorry to interrupt. I wondered, when she recovered, did they do anything for her, or did she get better on her own?"

Quincy shrugged.

His wife looked thoughtful. "You know, she actually seemed to get better after her dialysis treatment."

"Oh, she gets dialysis? That's for kidney failure, right?"

The woman nodded. "She's been getting dialysis for over a year now, every Monday morning. The doctor didn't want to delay her treatment, even though she was so sick Sunday night. She seemed a lot better Monday afternoon, although maybe it's a coincidence."

"Interesting. Well, thank you." I backed into the hall-way.

My foot landed on something and a grunt ruffled my hair. I shifted my weight to regain my balance and twisted toward the man I'd passed as I left the sunroom. I skirted around him. "Sorry," I muttered, although if he didn't want people stepping on him, he shouldn't hover so close.

He walked beside me and spoke in a low voice. "I would appreciate it if you didn't bother the other patients and their families."

"Excuse me?" I stopped and turned to face him head-on. He was about forty, wearing a button-up sweater over a dress shirt, which seemed a bit warm for Arizona, even inside in November. He wouldn't have stood out in a crowd—

medium build, brown hair, plain face, wire-rimmed glasses. He smelled like a type of laundry detergent I particularly hate because it reminds me of cat pee.

"I wasn't 'bothering' anyone," I said. "I was simply making conversation."

He lifted his chin. That was the only way he could look down his nose at me, since he was only a few inches taller. "I heard you asking about Mrs. Gregorian's illness. That was a difficult time for the family. You brought up bad memories."

"They seemed willing to talk about it. And I have a right to ask other patients and their families about their experiences here."

He gave a little hmph. It wasn't quite the same as the throat clearing from the fake Henry Wilson. I tried to compare his voice to the one I remembered and could only decide they might be the same, if he'd been trying to sound different before. This man seemed more soft-spoken and prim, less confident and blustery, but neither had a noticeable accent.

"In the common rooms, perhaps, but please stay out of patient rooms," he said. "If you have questions, you may ask me. We take patient confidentiality and privacy seriously, and I don't want to see anyone upset or disturbed."

"And you are?" I asked, even though I had a guess.

He frowned. "Norman Mendelson, memory care program coordinator. You can make an appointment to see me any weekday, and I'll answer all questions you have about patient care." He strode away.

So I'd met the man the receptionist mentioned, the one so concerned about confidentiality. I was generally in favor of privacy. Still, I had to wonder—was this obsession designed to protect the patients?

Or was it to hide wrongdoing?

Chapter Nine

I SHOOK MY head and returned to the sunroom. Joe
Washington was chatting with the nurse and her table of
patients. Mom, seated next to Marty Washington, looked in
my direction. Could she see me from there? Did she know
who I was?

I needed to sit. My leg trembled with fatigue. I headed
toward my family.

Marty rose. "Take my seat, honey. I'm going to find the
ladies' room." She winked as she passed by.

Dad got up as well. "I'll show you the way."

I sat next to Mom. "Have you been having a good visit,
Mom?"

"Oh yes. She's a very nice lady."

Did she actually recognize Mrs. Washington, or did she
think she'd met a nice stranger? "I guess you've been friends
for a long time."

"Since our husbands were in service together." She
looked vaguely around the room. "So long ago."

At least she remembered that. Didn't patients with Alzheimer's or dementia often have much clearer memories of
their pasts than of what had happened recently? I'd done
some research when I first got the news of Mom's diagnosis,

but that had been a couple months ago, and more recent events had knocked it out of my mind. More detailed research on Alzheimer's was another item for my to-do list.

In the meantime, how could I talk to my mother? I couldn't tell her most of what I'd been doing, and I doubted she'd been doing much of interest. News and current events weren't good topics either. I glanced at Jen, who simply crossed her arms and gave me a challenging look. No help there.

I mentally searched for an appropriate topic, until Mom said, "I'm scared."

Jen and I exchanged startled glances.

"What are you afraid of?" I asked.

"What if I don't have enough money? I don't want to tell your father. He'd worry."

"You don't need to think about money," I said. "Everything's taken care of."

In truth, I had only a vague understanding of the financial situation. I hadn't been involved with that from overseas. My meager savings wouldn't support me, let alone my parents.

But we'd care for Mom one way or another.

Mom leaned close and whispered, "But what if he wants more?"

When I raised my eyebrows at Jen, she shrugged and shook her head. I put my arm around my mother.

"Who, Mom? Tell me exactly what's bothering you." Maybe it was nothing, her imagination or some memory from the distant past.

She blinked at me. "The lady in my hall, Mrs. . . . I'm

not sure. She said that man told her she had to pay more, or she'd be kicked out."

"Kicked out of where?"

"Here, of course. Where else?" She squinted at me as if I was the one not making sense.

"Okay, one of your neighbors here at Sunshine Haven"—I waved a hand around the room—"one of the other people living here said this?"

Mom nodded. "The man told her he needed more money. Five hundred dollars!"

"Who is this man?"

Five hundred dollars was a relatively small amount. Maybe someone was late on her payments or had special costs. But surely, any employee would talk to the family, not the Alzheimer's patient, about financial problems.

"Oh, what's his name? Mr. . . . Mr. Brown? No, Rogers. That's it. I think."

I didn't remember either Brown or Rogers on the employee list. I'd have to take another look. Had Mom given me a clue to something shady at Sunshine Haven? Or was she merely confused? Even if Mom was relaying things accurately, the neighbor might have been mistaken or paranoid, or she might have really owed some money.

"Don't worry, Mom. If anyone says you need to pay more, you tell us. All right? We'll take care of everything."

She patted my hand. "You're a good girl. We were so worried about you."

Worried about my recent injury, or something else, maybe my entire career? She hadn't liked me being so far away in a dangerous job. I hugged her gently.

"I'm here now. No more worrying." Funny, my voice sounded odd as I said it. I blinked a few times and avoided looking at Jen.

Joe Washington wandered back over and entertained us with stories from the "old days." Mom was lively and laughing, and she seemed to remember the stories she'd heard before, as well as the events where she'd been present. Maybe when talking with her I should ignore today and reminisce about the past. That might help me connect with my mother now.

Of course, our past together was . . . complicated. We loved each other, but we hadn't always gotten along, and I'd spent most of my life working thousands of miles away in part so Mom couldn't nag and meddle as much.

Now I wished she could keep meddling for decades.

Marty Washington and Dad finally came back, but if either of them had been in the bathroom that whole time, they needed to increase their fiber intake. Mom seemed tired, so Dad escorted her to her room with the Washingtons trailing behind them.

Jen blocked my path.

"What was that all about?" she asked.

"The money thing? I have no idea. I take it you don't know of any financial problems."

She tossed her head. "We're fine. I studied the paperwork thoroughly. No, I'm talking about the fact that you come to visit Mom and spend half the time wandering around talking to other people."

I drew back. "I think that's an exaggeration."

I'd been with Heather five minutes or so, and I'd certainly spent much more time sitting with Mom than talking to the Gregorians. Granted, I hadn't *talked* a lot with Mom, but I'd been present.

Jen sighed. "I just think that if you're going to visit Mom, you should visit Mom. Isn't that why you're here?"

Well, no, not entirely. Unfortunately, I couldn't explain to Jen why I'd been interested in other patients. Secrecy was a lot harder with family around.

I tried to think of an explanation she might accept. "Look, you had a chance to check out this place before Mom got here. I didn't."

"Whose fault was that?"

I pried my clenched jaws apart. "So if I want to talk to some of the staff, or other patients, to make sure this is a good place for Mom, I'm going to do that, okay?"

"Now you don't trust my judgment."

I resisted the urge to pull out my hair—or hers.

"You want me to be involved. You don't want me to ask questions. Frankly, I'm getting a bit tired of what *you* want." I brushed past her and tried to stomp out of the room. It turns out stomping is hard when you have a cane and a weak leg.

The Washingtons headed down the hallway toward the front doors. I followed them. I should have said goodbye to Mom, but I needed to cool down before I saw Jen again. Plus, I wanted to find out what they had learned.

They waited in the parking lot until I caught up with them.

"Anything to report?" I asked.

"The woman I talked to is named Olivia," Joe said. "She

wasn't on our list. She's not a nurse. They call them 'attend-ants.' She's worked here six months. Seems to like it okay. She worked at another nursing home before this and it was a lot worse. Too many patients, not enough employees, so they could barely keep up with the patients' physical needs, let alone treat them like human beings. She thought she'd have to find another line of work, but this place is better. Strict standards for employees, but she thinks that's good. Less turnover than the last place. She seems to respect Heather Garcia, though she doesn't see much of her."

"You learned a lot."

Norman Mendelson, the guy who didn't like gossip, probably wouldn't be happy to hear that. You'd think someone in charge of training staff and supervising patient care would have more important things to do than nag visitors. You'd also think he'd have a better way with people.

Marty took her husband's arm. "Joe's a charmer. But I actually found Felicity Carver."

"The nurse without a past?" Shoot, I'd forgotten to ask Heather about her.

She nodded. "I only managed to speak to her for a mi-nute. As one of two RNs on the whole staff, she'll have a full workload in a place this size. But I have a theory about her."

"Oh?"

"I'm saving it until I'm sure." Marty gave a mischievous smile.

"Is that really necessary?" I asked.

Her husband frowned and shook his head. "Baby, you know what happens when someone says, 'I know whodunit and I'll tell you later.' That person *always* gets it next." He drew his finger across his throat.

Marty patted his arm. "Don't worry. This secret won't get someone killed. But if I'm right, it's something private, and I wouldn't want to embarrass the poor woman needlessly."

So far, our best guess about Felicity Carver had been witness protection, but that wasn't something I would have called "embarrassing."

"When do you think you'll know for sure?" I asked.

"I'll ask Mackenzie to check on something for me. I might have an answer tomorrow."

"Fine. We'll discuss it when we meet tomorrow. Until then, please be careful."

Joe gave me a salute. "I won't let her out of my sight."

They headed to their car arm in arm. I watched with a pang of loneliness. Serious relationships had been impractical in my career. I didn't mind. It meant I had complete freedom to make my own choices, and I'd never wanted kids. I'd had "friends with benefits" over the years. Near-death experiences tended to rev up the libido, and in my line of work, you ran into the same journalists and photographers in war-torn countries and disaster areas around the world. But I didn't have anyone who would be with me into old age, up to the end.

My thoughts flitted to Todd Paradise, now mayor and a father. How old were his kids? What was his wife like? Or husband, if he'd come out after I knew him. My high school classmates had thirty years to marry, have kids, divorce, remarry—some might even have grandchildren by now. The mind boggled. In fact, it staggered and collapsed in a dazed heap. We could not possibly have gotten that old.

I sighed and headed to the car to wait for Dad. Of course, my parents were a reminder that even if you found someone you wanted to marry and managed to stay married to them for decades, you didn't typically get to die peacefully in your bed at the same time. Was it worse to be alone from the start or worse to watch someone you love fade away?

No point in making choices I didn't have. I sat in the car with the door open, letting out some of the heat. I pulled a notebook from my shoulder bag and noted what we'd learned.

The information from the Gregorians seemed the most relevant. The strange illness was puzzling and potentially suspicious. She'd improved after dialysis. I looked that up on my phone to make sure I understood what it did. According to the all-knowing internet, dialysis purified the blood in patients who had kidney disease. It could remove waste products and chemicals. Had Mrs. Gregorian gotten some kind of poison or an overdose of a drug? Had the dialysis, by pure luck, removed the toxin?

If so, and if someone trying to kill her had administered the substance intentionally, the killer had not yet bothered to try again. He or she had, potentially, moved on to new targets with more success. That seemed to remove suspicion from her family members, who wouldn't benefit from the deaths of other patients. On the other hand, an "angel of mercy," or someone who thought God was commanding them to kill, might take the recovery as a sign to let Mrs. Gregorian live.

Dad joined me. "I figured you must have come out

here."

"Yeah, sorry. I hope Mom wasn't upset that I slipped out."

"To be honest, I'm not sure she noticed." After a moment of silence, he asked, "Fighting with your sister?"

I sighed. "It's not like I want to. But she has this huge chip on her shoulder." More like an entire tree. A giant redwood, maybe.

He nodded. I didn't want to put Dad in the middle of this, so I resisted the burning urge to complain at length.

"Oh, Heather gave me this." He squirmed in the seat until he could pull an envelope out of his back pocket. "She came out when we were taking your mother back to her room, slipped this to me, and said it was for you."

I opened the envelope and found two sheets of paper. They had obituaries printed from online sources.

"These must be the women who died," I said.

Heather had come through with the information I needed, while maintaining a rather sketchy plausible deniability to support confidentiality rules. She'd said she thought she could get official permission for me to interview the family members, albeit under the guise of researching an article. Maybe she hadn't been able to reach anyone yet and she was anxious to move forward before someone else died. Was her willingness to bend the rules simply a sign of how important this was to her? Or did it suggest a suspicious moral flexibility?

I leaned toward Dad and held the pages between us. He tipped his head up and squinted through the bottom of his bifocals. I had thus far avoided reading glasses, but it was a good thing the font wasn't any smaller.

One obituary was short, only about a column inch, and appeared to be from a smaller local paper. Brit Egland, a retired teacher, had died the week before at sixty-eight. At one time, I would have thought that old, but now, it seemed tragically young. I wondered how long she had been in nursing care before her death. She was survived by her daughter, Lisa Delacruz, and grandson, Ryan.

The other obituary, from the *Arizona Republic*, was longer, more detailed, and included a photo of a smiling face framed by tight curls. It stated that Penelope Valentine had passed away at age eighty-six, at sunrise, "joining her beloved husband in Heaven." She had a dozen descendants. Someone had made a mark in blue pen—casual enough to look accidental—under the name of her daughter Kellie Armstrong, who lived in nearby Chandler.

"What do you intend to do with this information?" Dad asked.

"Talk to the families. These women each had a daughter in the area."

"Will you schedule appointments or just stop by their houses?"

"If I call, they can say no, so I'll stop by. Even if they won't talk to me, you can sometimes learn a lot by getting a look at a person and their house. But of course, we risk them not being home."

"At least it's Saturday."

Was it? I didn't normally worry too much about the weekend, since warlords, terrorists, and military personnel didn't stick to a five-day workweek, and the days designated as the weekend varied in the Middle East. But here, most people would work a regular schedule with a Saturday-Sunday weekend.

"No time like the present," I said. "Do you mind if I take the car this afternoon?"

"Of course I mind. I'll be going with you. Don't worry. I'll let you handle the interviews, but I can drive and be there in case you need me."

"Thanks, Dad." I chuckled. "You know, sometimes when I travel in risky areas, I have a fixer, a guy who speaks the language, knows who to bribe, knows the safest routes and so forth. Here, I guess you're my fixer."

"Works for me. It's a father's job to fix things for his daughter when he can." He smiled as he started the car.

I'd been right to bring Dad into this. I hadn't realized how much he still needed to feel useful, and how much I still needed my dad.

"I'll see if I can find addresses." I searched on my phone. "Here's Kellie Armstrong in Chandler."

Dad punched the address into the GPS as I read it aloud. Then I found the second address, for Lisa Delacruz.

"Let's do Chandler first," he said. "Then, depending on how long that takes, I know a good place to have lunch, and we can swing by the second address on the way home."

"Perfect." My stomach grumbled at the mention of food. I hadn't had much appetite since my injury, and food had tasted bland. Maybe that had been another side effect of the prescription painkillers, or maybe my body simply wanted more food now that I was back in action.

As Dad drove, I explained what the Washingtons and I

had found. "Do you have anything to add?"

"I'm not sure who told you not to talk to people, but I noticed a fellow watching us all from the doorway before you left the room."

"Medium height and build, brown hair, dressy clothes?"

Dad nodded. "I don't recall his name, but we met with him before moving your mother in. He talked to Jen as if I wasn't even there."

"What a jerk."

"It happens a lot now. You get old, and people assume you can't see, hear, or think. I suppose he has some reason, working in a place like that, but other doctors do the same thing."

I'd witnessed women being treated that way, as if they had no brains. I hadn't realized it happened to elderly people as well.

"Does Jen usually go to doctors' visits with you?"

"She insists. She says it's good to have someone else along to take notes, and your mother can't do that anymore. Jen isn't wrong about having an extra pair of ears, but I don't understand why the doctors assume that person is in charge."

I tried to think of a reason that wasn't offensive to the patient. I couldn't. "Did anything else happen when you were, uh, showing Mrs. Washington the way to the bathroom?"

"Not really. I took a good look around the place. Didn't find much security. It's designed to keep patients from going out unattended, not to keep people from coming in. Besides the front door, there's a loading dock in the back. The door says it's alarmed, so I didn't try it. No one stopped me from wandering around. I could have walked into any of the patients' rooms. Of course, I probably look like a patient myself, so I blend in."

"No, Dad." Although, in truth, I'd have trouble telling the patients from some visitors.

More relevant to our investigation, it appeared that anyone—patient, staff, or visitor—had a good chance of wandering into a patient's room without being noticed. On the surface, that made sense. The home didn't want patients to feel like prisoners. The whole place had the look of a hotel or furnished apartment building rather than a hospital. But if someone was killing patients, it left the field wide open.

"There's something else we should maybe talk about," Dad said.

"Oh? What now?"

"I think we're being followed."

Chapter Ten

I RESISTED THE instinct to turn. I didn't want the person following to know we'd spotted them. "What did you see?"

"I think that silver car has been behind us since we left Sunshine Haven. I wouldn't have noticed, except you said the car that almost hit you was silver or gray."

I leaned toward the side mirror. We were on a moderately busy street, two lanes in each direction.

"It's two cars back, behind the Ferrari," Dad said.

I assumed the Ferrari was the sporty-looking red car. I couldn't see much of the car behind that, but it was silver, and a car rather than a truck, van, or SUV. An exact match for the one that had almost hit me!

Maybe I needed to learn a bit more about cars.

Dad turned the corner. This brought us into a more residential neighborhood with less traffic. A stern voice with a German accent came from the GPS, demanding that we make a U-turn.

The red car kept going, but the silver one turned after us. It also slowed to a crawl. Unfortunately, Arizona doesn't require a front license plate, and sun glared on the window, hiding anyone inside.

"Can you tell what kind of car it is?" I asked.

"Toyota Corolla or maybe a Chevy Prizm, I'd guess. Hard to tell at this distance." Dad slowed more, but the other car turned at a side street. "Maybe it's a coincidence."

"Or they realized we spotted them. Try to get behind them."

Dad pulled into a driveway and turned around, but by the time we reached the side street, the silver car had vanished. We drove a couple of blocks, with the GPS voice complaining the whole way. We passed a silvery car in a driveway and one on the street, but both were empty. The driver could be hiding, but more likely, someone trying to avoid us would simply have turned back toward the busy main road and disappeared in traffic. This would be a lot easier if our suspect drove an orange VW Beetle or a purple Humvee.

I sighed. "Another dead end."

"No, this street goes through," Dad said.

I narrowed my eyes at him.

He laughed. "Now what?"

"I don't know what we can do about someone following us, except try to catch them next time. From now on, we can have the Washingtons leave after us and check for anyone following. Should have thought of that sooner."

"How could you guess this would happen?"

"Yeah, I suppose." I pressed the heel of my hand against my forehead. I had to keep track of too much. I'd covered more complicated stories—okay, as complicated anyway—a hundred times before. But just as my body kept reminding me I wasn't at full physical strength, I had to remember my mind wasn't back to normal either. "We might as well stick to our plan."

"Helga will be pleased," Dad said.

"Who?"

"That's what I call the voice on the GPS. She sounds like a stern German nurse."

Even knowing it was an automatic recording, I had to admit "Helga" seemed mollified when we got back on the street she wanted.

We drove for about half an hour. I recognized things here and there, but so much had changed since I'd left the area. Towns that had once felt separate were now linked by endless strip malls and planned communities of identical homes.

While Dad drove, I checked what the internet could tell us about our targets. Kellie Armstrong, daughter of the much-beloved Penelope Valentine, apparently lived with her husband and was the office manager for his CPA firm. They had two children in college and an older daughter who was a stay-at-home mother of two young children.

The Armstrongs lived in one of those bland, planned communities that had popped up everywhere. Large houses on small lots, carefully controlled shades of tan and beige, with xeriscaped yards. Only a few things differentiated the houses: the types of cacti or bushes in the yards, and whether they had Christmas decorations up already. Apparently, a few people thought you didn't need to wait until after Thanksgiving.

Without the GPS, we might have gone in circles and run up against dead ends for a lot longer before finding the

Armstrong house. Dad parked in the street and we peered at the house.

"Nice place, I guess," he said.

The people who owned it must have money, but if they had personality, it wasn't showing.

The only signs of life in view were a couple of men working in a yard across the street two houses down, and the cactus wrens flitting in and out of the saguaro next door. All the houses had two- or three-car garages, so the streets and driveways were nearly empty. A white truck across the street probably belonged to the gardeners, and a boxy, pale blue car sat by the curb a few houses down. Why couldn't that have been the one trying to follow us?

I glanced at Dad as we got out of the car. I wanted him to feel included, but bringing my father on an interview felt weird.

"I'll stretch my legs." He wandered toward the men gardening.

Was he psychic? Because I appreciated his actions, but no one needed a mind-reading father.

I went up the walk and rang the doorbell. The air was dry and still, quiet except for the chirping of a bird and a background hum from some kind of insect. After thirty seconds, I rang the bell again. I cocked my head to listen for sounds from inside as a curtain in the front window twitched. Something was in there, though it could be a pet. More likely a cat than a dog, given the lack of barking.

Finally, the door cracked open and out peered a woman, fine-boned, blonde, and pretty. "Yes?"

I recognized her from her social media profiles. Given

that she had children in their twenties, she had to be near my age, but she looked no older than thirty-five.

"Kellie Armstrong? I'm Kate Tessler. I'm working on a story about Sunshine Haven. I understand your mother lived there until recently."

"That's right. But she's . . . no longer . . ."

"I know she passed away. I'm sorry for your loss." I brushed hair and a drop of sweat off my forehead. "May I come in and ask you a few questions?"

She glanced back into the room. "I guess. Wait a minute." Kellie closed the door on me. Was she a neat freak who couldn't let a stranger in without tidying up first, or was she hiding something?

A soft thud came from somewhere not far away. It might have been another door closing at the back of the house or at a neighbor's house. Half a minute later, Kellie returned and waved me in. The front room looked like a professional had decorated it for inclusion in a magazine. Kellie didn't fit the room. She wore yoga pants and a wrinkled T-shirt with the tag sticking up in back. Her short blond hair was tousled—randomly, not artistically—and her mascara had smudged. Maybe I'd interrupted a nap. She waved me to a seat and as I passed close by her, I caught a whiff of men's cologne, sweat, and sex. She might have been napping but not alone. Yet the rest of the house was silent.

"What's this about?" she asked.

I'd prepared a story that I hoped would be plausible and not cause suspicion about the nursing home or me. "Two years ago, Sunshine Haven faced lawsuits over the treatment of patients. Since then, they claim they've made a lot of improvements and things are much better. I'm following up on the original story by talking to some of the families of patients."

She nodded.

I waited, but she didn't launch into complaints or a confession. I pulled out a notebook and pen.

"I'm sorry to bother you at a difficult time, but I thought the people who could best address my questions were those who'd recently lost someone who'd been living at Sunshine Haven. Were you satisfied with the treatment your mother was getting? Did you have any concerns or suspicions about her death?"

"I thought they did a fine job," Kellie said. "Mom was only there for a year, sixteen months, so I don't know anything about the earlier problems. We heard about them, but everything was fine by the time Mom moved in. We wouldn't have sent her there otherwise. I visited almost every day, and I never saw any problems."

"You thought the place was adequately staffed? Did you get to know any of the people who work there?"

Her gaze avoided mine. "I thought the staff was very nice." She spoke more quickly. "Not that I really know any of them, but everyone seemed competent."

She was hiding something, or perhaps felt guilty about something, but what? A little defensiveness was understandable. No one would want a reporter to think they'd put a parent in an unsafe or unpleasant home. But her anxiety had seemed to increase when I asked about the staff. "Was anyone working there especially helpful?"

She stared at me as if trying to read my thoughts. Fair

enough. I was doing the same to her.

"I thought the physical therapists next door were really good. Mom had to have a knee replacement last year and they helped her with rehabilitation."

She glanced at my notebook so I dutifully jotted down *good therapy*.

"Of course, if we'd known she had less than a year to live, maybe we wouldn't have bothered with the surgery." She sighed. "But you never can know, right?"

I nodded. "I guess you do the best you can with the information you have. I'm dealing with aging parents myself, which is why stories like this are important to me."

She gave a slight smile, and for a moment, we connected in shared experience.

But that wasn't helping my investigation. "Who worked with your mother at the physical therapy clinic?"

Kellie twitched. "Oh . . . I don't remember his name."

A man anyway, which narrowed it down. I had a feeling she did know the name, but why would she lie about that? Had he been "napping" with her?

The only person from the PT clinic we had on our suspicious list so far was Berta, who was spending too much money. But I'd seen one man at work during my visit, and there could be more. At first glance, a physical therapist didn't seem like the best candidate to murder a patient, but maybe it wouldn't be that hard to offer someone a "vitamin" or nutritional drink spiked with poison. As long as the poison took a few hours to work, the death wouldn't be connected to the therapist. I tried another tack. "Places like Sunshine Haven can be quite expensive. That puts a burden on family members."

Kellie relaxed back against the sofa cushions. "Fortunately, that wasn't a problem for us. Mom got a good life insurance payout when my father died. We're lucky he died first." She scrunched up her face. "That sounds terrible. I don't mean we're lucky he died, but things would've been different if he'd been the one in nursing care. As it was, Mom was able to take care of him at home, and his life insurance helped her. That, plus their house sale, covered her."

"It used up any inheritance, though."

She gestured around the room. "As you can see, I'm managing." She scowled at a vase on the coffee table as if she'd like to smash it. "Everything a girl could want, right?" She shook herself and looked up. "We didn't expect any inheritance. They had a nice, middle-class life, but they weren't rich, and with money split between several children and grandchildren, we wouldn't get much. I know it's harder for poor people, though."

She said the last sentence in the offhand way of someone who never had to worry about money, and only knew that other people did as an abstract concept. But she seemed sincere enough about the inheritance, and she spoke of her mother with affection.

"Seeing someone you love fade away must be so hard." I thought of my mother and let the sympathy and worry show on my face. "Did you ever get to the point where you wished it was all over?"

Tears glistened in her eyes. "Never. She was my mother. Even with her health problems, she still took joy in seeing her grandchildren and great-grandchildren. I had to nag my kids to visit. You know how young people are, so busy. But Mom loved it, especially when my daughter brought her baby in. I'm sorry for the little ones who will never get to know her."

I'd interviewed plenty of people who had lost a parent, spouse, child, or comrade in arms, often too young and through violence. Grief expressed itself differently, but underneath, it had the same flavor. Kellie's grief was real. I doubted she'd had anything to do with her mother's death, but what about another family member?

"I guess you have a large family. Is everyone local, so they could visit your mother often?"

"No, I'm the only one in Arizona. Most of my siblings tried to visit once or twice a year. It would've been nice if we'd known Mom was . . . was at the end, so they could've been there, but it happened too fast."

"None of them were in the state when your mother died?"

"No." She gave me a puzzled look. "They came for the funeral, of course."

I offered her one last chance to complain about anyone at Sunshine Haven. "Well, it sounds like you were satisfied with the care your mother got. No one could have done anything differently to prevent her death, right?"

She sat up straighter and glared. "If you're looking for scandal, you're not going to find it. My mother was a wonderful person, and I have no complaints about Sunshine Haven or anyone there."

Whoops. I'd gone too far. I tried to soften my voice and

stance, less tough reporter and more sympathetic friend. "I'm glad. I hate to think of seniors being mistreated. I'm sorry to bring up all these memories."

She looked away. "They're always there. It's good to talk about them. I'm sorry I can't help with your article, though."

"I'm not sorry to hear people are treating patients well. You can take comfort in knowing you did the best you could for your mother."

She bowed her head and her bangs fell, screening her eyes. "We thought we'd have a few more years." She sighed and looked up at me. "I'm trying to tell myself that in the long run, sudden is better. She didn't suffer much at the end."

"Thank you for talking to me." I stood. "If I think of any more questions, may I call you?"

"Sure." She scribbled her number on a scrap of paper.

Her handwriting was girlish with large, loopy letters. I'd be willing to bet that as a teenager, she'd dotted the *i* in her name with a heart. Overall, I liked Kellie Armstrong. Yet, I suspected she was hiding something.

We shook hands at the door and I headed for the car. Dad waved from across the street, where he was chatting with the gardeners, and joined me. As we pulled away, I described my visit.

"She acted odd at times, but I don't think it has anything to do with murder."

Dad grinned. "I might be able to explain that. Right after you went in, a man came around the side of the house. He got in that light blue car and drove away."

"The car parked a couple of houses down? Interesting. I

thought I heard a door close before she let me in. So someone might have snuck out the back, and he'd parked down the street instead of in her driveway."

"What's more, those fellows across the street are here every Saturday morning. They say a man leaves the house early. How early depends on how hot it is, earlier in summer than in winter, but they often see him either leave or come home. My guess would be he's golfing. And while he's gone, the guy with the blue car comes for a couple hours. It's been going on for three or four months."

"Aha. So maybe Kellie is hiding an affair." That would explain her disheveled state, her smell, the delay in answering the door, and the peculiarities of her behavior during our interview. She'd been both anxious and helpful, both sincere and guilty. She had something to hide, but it didn't relate to her mother.

Or did it? Cheating on one's spouse was a far cry from murder, but the two occasionally went together. More often, it was the spouse who was killed, though. I couldn't see any reason Kellie's affair would lead her to kill her mother, but I might be missing something. A husband who had uncovered the affair and was getting a bizarre revenge by taking away her mother? A lover who mistakenly thought he was doing her a favor? Could his car have been the one that tried to run me down? I hadn't noticed any blue tint to that vehicle, but the pale blue might have looked silver with the sun glaring off it. I thought the "attack car" had been a regular car, though, not one of those boxy things.

"I'd like to find out who the man was," I said.

"I got the license plate. Can you look up the name

somehow?"

"I'll put it on my to-do list. Thanks, Dad. What would I do without you?"

"I suppose you'd manage somehow. Eventually."

I smiled. "I'm glad I don't have to find out."

"How about lunch before we tackle the next suspect? I know a place near here."

"Sounds good. I need to think about my approach anyway. I have to get more answers, faster, if we're going to solve this thing quickly. But how?"

"Pretend to be something other than a reporter?"

"That wouldn't be ethical." I frowned. "Not if I'm acting as a reporter. Maybe it's okay if I'm acting as a PI? I don't know the rules there, but I'm not a licensed PI so I'd better play it safe. I'm skirting the edges of ethics enough as it is."

"The ends do not justify the means. I'm glad you feel that way." Half a block later, he said, "Still. Your mother is there."

"I know." I resisted the urge to whine that I was doing the best I could. That was little comfort if you failed. I sighed. "Maybe Lisa Delacruz holds the key. We might get lucky this afternoon."

Luck could make a difference. I'd never broken a major story without a stroke or two of luck.

Unfortunately, "luck" tended to appear only after days of hard work.

Chapter Eleven

D AD DROVE TO a soup and sandwich place he knew. When I got out of the car, I paused in the open door, facing outward, one hand clinging to the door and the other to the side of the car. I propped my foot on the seat behind me and stretched my quad. The pain radiated up my back and down to my foot. Meanwhile, aches and twinges danced all over my body.

After half a minute or so, the pain receded to a dull ache and I could move again.

Dad waited for me without speaking, but once we sat and ordered the baked potato soup he recommended, he asked, "How is your leg?"

"Much better." Where had that come from? Even at that moment, I was absently massaging the leg under the table. But it had improved. "I stopped taking the serious painkillers during the day, and my leg hurts about the same amount as before. I've been afraid to ease up on the meds, but maybe I've improved more than I realized."

"It's been two months," Dad said. "Sometimes after surgery it seems like you don't get better and don't get better, and then within a few days you suddenly improve. But, of course, recovery always has ups and downs."

"It still hurts all the time. But I'm getting used to it."

Dad nodded. "It's amazing what you can get used to if you must."

"Mm." How many things had he gotten used to, physically and mentally, as he and my mother aged? Was I already starting down that path of accepting more pain and less function, because I couldn't do anything about it?

My gut reaction was refusal. I'd fight and claw my way back to how I was before this injury, back to what I still believed to be normal for me. Was it a strength or a weakness to fight what was probably a losing battle?

Fortunately, the waitress came by with our water, interrupting my dark thoughts, and I took some ibuprofen. For weeks, I'd had nothing to do but think about the pain from my injury, the things I couldn't do, and how this would affect my career. Now, I had pain, but I was too busy to focus on it all the time. I could still tackle a difficult investigation, which gave me hope that my career wasn't over, even if I'd slowed down.

Conversation turned back to the investigation while we waited for our food. It was fun. Dad and I had always gotten along, but we hadn't spent much time together since I'd become an adult, especially not the two of us alone. Mom and Dad had met me in Europe a few times, but those trips focused on seeing the sights, and Mom was the chattier one.

I'd tried to come home at least once a year, but holiday visits involved bigger family gatherings—my parents, Jen and her husband and kids, and sometimes other social groups like neighborhood parties.

I'd never spent much one-on-one time with my father,

but now I could. If that was the only good thing to come out of my injury and Mom's disease, I'd appreciate the silver lining.

The baked potato soup was rich with cheese and sour cream. Living someplace with a dozen restaurants on every block had advantages.

As we headed to the car, Dad asked, "What do we know about this woman you're going to see next?"

"Not a lot. Lisa Delacruz isn't a terribly common name, but the ones I found don't seem to be the one we need. As far as I can tell, our local Lisa isn't on social media, which is unusual these days but not suspicious. Her last name is different from her mother's, so presumably she got married and changed it, but I can't tell if she's currently married. Lisa's mother, Brit Egland, was the second person to die. That makes her the third victim, if you assume our villain also caused Mrs. Gregorian to get sick."

"So Brit Egland was the most recent death."

"Right, less than a week ago."

"Her daughter's feelings will be fresh."

I shrugged. "That's not necessarily a bad thing. People are often more honest when they're more emotional."

While stopped at a light, Dad gave me a long, considering glance.

"What?" I asked.

"Do you ever find it hard? Poking into people's lives, getting them to talk about things they might not enjoy?"

"Of course it's hard, but it's important. I'm not harassing people for fun or to get a titillating story about celebrity sex scandals. We're trying to find out if there's a murderer on the loose! The truth is important, and sometimes you can't get to it without upsetting people."

"I didn't mean to sound judgmental. I admire what you do, but I'm sometimes amazed that my daughter is doing it. Your mother and I used to wonder where you got that drive, to travel around the world, go dangerous places, do things that would terrify most people."

"I don't know, but I'm pretty sure I got my passion for the truth from the two of you."

He chuckled. "I guess we'll take some credit."

Helga the GPS announced that our destination was on the right. Lisa Delacruz's neighborhood had little in common with Kellie Armstrong's. We were in a much older community with houses that had probably been considered quite nice in the 1950s, but they would now seem outdated, rundown, and too small. Some residents had tried hard to keep up appearances, with fresh paint and carefully tended bushes and flowers in the yards. Other houses had peeling paint, sagging porches, and hard-packed dirt yards scattered with toys or random junk. A group of children played in one yard, while an older woman in a flowered dress watered bushes in another.

Lisa Delacruz had a tiny house with fading paint, but the yard was tidy, and pretty curtains hung in the windows. The old brown sedan parked in the driveway had some scratches and dings but no dust or mud.

"Are you going to chat up the neighbors again?" I asked Dad.

"We'll see. It's harder to approach women and children without seeming creepy."

"Good point. Don't get arrested." I left him in the car and headed up the walk.

Voices filtered through the door as I reached the porch. It sounded like a TV show. I knocked, and half a minute later, the door opened, revealing a tall, skinny teenager with dark hair hanging over one eye. Probably the grandson, Ryan.

"I'm looking for Lisa Delacruz. Is she home?"

He glanced at my cane, turned, and yelled, "Mom!"

The teen retreated to the couch, leaving the door half-open. I waited in the doorway until a woman came out from a back room. She was somewhere between forty and fifty, short and plump. Her shoulders hunched and wide eyes peered at me from under bangs that showed graying-brown roots at the base of the honey-blond strands.

"Yes? Can I help you?"

She looked ready to flee, so I gave her a reassuring smile and spoke softly.

"Ms. Delacruz, my name is Kate Tessler. I'm writing a story about Sunshine Haven." I avoided using the words *reporter* or *journalist*, as they often made people anxious, and she already looked anxious enough. "I'm sorry to hear about your mother passing away so recently. I know it's a difficult time, but could we talk?"

"About Mother?"

"About her experience at Sunshine Haven, and your experience as relatives." Judging by the house, paying for the care facility would have been a burden for this family, so I said, "I know how hard it is for families to pay for end-of-life care, especially for someone who has health or memory issues. We need better options."

She nodded and stepped back from the door, waving me inside. "We were lucky to find Sunshine Haven. Some of the other places were simply awful, but most of the good ones were much too expensive. And I couldn't take care of her at home and keep my job." She glanced at her son and the blaring TV. "Let's go into the kitchen. Would you like a cup of tea? Or some lemonade?"

"Lemonade would be nice. Thank you." I didn't particularly want anything, but sharing drinks would make this seem more like a friendly visit.

I followed her slowly, studying the room. Faded furniture, worn carpeting, an old TV, and a can of soda on the coffee table. The boy slumped on the couch, eyes fixed on the TV, which showed racing cars zipping around a track. I noticed a smell I couldn't quite identify. Pine-scented furniture polish and burned toast?

Lisa mixed spoonfuls of powdered drink mix into glasses of water and added ice. I sat at the scarred Formica table and glanced around the room. A door led into a small backyard. Several coats hung next to the door, including a man's jacket that had to be huge on skinny Ryan, but maybe he thought loose clothes were a fashion statement.

"I take it the young man was your son, Ryan? He was mentioned in the obituary. Is it only the two of you here?"

With her back to me, Lisa hesitated until the moment grew awkward. Finally, she turned and put drinks on the table. "Yes."

It hadn't been a hard question. Still, a single mother might be cautious about admitting that she didn't have a burly husband around the house.

She didn't seem inclined to elaborate, so I thanked her for the lemonade and took a sip. I managed not to make a face at the overly sweet, artificial taste. "And your father? He passed away before your mother?"

"Yes, he's been gone for some time now."

"That must have made your mother's passing especially hard, leaving only you and your son."

"It was such a shock. She seemed fine one evening, and the next morning, they called to say she was gone."

I turned the questions toward Sunshine Haven and managed to drag out some answers. The place was nice, the staff seemed competent, and Lisa didn't have any complaints. She was lucky to get her mother in there. The prices had dropped after the trouble two years before, but they'd been rising again. Lisa slowly warmed up.

"Mother's memory was going. She'd try to run errands and forget how to get home. I'd stop by every day before and after work, but it wasn't enough. I was going to move her in here, but—" Her mouth snapped shut.

"But what?"

She shook her head. "It wouldn't have worked."

I gave her a questioning glance.

"I'm at work all day, and Ryan's at school, and we couldn't have left my mother here alone anyway. Sunshine Haven was better."

I forced down another gulp of lemonade. If I managed half of it, it wouldn't be too rude to leave the rest. I dried my mouth with the back of my hand. "Even with the lower prices, a place like that is expensive."

"I was shocked when I first saw the amount they wanted. Medicaid alone wouldn't cover it, but with the money from selling Mother's house, and her social security payments, we managed to make it work." Lisa sighed. "Of course, she was only there for three months."

"Really? Your mother wasn't very old. Did she have a lot of health problems?"

Lisa turned her glass around and around in her hands. She hadn't taken a sip yet. "I didn't think so, but heart attacks can be so sudden."

"Was it a heart attack? The obituary didn't specify."

"I think they called it cardiac death or something like that. Some fancy term that means her heart stopped."

Heather had said no autopsies were done. The doctors probably put the simplest reason on the death certificates. When one died, the heart did stop, even if that wasn't the reason for death. "Did your mother have heart problems?"

"Not that we knew, but you know how doctors are. Half the time, you can't understand what they mean." She glanced at my cane and away. "If we'd known . . ."

"What would you have done differently?"

"Nothing." She shook her head. "It's only that Mother's house was worth a fair amount, so I could've quit my job and stayed home with her, and she would've been happier too. But now Sunshine Haven keeps the money, even though they only had her for a few months. It doesn't seem fair."

"You would have inherited more if you hadn't signed over the house?"

She nodded. "If Mother had been in Sunshine Haven for

a year or more, that would have been different. If we'd known it would be this short, we could have sold the house and kept the rest of the money. Ryan graduates in another year, and unless he gets scholarships, I don't know how he'll go to college. I want him to do better than I did."

We chatted a little longer, but I didn't hear anything useful. Lisa checked the wall clock every few minutes. Twice, she jumped at a shout from the TV. I decided to stop tormenting her.

"Well, thanks for your time." I rose and picked up the glass for a last sip of lemonade. "Where should I put this?"

"I'll take it."

I called a thank you as I left the kitchen. I paused in the living room behind the couch. Ryan held a phone with some kind of racing video game playing. He glanced between it and the TV race.

"You're a race fan, huh?" I said. "Who's in the lead?"

Ryan mumbled a name I didn't recognize. I couldn't see any way to get a surly teen talking without making his mother suspicious, so I left.

Dad started the car as I got in. "Where to now?"

I pushed the seat back so I could stretch out my leg. "Home. I need a rest, and I need to think. I feel like we're on the wrong track and wasting time."

He headed down the street. "You didn't learn anything useful?"

"She didn't have any complaints about Sunshine Haven or its staff, and she doesn't seem to consider her mother's death suspicious. As for Lisa Delacruz herself, she has the opposite of a motive. If she'd killed her mother instead of putting her into Sunshine Haven, she says she would've inherited some money. As it is, Sunshine Haven got the money from Brit Egland's estate. Unless the home killed patients to get their funds without having to care for them, I don't see how money could be a motive here. It's looking more like mercy killings, or else we're on the wrong track entirely. If we're after an 'angel of death,' I'm not sure how to identify the person."

Dad stopped at a light. "What about the guy who called you pretending to be Henry Wilson?"

I rubbed my hands over my face. "That would fall under the category of 'we're on the wrong track entirely.' I have no idea how it fits into the deaths, or if it does. If a board member really made the call, I might suspect a conspiracy to kill patients and embezzle the money. But the call could have been from anyone. An employee trying to deflect attention from his own crimes? Someone trying to set up Henry Wilson? Someone who wanted me to investigate Sunshine Haven and correctly assumed this would make me suspicious?"

"That's a lot of questions."

"And no answers." We needed more clues. But how could we find them without waiting for another patient death?

Chapter Twelve

THE NEXT MORNING, the Washingtons brought home-made cinnamon rolls, which smelled like fresh-baked heaven. Apparently, Joe had become quite the chef in his retirement. I should have gotten myself some assistants years before.

I didn't tell the others about my interviews with the daughters of the deceased patients, since I hadn't told Mackenzie or the Washingtons that I was investigating suspicious deaths. Instead, we reviewed what we'd learned about the Sunshine Haven employees.

"Marty, did you follow up on Felicity Carver?" I asked. "Glad to see you didn't get bumped off last night, by the way."

She laughed. "I told you it wasn't anything dangerous." Marty turned to Mackenzie and nodded.

Mac looked from me to Dad. "It's nothing suspicious."

We waited.

"It's private, though," Mackenzie said.

"It can't be that private if you uncovered it," I said. "But we won't tell anyone else, unless it's relevant to this investigation."

"All right. Felicity Carver used to be Franklin Carver."

"He had a sex change?" Dad asked.

"We don't call it that anymore," Mackenzie said. "But yes, *she* changed her name after transitioning."

I turned to Marty. "How did you figure that out from talking to her for a minute?"

Marty shrugged. "I grew up in San Francisco during the early era of gay rights and transgender riots. I used to visit some of the drag queen clubs with a friend of mine. Felicity had the most perfect makeup I've seen in years, and way more makeup than you usually see in this part of the country. She reminded me of the clubs, and that made me wonder."

"How did you confirm it?" I asked Mac.

"I checked some of her friends' pages, went back several years, and found some group photos with Felicity before she began her transition."

"Clever investigating," I said. "I don't see how Felicity's gender would have anything to do with problems at Sunshine Haven. Let's drop her off our investigation list for now." I frowned at Mackenzie. "Did you think we were going to be shocked or offended?"

"Well, you're . . . of a different generation. My parents would be uncomfortable, and my grandparents wouldn't get it at all. I wasn't sure about you."

I felt ancient. I resisted the urge to defend myself or my generation, or to point out that people of any age could be prejudiced, or not.

"Let's move on," I said. "Do we know anything yet about Ana Marija Jurić, the Bosnian immigrant whose work visa is running out, or Maximilian Richards, the attendant who was on probation for drug charges?"

We hadn't made any progress there, and, of course, we hadn't even looked at a lot of the other employees. I leaned my elbows on the table and stared at the plate of cinnamon rolls as if I could move it closer by the force of my mind.

The plate edged toward me.

I took one. "Thanks."

Dad had read my mind again. At least he used his psychic powers for good.

I savored a rich bite. "We need to find out more about these people. I'm not sure deeper background checks will help, though. We might need to talk to them, or their friends and neighbors."

Joe said, "If you can get their work schedules, that would help."

"I'll ask Heather for work schedules, and then you can focus on Ana Marija and Max. Leave Berta Lopez to me. I have a PT appointment with her tomorrow. I'll see what I can learn about her fancy car and expensive vacations. Mackenzie, I'd like you to look into Heather Garcia."

"The director?"

"Right." I had to figure out how to explain based on the limited amount Mac and the Washingtons knew. I had told them about the phone call from the man claiming to be Henry Wilson. "She says Henry Wilson, the board member, is a great guy. I don't think he's the one who called me, but I'm basing that on his denial and his accent, which was different from the man on the phone. He could have disguised his voice, though. Maybe Heather and Wilson are up to something together. Or Heather and someone else. She's the one person who would definitely know I was in the building, and that I'm a journalist, so she might have warned someone about me."

That didn't really fit with her request that I investigate, but I'd learned long ago that people could be baffling. Maybe she'd asked me to investigate the "suspicious" patient deaths in order to distract me from another crime, such as embezzlement. Sure, she'd have been better off not drawing attention to herself, but people often assumed everyone noticed and judged them. Otherwise we wouldn't freak out over acne and bad hair days. I couldn't give Heather a pass simply because I had known her slightly in high school, or because she had asked for my help.

"What are our chances of tracking the phone number that called you?" Mac asked.

"It was blocked," I said. "I doubt the phone company would reveal it without more evidence of a crime committed. Anyway, a smart crook would've called from a prepaid phone he bought for cash. Of course, if he was smart, he wouldn't have called me in the first place and made me suspicious."

Joe looked at his watch. "We'd better go if we're going to make the second church service. I'll leave some of these." He grabbed a plate from the cupboard and put a few extra cinnamon rolls on it. "Let us know when those two people work. Maybe we'll arrange to run into them in the parking lot and chat for a few minutes, and then we can follow them."

"All right. Be careful, of course."

Marty winked. "Don't worry. I'll look after him."

They headed for the door. We called out our thanks for

the delicious breakfast. They both smiled at me with something like sympathy.

"I'll go home to research Ms. Garcia, if you don't mind," Mackenzie said. "My internet is faster."

"Let me know what you learn," I said.

She downed the last of her coffee, put her mug in the sink, and left Dad and me alone at the table.

"Do you think they're getting suspicious about what we're really doing?" I asked. "Since they don't know about the patient deaths, some of this must seem pretty weird, like we're fussing over nothing."

Dad looked guilty. "I may have hinted to Joe that you weren't dealing very well with being injured and out of work, so we're trying to distract you and make you feel useful. Only because I wanted to keep them from asking too many questions."

He grabbed the coffeepot, topping off my mug and his own. "Oh, and something Jen said made Marty think you might be feeling guilty over not being here when your mother went into Sunshine Haven."

I gave a short laugh. "Great. Though I can't say you're wrong on either count."

"You had a good reason not to be here right away."

I nodded. I'd been covering a big story when Jen first informed me that Mom had heated up a can of soup in the microwave—the soup still in the can, thereby destroying the microwave. That was the last straw. For months, Mom had been leaving food in the oven to burn, wandering in the middle of the night, and putting her purse, glasses, and other items in odd places and then claiming someone had stolen them. Jen decided Mom could no longer live at home, and Dad had reluctantly agreed that he couldn't take care of her anymore. He'd given up his coffee group and other social activities, but even then, simple tasks such as grocery shopping were hard if he couldn't leave Mom alone.

When I'd heard, I started making plans to come home, but I thought I could take a few weeks to finish the story, schedule vacation time, and make travel arrangements. Then the explosion had delayed my return another two months.

Having a reason to be gone, even one involving a long hospital stay, didn't lessen my feelings of guilt. Plus, if I had returned as soon as I heard about Mom, I wouldn't have been in Syria to be injured. It almost felt like a punishment for not being a good daughter.

Dad patted my arm. "What would you like me to do today?"

"I'm not sure yet." I sighed.

"What's wrong?"

"It's frustrating. We keep learning things, but we're not getting anywhere. When I'm investigating for a news article, I expect that. Life is complicated, and politics are insane, so I don't hope for easy answers, no matter how much the paper and the public want things simple. But here, it's not enough to simply find out all the weird random things happening, or to uncover everyone's secrets. We need one specific answer. We need to know who is responsible for patient deaths, so we can stop it from happening again."

"We're making progress."

"I feel like we're going in circles. We look into person A and find a secret or something suspicious. Then we figure out what the secret is, and it has nothing to do with killing patients. But that doesn't mean person A isn't *also* killing patients, or that the secret isn't connected in some weird way. For example, I don't think Kellie Armstrong would have killed her mother, but would her lover or husband have done so for some reason? Knowing her secret is an affair doesn't clear her family from suspicion."

"We don't even know for sure that someone is killing patients," Dad said.

"Right. We know Mrs. Gregorian got mysteriously sick but recovered. A week later, Penelope Valentine died. She was eighty-six but not expected to die so soon. In another week, Brit Egland died at sixty-eight from heart failure when she didn't have known heart problems. I wonder how long the average patient lives at a place like that."

"Eighteen months to two years."

I raised my eyebrows.

"Jen researched it. I think there are about fifty patients at Sunshine Haven."

I shoved aside the thought that *Mom* was in there, and two years was no time at all. That was the average, and surely some patients had many more health issues before they got there. Mom was healthy, except for her brain.

Don't think about the future. Focus on now.

"Let's see . . . to make the math easy, if each of those fifty patients lived two years, you'd have twenty-five deaths per year, or two per month. Two within a week on occasion is within reason."

"But fifty includes everyone," Dad said. "Short-term nursing care, assisted living, and Alzheimer's care. Mrs.

Gregorian is in Alzheimer's care, and I think that wing only has fifteen beds. Do we know what unit the other women were in?"

"Brit Egland must have been in Alzheimer's, because her daughter mentioned memory problems. But I'm not sure about Penelope Valentine. It would certainly be suspicious if they were all in the same small unit." Suspicious and terrifying, since Mom was there. If someone was targeting Alzheimer's patients, and only had fifteen to choose from . . .

The delicious cinnamon roll threatened to come back up. I forced it back down with coffee that burned in my gut.

"I'll ask Heather where Penelope Valentine was," I said. "Heather must have had some reason for worrying. I guess I should also ask Heather who else has died in the last six months to see if any of the deaths look suspicious now that we have some leads. On the bright side, it's been a week since Brit Egland died, and I haven't heard of any more deaths."

"It was a full week between the two deaths, right?"

"I think so." I glanced at the calendar on the wall but getting up to go four steps was a lot of work these days.

Dad retrieved it, placing it on the table so we could both see the month of November. I double-checked the death dates from the obituary.

"The most recent death was Monday of last week. The first one was the previous Monday." I frowned. "I'm not sure when Mrs. Gregorian got sick, but her daughter said . . ." I searched my memory, since I hadn't taken detailed notes of that conversation. "Her mother always has dialysis on Mondays, so that's the day she recovered. Which means she got sick Sunday evening."

"I don't like the sound of this," Dad said.

A shiver ran up my back. "I'll say. Penelope Valentine died at dawn, according to her obituary, so if she was poisoned it probably happened Sunday night or early Monday. And Brit Egland's daughter said her mother was fine in the evening and dead in the morning."

"All three of them got sick sometime Sunday night."

We stared at each other. I could barely force the words out. "So if the killer is on a regular schedule, they'll strike again tonight."

Dad shot out of his chair. "We need to get to Sunshine Haven."

"Yes." I struggled to my feet, one hand clinging to the table for balance. "Someone should stay with Mom all day. We need to keep an eye on the wing overall. We have to solve this fast. In the meantime, we need to protect the current patients."

"Is it time to call in the police?"

"Yes. No." I groaned. "We don't have any evidence. Would they believe us?"

Dad shrugged. "I'm still having trouble believing it. If we could convince them to send someone over, having an officer around might stop the killer from trying again."

"Yeah. But it wouldn't tell us who the killer is. It might drive them away for a while, until things settle down. It might create enough chaos that we never learn the truth."

"I can't leave your mother there if we don't solve this."

We stared at each other for a minute.

Dad said, "You have to keep investigating. I'll stay with

your mother today. I'll ask Marty and Joe to come over after church, and I don't think Simon's shop is open on Sundays. They can take turns watching the hallway and keeping an eye on anyone who goes into one of the patient rooms. You and Mackenzie should focus on finding answers. But I don't know how we'll do this without telling all of them what we're really doing."

"You're right." I closed my eyes. My fingernails dug into my palm. Panic battered my mind, screaming, *Run, run!* But I had to be stronger than my body's instinct. We wouldn't save Mom, and the others, by irrational action.

Don't run. Think!

We needed to solve this fast. The police might not believe us, and they almost certainly couldn't afford the resources to protect everyone and track down clues quickly.

Confidentiality be damned. I opened my eyes. "It's time. Marty and Joe, Mackenzie, even Simon, I guess. We need a full squad."

We grabbed our things and headed for the car. As we pulled out, Dad asked, "Would it help to know who is on duty Sunday nights?"

"It might. If the patients were suffocated, that narrows it down to who might be there early on a Monday morning. But a doctor would notice signs of suffocation, even if without a thorough autopsy, I think." I shook my head. "Anyway, they got sick, which doesn't fit with suffocation. If the women were poisoned, it might take time for the poison to work."

"Mrs. Gregorian's illness and recovery after dialysis suggest poison."

"Right." At a red light, I leaned forward as if my glare could force the color to change. "Poison might take hours to work, so that opens up all day Sunday. You'd think the killer would want an alibi for the actual time of death."

"But if an employee is killing patients because he has some kind of God complex, he might want to see it happen."

"Good point. There's another reason to ask who was around when the patients died. An attendant might have noticed symptoms that were gone by the time the doctor determined the cause of death."

"It will be hard to ask the staff questions like that without making people suspicious," Dad said. "But if it turns out that Penelope Valentine was in the Alzheimer's unit . . ."

I nodded. "It's getting harder to believe in an innocent explanation. Protecting the patients takes precedence over protecting Sunshine Haven's reputation."

We didn't have to say it: this was getting too close to Mom.

Chapter Thirteen

D AD AND I sped to Sunshine Haven. Once we arrived, Dad raced across the parking lot on foot, while I hobbled behind. When he gave an anguished look back, I waved him on. If our analysis of Sunday night being the killer's prime time was correct, everyone was safe for a few more hours. But that didn't lessen our need to check on Mom *now*.

I got to the Alzheimer's unit hallway as Dad burst out of Mom's room. He stared at me wild-eyed. "She's not here!"

I leaned on my cane, dragging in breath.

"Don't panic." Was I telling him or myself? "She could be in one of the common rooms, at breakfast . . ."

Dad glanced at his watch. "It's after ten!" He drew in a breath and gave me a shaky smile. "I'm sure you're right. Let's check the sunroom."

A buzz of cheerful voices filled the large, crowded room. I didn't immediately spot Mom among all the other white- and gray-haired heads, but Dad made a beeline to her.

"Isaac!" She scooted forward in her seat and lifted her face for his kiss. Dad took her hand and stood beside her.

Mom greeted me with a smile, but she squinted with her eyebrows pinched together, as if puzzled.

"Hi, Mom."

"Hi, sweetie. You look tired. You ought to get more rest."

"Thanks, Mom." I'd slept eleven hours the night before, and when I looked in the mirror that morning, I'd thought I seemed healthier, not so drawn and haggard. Mom might be thinking of me as a young adult, although she often suggested I ought to color my hair and take better care of my skin. This time, I was too relieved to take offense.

"Is this a party?" Dad asked.

Mom beamed. "We had a lovely concert. Such nice singing."

I glanced around the room, and a nearby woman caught my eye. She stepped closer and said, "It was the weekly church service, but it's mostly singing and reading a few passages. The choir from a local church comes here after their regular service."

I thanked her, and she rejoined an older couple. Dad was a secular Jew and Mom was a lapsed Catholic, more or less agnostic, but Mom had always enjoyed exploring various religions. It was nice that Sunshine Haven had activities like this for the residents. Visitors must enjoy the service as well, since almost half the people in the room looked too young and healthy to be residents.

I sighed, my muscles trembling as the tension faded. No seats were empty near Mom, and standing was making the pain in my thigh radiate up into my back and down to my foot.

I told Dad, "I'm going to see if Heather is in."

He nodded without taking his eyes off Mom. I glanced

around the room as I made my way toward the doorway. With this many people here, would that make it easier or harder for a killer? If Sundays were always like this, with lots of visitors throughout the day, an outsider could easily sneak in. But the crowd also meant more eyes on the patients.

Still, most visitors wouldn't stay all day. At some point, the residents would head back to their rooms. Would anyone notice if a visitor slipped into one of those rooms? I wouldn't know who was supposed to be visiting each patient. Someone might have witnessed the murderer at work but not realized what they saw.

I blew out a frustrated breath as I got back to the front room with the reception desk. All I could do was keep investigating the mystery and hope we'd uncover a clue.

I searched my memory for the receptionist's name. "Carla, right?"

"Yes. You're Mrs. Tessler's daughter?"

"Yes, Kate. Is Heather in?"

"No, she doesn't work weekends."

Oh, right. It made sense that the director would work a regular Monday through Friday schedule. But I didn't want to wait until the next day to get information, not when a killer might be at work that evening. I thanked Carla and moved to the far corner of the lounge before calling Heather's cell phone. It rang six times before she answered.

"Kate, what's up?"

"I'm at Sunshine Haven. Can you join me here as soon as possible?"

"I'm meeting someone shortly." The sound of running water came from the background.

"How about this afternoon?"

Heather sighed. "Today isn't good. I'm not sure when I'll be free."

I heard a muffled swear and the loud bang of her phone hitting a hard surface. I flinched.

"Sorry, sorry. Look, I'm in a rush. If it's urgent, can we do this over the phone? I can call you from my car in about fifteen minutes."

I had another idea.

"How about if you tell Carla to give me some information?" When Heather didn't answer right away, I said, "It's important. Maybe not an exaggeration to say life or death."

She gave a sharp intake of breath. "If it's that important, I can cancel my . . . appointment."

"No, that's all right. I'm sure Carla can help, but you need to tell her it's okay to talk to me."

Another long pause before she said, "Fine. Put her on."

I crossed to Carla and handed her the phone. Heather talked for about a minute, but she'd hung up by the time Carla handed my phone back.

"She says I'm supposed to give you any information you need."

I didn't blame her for sounding skeptical. It wouldn't be legal for Carla to give me access to confidential files.

I said, "I want to know who's on duty here on Sundays, especially Sunday night through Monday morning. Also, what regular activities are scheduled on Sundays?"

"All right. Give me five minutes." She turned to her computer.

I backed away while dialing Mackenzie. "Mac, I need you to do something right away."

"Sure."

"Heather has a meeting soon. It sounded like she'd be getting in her car within fifteen minutes. Any chance you can get to her house and follow her?"

"On my way. Am I looking for anything special?"

"See who she meets." The sound of a door slamming came through the phone. "If it's someplace public, try to get close and listen to their conversation. She doesn't know you."

"Got it." A car engine started. "Leaving now."

The girl moved fast.

I said goodbye and hung up so she could concentrate on driving. I wasn't sure where either Heather or Mackenzie lived, and the greater Phoenix area was huge. But if Mackenzie had been researching Heather, presumably Mac knew where her target lived and thought she might get there in time. It was worth a shot. Heather was meeting someone on a Sunday afternoon, and she had hesitated before calling it an appointment. She could simply be meeting a friend, but she'd spoken like someone trying to avoid questions. Which, of course, made me ask questions.

In the meantime, I could get what I needed from Carla and take advantage of the Sunday chaos at Sunshine Haven to poke around. I lowered myself into one of the lobby chairs. It was a wide padded chair with arms, but fortunately, the cushions were firm and it kept my butt above my knees instead of the other way around. I now struggled to get out of soft chairs, especially if they had low seats. I never used to think about these things, but I suppose any place serving an elderly population knew which chairs made it easier for people to get up again.

I concentrated on my breathing, using the meditation techniques the German physical therapist had taught me. Normally, I hated meditation. It was so boring I got mad rather than relaxed, but it did seem to calm my reaction to pain.

Carla crossed the room, carrying some papers. I smiled my gratitude that she hadn't made me come to her instead.

"Here's the work schedule and the social schedule for today and last Sunday," she said. "I put an X next to the one-time events. The others are all regular except for holidays."

"This is great. Thanks. Do you know if all the employees were here as scheduled the past two Sundays?"

"I can double-check the time cards, but I think so. The cleaning crew rotates, though. It's an outside service. They take care of the staffing, and I think turnover is pretty high." Carla shrugged. "Not that I blame them, a job like that."

"The cleaning crew comes at night?"

"They clean the patient rooms during the day, and a separate group comes every night to clean the public rooms and bathrooms. But the big cleaning crew comes Sunday night, for things that don't need to be done daily."

I groaned. Carla didn't even blink. Apparently, she'd decided someone with her cool, professional demeanor ignored bizarre behavior.

"Can I get you some water or a cup of coffee?" She gestured toward a counter with coffee urns.

"A cup of coffee would be amazing. Thanks. With a

good splash of milk or cream." I hated to make someone wait on me, but at the moment, I hated the idea of getting up and down more. While she took care of the coffee, I pondered the cleaning service. They hadn't been on Heather's list of employees, no doubt because they weren't actually employees of the home. This new information widened the field of suspects considerably.

On the other hand, the Sunday night crew wasn't supposed to go into patient rooms. That didn't necessarily mean they couldn't. Were the rooms locked at night? Probably not, since the night staff would need access in case of an emergency.

Still, they wouldn't gain anything from killing patients.

But people did crazy things. When you made assumptions about how someone *should* behave, you got into trouble. Every bell curve had outliers.

I closed my eyes and groaned again. If people weren't acting logically, or if I couldn't guess at the logic they were using, anything could be true.

A throat cleared. I glanced up at Carla. Her wide eyes suggested my nuttiness was starting to crack even her well-polished facade.

She handed me the coffee as the main doors whooshed open and someone crossed the lobby. I couldn't see past Carla at first, so I didn't identify the new person until he turned down the hallway.

I said, "That man who just came in, he's a physical therapist?"

The one who was possibly having an affair with Kellie Armstrong, daughter of one of our dead women.

Carla glanced back and nodded.

"Would he be working here on a Sunday?" I asked. "In this building?"

"Probably not. They sometimes visit patients in their rooms, instead of making them go next door. But I don't think any of the PTs work on Sundays."

I stared at her. "So what would he be doing here?"

"It's possible he's visiting a friend or family member, but most likely he's here for the dogs."

My head throbbed. I took a sip of coffee. "Dogs?"

"A volunteer group brings therapy dogs in on Sundays. They're a lot of fun, and sometimes staff who aren't working drop by for that."

"You're kidding me," I whined.

"No." Carla backed away. "If that's all . . . ?"

"For the moment. Thanks."

I lifted the mug and simply inhaled the scent for a minute. The whole "breathe in and out" part of meditation was more interesting with a delicious smell.

I couldn't let the weight of the problem crush me. It was looking like anyone, literally anyone at all, might be in the building on a Sunday. Staff who were scheduled to work that day, and those who weren't. Friends and families of patients. Random strangers. What were they thinking, not having better security in this place?

I slumped back and sighed. They were trying to make it like a real home, not a prison or even a hospital. And granted, they usually wouldn't need security. The receptionist was there to help people, not to stop them.

I looked over the papers Carla had given me, but I'd almost lost hope of finding clues. The names were familiar because they'd been on Heather's original list, but none of the employees scheduled for Sunday nights were on our shortlist of suspects.

I was questioning that list anyway. Family members might have killed a patient for an inheritance. They wouldn't need to kill additional patients on a weekly schedule. A staff member who wanted money, to support a drug problem or a lavish lifestyle, would steal cash or valuables, or try to extort money from the patients. That went with what Mom said about someone asking for more money. But then why kill the patients? That would eliminate the source of cash.

Unless they were trying to get rid of witnesses? But that wouldn't explain the regular weekly schedule. Plus, targeting Alzheimer's patients made sense if you wanted to trick people and knew any complaints they made afterward might be blamed on their poor memories and confusion. They were the one group a thief *didn't* need to kill.

I felt like I'd gotten the pieces for three or four different jigsaw puzzles and I was trying to make them fit into one picture.

Maybe it was time to focus on the angel of death theory. Ignore any pieces that didn't fit that image. But if we had someone killing for the sake of killing, how could we identify that person? I'd hoped that hadn't been the answer, because an angel of death would be almost impossible to uncover. Short of setting up hidden cameras in every hallway and waiting for the killer to strike again, how could we stop the murderer?

I needed new clues. Preferably ones that simply showed

up and dropped into my lap.

A young woman came in the front door and crossed to Carla, who gestured toward me. The girl turned and headed for me.

She was blonde and plump, maybe sixteen. She stopped in front of me and smiled, showing dimples in her cheeks. "Hi. I'm Zinnia."

"Like the flower?"

"Right! My grandpa said I should help you."

"Okay . . . who's your grandfather?"

"Henry Wilson."

Ah, this must be one of the granddaughters who volunteered at Sunshine Haven. "What did your grandfather say you should help me with?"

She looked around the room carefully. It was empty except for Carla, who was at least twenty feet away and tapping at her keyboard. Zinnia leaned toward me and whispered, "He asked if I've seen anything suspicious. I thought about it and came up with some things so he said to let you know what I found!"

"You have noticed suspicious things?" Could this be a clue dropping right into my lap?

She sat in the next chair and arranged her short skirt. She bit her lower lip and scanned the room as if checking for enemy spies. "I think someone is giving the patients the wrong medicine."

The wrong medicine? No, that didn't fit with our theories at all! I wanted new clues to the deaths, not a brand-new path to follow. I should have been more specific with my wish.

Wait, maybe the deaths were accidental overdoses, or

intentional ones. It would depend on when the wrong medicine was administered. "Tell me about it."

"I've been volunteering here since I was fourteen, you know? Almost two whole years! I have a lot of experience. I know what the patients are supposed to be like."

"Isn't there a lot of variety? Even the Alzheimer's patients won't all be the same, and other patients have different problems."

"Sure, but some of these people I've known the whole time. I've seen *changes*."

Interesting, but I didn't want to give too much credit to a teenager's medical diagnosis. "People are likely to change as they get older and sicker."

She huffed out a breath. "But they don't go back and forth!"

I imagined they could have up and down days, but maybe she was onto something.

"Why don't you tell me exactly what you've seen, in detail?" I pulled out a notebook.

"About three months ago. That's when it started. One of the ladies had always been real lively. Like, her mind wasn't all there, but she was fun, you know? But then one week, she could hardly talk. I thought, like you said, she'd gotten worse. But the next week, she was okay again, and I remembered how her eyes looked. I see a lot of people when they're in pain, and when they've had painkillers. They get a look, right? It's in the eyes."

"You think she was in more pain the week before?"

She shook her head. "I think she was on more painkillers. Too many. I think someone has been giving patients the wrong amounts of drugs."

Chapter Fourteen

I T TOOK ANOTHER ten minutes to get all the information from Zinnia. She tended to ramble and go in circles, but she seemed observant and clever. When I glanced back over my notes and put stars next to the main points, I went light-headed. Mrs. Gregorian, who had gotten sick but recovered, and Brit Egland, the most recent death, were among the patients Zinnia thought had been affected. I reminded myself to breathe and to think logically. I didn't want to make assumptions.

Zinnia mostly worked with the Alzheimer's patients. About half of them, in her opinion, had shown signs of oversedation in the last three months. Zinnia confirmed that Penelope Valentine had been in the Alzheimer's unit, which meant both dead women and the one who recovered were in the same wing. That definitely suggested something wrong.

However, Zinnia hadn't noticed any problems with Penelope Valentine's sedation level. So far, my mother hadn't been affected either, but she was the most recent addition.

Alzheimer's patients could be difficult. They got confused and tried to wander. Sometimes, they got violent. Giving such patients extra sedatives could simply be a nurse's way of making their job easier. That might be unethical, or even illegal—Jen had said something about that—but it didn't necessarily mean someone wanted to kill patients. Had the deaths been accidental overdoses?

But it was weird that the extra medication seemed to affect one patient at a time, according to Zinnia. If a nurse had been overdosing patients to keep them calm, why not overdose all the patients on their shift? Maybe they couldn't get enough medicine? Maybe they targeted the one who seemed most difficult that day?

Zinnia had estimated the dates she'd noticed problems, and each episode seemed to be about two weeks apart. Was that significant, and if so, why? The overmedicating didn't seem timed to the deaths, but it wasn't like the girl had been keeping a record. She was basing her recollections on things such as "the week after school started" or "the day they had Halloween cupcakes with lunch."

"Did you tell anyone about this?" I tried to keep the censure out of my voice, but questions about patient care should be reported.

"Uh-huh. I told Mr. Mendelson a while ago. He said he'd look into it, and I shouldn't tell anyone else."

"He's the one who doesn't like gossip?"

She rolled her eyes. "I guess I understand, but he acts like I can't keep my mouth shut because I'm a girl. I'm glad you're here today, because he doesn't work weekends. If he saw us talking . . ." She scrunched up her face. "And maybe I'm not keeping my mouth shut right now, but Grandpa said I should talk to you."

"I'm glad you did. This could be important." I'd have to take a closer look at Norman Mendelson. Had he ignored

Zinnia's complaint, assuming she was wrong because she was young and female? Had he actually investigated? If so, wouldn't he have told Heather?

Or was he involved?

"It's not gossip if you're investigating, right?" Zinnia asked. "But you don't really think this has anything to do with those women who died, do you?"

"What do you mean?"

She and I hadn't talked about the deaths, other than acknowledging that Brit Egland and Penelope Valentine were no longer with us.

She shrugged and glanced around. After a family passed through the room, she turned back to me and lowered her voice. "Grandpa said you were investigating and that's why it was so important to tell you what I saw. But no one would want to hurt these people!"

"You're probably right. Either way, it's definitely something you shouldn't gossip about. Your grandfather told you I was investigating the patient deaths?"

She frowned. "Not exactly. He asked about Mrs. Valentine and Mrs. Egland. They both passed away recently. Then he told me you were looking into some things here and I should help you if I could."

"I see." Except I hadn't told Henry Wilson about the deaths. I'd only told him I was suspicious because of the phone call warning me to mind my own business. As a board member who didn't work at the home, I doubted he'd even hear about every death.

As far as I knew, the only other person who knew the deaths were suspicious was Heather Garcia—and possibly a murderer.

My mind whirled, but Zinnia was starting to fidget and I needed to finish my questioning. "Can you tell me anything about Mrs. Valentine or Mrs. Egland, or their families? Did you get to meet any family members?"

"I saw Mrs. Valentine's daughter a few times, but I didn't hang around. Mainly, I spend time with patients when their families aren't here."

"And Mrs. Egland?"

Zinnia's cheeks went pink. "I know her grandson, Ryan, from school."

"Are you friends?"

She bit her lip as her blush blossomed. "Not really."

"But he's cute?"

She nodded. "I'm sorry his grandma died. He must be really sad. I wanted to say something when I saw him in school, but I didn't know what."

"Just try to be nice, I guess."

"He's really shy. His mom seems sweet, but his stepfather is kind of a jerk."

"He has a stepfather?" Ryan's mother, Lisa Delacruz, had said she and Ryan lived in that house alone.

"I guess, or maybe it's his mom's boyfriend. He came here to visit Mrs. Egland with them a couple of times." Her expressive face showed her dislike of the man.

"Did he do something that bothered you?"

"He asked me a lot of questions, all jolly like. It was weird. Like he was *flirting*. And he must be at least forty!"

"What kind of questions?"

"About what I do here, how things are run, stuff like

that. Nothing too personal, but why would he talk to me at all if he didn't want something?"

Why indeed? Was he simply a perv creeping on a pretty teenager? Or was he trying to learn more about the home's operations? Maybe it wasn't yet time to give up on investigating the patients' family members. My head throbbed with all the possibilities.

Zinnia sat up straight and clapped her hands. "They're here."

"Ryan and his family?" I glanced toward the door.

"No, the dogs." She bounced to her feet but turned back to me. "If you want people to talk, do it while the dogs are here. It's like they wake up."

I assumed she meant the patients woke up in the presence of the dogs, rather than the other way around.

"Thanks for the tip. And for all the other information. You've been a big help." I gave her my card. "Please call if you think of anything else, or if you see anything suspicious."

She flashed me a bright smile and dashed after the group of humans and dogs passing through the room. I took a minute to finish my coffee and stretch my leg before crossing to Carla.

"Zinnia seems like a nice girl," I said.

"She is. A real natural with the patients. We get teenage volunteers in here fairly often, but few of them are as friendly and outgoing as Zinnia."

"Sundays seem chaotic. Church service, lots of visitors, and then the dogs. I'm surprised you don't spread out the activities more."

"They have activities during the week, crafts and games and things like that. Some of the therapy dog handlers visit during the week as well and stop by patient rooms one at a time. But several of the handlers work during the week, so they can only come in on weekends." Carla studied me for several seconds. "Also, they schedule extra activities on the weekend because so many family members are here."

"You mean so visitors can enjoy them as well . . ." I paused. "No, you mean because visitors get to *see* the patients having a good time."

She nodded. "I'm being honest, since Ms. Garcia said I should help you. You must know that Sunshine Haven is struggling to rebuild its reputation. It's important that people see the positive things."

"That makes sense. There's nothing wrong with a little good marketing, as long as it's not trying to cover up nasty secrets."

Carla shook her head and chuckled. "There's nothing like that here. It's a nice place to work, and Ms. Garcia is good. Sure, some of the employees are annoying, but you get that anywhere."

"Like Mr. Mendelson?"

"Mm. Fortunately, I don't have to deal with him very often, since I mainly work weekends."

"Lucky you. He sounds . . ."

"Uptight? He's one of those petty tyrants who acts like the whole place belongs to him. He even stops in on the weekends to check up on us."

"Really? So he might be here on a Sunday?"

"In theory, he works eight to five, Monday through Friday. I've seen his time cards. But I've also seen him here on Saturdays and Sundays. He doesn't stay long, just bustles in, asks questions, like he's sure you've been up to something scandalous, pokes around for an hour checking on everyone, and leaves again."

"And he's afraid of gossip."

Her cool, professional demeanor slipped back on, and she eyed me for a moment. "He's right about that. Gossip can be dangerous to a place like this. I trust you won't repeat what I've said."

"Of course not. I understand the importance of protecting the business's reputation. But it seems like Mr. Mendelson has an obsession."

"I suppose you could call it that. In my opinion, he's a control freak."

Did Mr. Mendelson get an ego boost from throwing his weight around? Or was he terrified of gossip because he had secrets? One more question that needed answering, especially since he was now on the list of people who might be there on a Sunday afternoon.

"Well, I guess I'll check out the fun. Thanks for your help."

By the time I got to the sunroom, the dogs and their handlers had spread out with different clusters of patients and visitors. Happy chatter and laughter filled the room as elderly residents and young grandchildren bonded over the dogs. The room smelled a bit doggy, a nice change from medicinal cleaning products and air freshener. I spent a few minutes with Mom and Dad as she stroked the ears of a panting beagle and spoke to it in baby talk. Then I wandered around the room, listening in on other conversations. Good thing Jen wasn't there to scold me for neglecting my daughterly duties.

The male PT was chatting with a group of people I didn't know. Not a great time to talk to him. In a far corner of the room, I lingered by a skinny man in a wheelchair. His scalp showed splotchy age spots through his sparse hair. He didn't seem to have any family visiting. The only people nearby were a gray-haired woman with her eyes closed, and the burly, fortysomething man crouched beside the dog. The man in the wheelchair hunched forward, his hand on the dog's head. The beautiful Irish setter rested her chin on his knee, looking up adoringly. I moved closer so I could hear the elderly man's hoarse voice over the background murmur. He was telling war stories, remembering the military dogs.

A minute later, he glanced at my cane, then up at me. "Well hello, young lady."

I grinned. "Don't mind me. I'm just enjoying your stories."

"Oh, no one wants to listen to my rambling. Except Sasha here." He stroked the dog's ears.

"She seems like a good listener."

The dog handler said, "He's one of her favorite patients. But I should spread the love around, if you're going to keep him company."

"Oh, uh, sure." I glanced across the room at my parents. Jen's voice in my head scolded that I should be spending time with them, not a random stranger. But Mom had Dad, plus a circle of chattering patients and visitors. Besides, I was trying to learn more about Sunshine Haven, and this patient looked like he could have lived there for years.

We introduced ourselves. His name was Tommy, and we chatted for several minutes about his life and mine. I guessed he wasn't an Alzheimer's patient, because he seemed mentally sharp, if physically frail. I pointed out my mother and asked questions about the home. I finally got one interesting nugget of information.

"I had a friend in your mother's hallway. Penelope Valentine. Beautiful lady." Tommy sighed.

"Oh, I'm sorry. I know she passed away two weeks ago."

"Nearly everyone I know has died."

"I gather she went suddenly." I wanted to get information but not make him suspicious or upset. "Did you notice anything unusual in the day or two before she died?"

"Unusual?"

I shrugged. "Anything to suggest she was unwell? Any . . . extra attention from the staff?"

"I did notice a strange man come out of her room as I was on my way to visit her. Not one of the staff, because he wasn't in uniform. At least, I'm pretty sure it was her room. I had barely turned into that hallway so I could have been mistaken. When I asked her about her visitor, she seemed confused, but poor Penny was often confused about things that had just happened. We mainly talked about the past."

"When was that?"

"The evening before she died. I don't remember the date."

The perfect time for a poisoner, if the poison took several hours to work. "Could it have been Mr. Mendelson? He works here, but I don't think he wears a uniform."

"No, I know him. This was a big guy."

"What else do you remember about him?"

"My eyes aren't so good anymore. He had short hair, light-colored, gray or maybe blond."

"Any idea how old he was?"

"Younger than me." He chuckled. "Maybe forty or fifty? I can't recall his face. Now, why is that?" He thought for moment. "Oh right, he put his hand up, kind of rubbed his face and turned away. Not friendly at all. But some people are nervous around us old folks in wheelchairs. They'd rather ignore us than have to interact."

My heart pounded, but I smiled and kept my tone mild. "You said he was big. Tall?"

"Hmm. It's harder for me to judge from down here." He gestured at the wheelchair. "But he didn't strike me as especially tall. More bulky, you know? Like someone who does physical work. Maybe average height or a bit more." His shrewd eyes studied me. "What's this about?"

I glanced around. My gaze met that of Mr. Mendelson across the room. The gossip-hater was here, and he was glaring at me.

Chapter Fifteen

M ENDELSON STARTED TOWARD us.
I put a hand on Tommy's wheelchair and leaned down. "I'll tell you all about it sometime, if I can. But for now, please pretend we've only been chatting about times long past."

Mendelson joined us, his hands on his hips. "Miss Tessler, I see you're here again. I hope you aren't bothering the residents with your questions."

"I prefer *Ms.* Tessler, and I was having a lovely chat with a very interesting man."

My new friend beamed at Mendelson. "Not many people want to listen to my war stories, but this young lady has been humoring me."

I nodded. "It's wonderful to see how excited everyone is about the dogs."

He gave a harrumph. "Waste of money."

"You pay the handlers to bring in the dogs?"

"Well, they're volunteers, but there are expenses. In any case, look at this, this *disorder.*" He gestured around the room as if people were shooting paintballs and Silly String instead of petting dogs.

"I see people having a good time. Don't you want that?"

"We want people to be satisfied quietly and calmly."

I wasn't sure whether to laugh, be annoyed, or feel sorry for the guy, forced to deal with actual human beings in all their complexity and messiness. Maybe he should get a job restocking the shelves at a container store instead. But why did he come in on the weekends if he didn't enjoy it? Did it bother him more to be at home, knowing the chaos here?

If I'd been feeling generous, I might have tried to placate Mendelson. But where was the fun in that? I could confront him about the pain medication, but I'd have more ammo after I talked to Heather. Besides, I didn't want to get Zinnia in trouble, or make my new friend Tommy more suspicious.

I spotted Mrs. Gregorian and her family. I'd probably learned all I could from them about Mrs. Gregorian's illness and recovery, but Zinnia had named Mrs. Gregorian as one of the overmedicated patients. The girl thought that episode had been at least six weeks earlier, so not related to the illness, but it opened up a new line of questioning.

And another thing: Mom had gotten worried about money shortly after seeing Mrs. Gregorian. Could that have been the neighbor she meant, the one who claimed she'd been asked for more money? Could "Mr. Brown—no, Mr. Rogers" actually be Mendelson? He'd been wearing a brown button-up sweater, so maybe that triggered Mom's memory but sent it in the wrong direction.

I turned to Tommy. "It was lovely talking to you. I hope we'll meet again when I'm here visiting my mother. I need to speak to some other new friends now."

Mendelson scowled and shuffled his feet.

I grinned. "Have a great day."

I felt his gaze on me as I turned to cross the room.

Between the residents, visiting family members, dogs, and their handlers, the spacious room was a swirl of activity. I waited for a woman using a walker to cross in front of me. My leg ached, so I shifted more of my weight onto my good leg and the cane. A man to my right half turned, gesturing wildly with his arms while he told a story. I flinched back to avoid being hit.

Something slammed into my left leg. I grunted in pain as my leg collapsed. My cane swung upward, goosing the gesturing man and tangling in his legs.

The next thing I knew, I was sitting on the floor in a heap. I looked up at the wheelchair that had hit me, and into Tommy's distressed face.

"Oh, Kate, I'm sorry. I don't know what happened." He twisted in an attempt to look over his shoulder, but he didn't have much range of motion. "Someone pushed me forward."

People circled us, watching. Nobody stood behind Tommy's wheelchair at the moment.

I said softly, "Did you notice anyone behind you?"

He glanced around at the crowd and murmured, "I didn't look back. I'm really sorry."

Had Mendelson, or someone else, intentionally pushed Tommy's wheelchair at me? Or was it merely an accident from the crowd?

"It's not your fault." I straightened my leg and massaged my thigh.

The woman with the walker asked if I was hurt, and a voice behind me said, "Do you need help?"

I shifted to look at the person, but Mendelson pushed in

front of them. "Don't move," he said.

"Excuse me?"

"Stay right there until the ambulance arrives."

"I don't need an ambulance." I needed people to stop staring at me. "I'm fine." Except for being stuck on the floor.

"If you are injured, you must go to the hospital to be checked. Otherwise you will have to fill out a form absolving Sunshine Haven of all liability." The light reflected off his glasses, hiding his eyes, but his mouth twitched like he was trying not to smile.

I groaned. "I'll sign the form."

I probably had new bruises on my old bruises, but I wasn't about to go to the hospital for that. Any strained muscles could be dealt with at my PT appointment the next day.

"Get a form from Carla at the front desk," Mendelson snapped at a woman in an aide's uniform. He looked down at me, his hands on his hips. "You'll have to stay there until you sign it."

Dad pushed his way through the crowd. "Don't be ridiculous. She can get into a chair."

We ignored Mendelson's protests as Dad and another man helped me up. Someone vacated a nearby seat, and I limped to it. Mendelson walked away. I was willing to bet he had pushed Tommy's wheelchair at me in order to distract me or prevent me from talking to the Gregorians. But with everyone's attention focused elsewhere, no one witnessed the event. Now, Mendelson was with the Gregorians, probably warning them about the dangers of gossiping with me. I hoped he could feel my glare, because I couldn't do anything else at the moment.

The aide came back and I signed the paperwork. I rested for a few more minutes, largely because I didn't want to walk through the crowd. Finally, the dog handlers headed out. Some patients drifted toward their rooms, while others settled in with family members. I hadn't noticed Mendelson leaving, but I didn't see him anywhere.

I heaved myself to my feet and headed toward the Gregorians, trying not to limp more than necessary. When I got close to the family, the son-in-law I'd spoken to before blocked my way, his arms crossed. He didn't look friendly.

I smiled anyway. "Nice to see you again."

"We don't have anything to say to you."

Mentally, I sighed, but I kept my smile in place. "I'm not sure I understand."

"We know you're a journalist trying to dig up dirt on this place. You won't get any from us."

"I'm not here as a journalist."

"Yeah, right." He leaned closer. "Do you know how hard it was to find a good place? We can't afford to start over."

"I think there's been a misunderstanding. Mr. Mendelson obviously warned you about me, but I'm honestly not here for a story. What did he say I'm trying to do?"

"He said shocking stories sell papers, and you'd turn any little problem into a big deal to get a good story. But if this place gets closed down, all these patients are out of luck." He lowered his voice. "Including my mother-in-law, and I *cannot* have her living with us again."

I gestured toward my parents. "My mother is here. Do you think I don't know how hard it is to find a good place?

Do you think I'd want to start over?"

He looked more confused than angry. "Then why are you asking questions about Mom's sickness?"

It was hard to explain without explaining everything, but it wasn't yet time to reveal the potential danger. In any case, I didn't have more questions about the illness. I had questions about whether someone had been overmedicating patients, and whether someone was pressuring them for money. It would be hard to get proof of any drugging that might have happened six weeks before, but extortion could leave a paper trail.

"I am a journalist, but my mother is more important to me than any story. I don't want anything to be wrong here. I'd love to prove that this is the best, safest place ever, for her sake. But I need evidence. I'm not going to believe everything is great merely because I want it to be true."

"That makes sense. But our experience here has been as good as you could expect."

"I'm glad to hear that. I promise I don't want to shut down Sunshine Haven. I want to make sure no one is taking advantage of the patients, though."

"What do you mean?"

"Something I've learned suggests patients are being asked for money. It could be a misunderstanding, but I'd like to check. Do you know if anyone here, perhaps a staff member or even another patient, has pressured your mother-in-law for money?"

"No. At least, I don't think so." He glanced back at his mother-in-law. His wife chatted with her but watched us. The guy gave her a smile before turning back to me. "My wife has power of attorney for her mother's bank account. We don't use it very often, though."

"Please ask your wife to check the account. See if anyone has withdrawn money. It might be a check or even an ATM withdrawal. It sounds like a couple hundred dollars here and there might not be missed."

He studied me, clearly still wary, but nodded. "I'll take a look. I guess that can't hurt."

"Thanks. If you find anything suspicious, you can tell Ms. Garcia, Sunshine Haven's director." I figured he'd feel more comfortable with that than with trusting me. "We all want the same thing, to make sure this place is safe and comfortable and the patients are happy."

He studied his wife and mother-in-law. "Yeah. Nobody should have to see someone go through Alzheimer's. If someone is stealing from these people, that's sick."

I thanked him and joined my parents.

"Your mother is ready to go to her room for a rest," Dad said. "You look like you could use a nap too."

"Yeah, but . . . I'll stick around."

Dad helped Mom to her feet. "She only has one chair in her room. No need for both of us to stay."

Dad wouldn't feel comfortable unless he could keep Mom under his gaze. But what about the other patients in the Alzheimer's unit?

"I'll move one of the lobby chairs so I can see the hallway entrance."

I didn't want to say too much in front of Mom, but Dad nodded, so he understood. We couldn't watch every patient individually, but I could see who went into that unit and have a good idea of what room they visited. Knowing they were watched should discourage the killer. If the murderer did strike, at least I'd know who had been there. It wasn't the best way to solve the mystery, but I couldn't think of a better one. Even if we decided it was time to tell the police, that would involve long, complicated explanations. Who knew if they'd take us seriously? We had some odd coincidences but no proof.

I hugged Mom and headed for the lobby. The front desk had a good view down the hallway of the Alzheimer's unit. A waist-high gate blocked off that hallway, and the person at the front desk had to press the buzzer to unlock the gate. No doubt it was meant to keep the Alzheimer's patients from leaving the building without anyone noticing. It would also help me make sure I didn't miss anyone pretending to go toward the solarium and darting into the Alzheimer's unit instead.

None of the lobby chairs were situated to see the hallway, so I asked Carla to move one for me. She blinked a few times but complied. She even brought me another cup of coffee.

I settled into the chair, rubbing my thigh and thinking about everything that had happened. I now had three threads to follow. First, an illness or death on three consecutive Sunday nights. Second, the possibility that someone had been drugging patients. And third, the question of money. Had Mom's worry been a misunderstanding, or was somebody extorting money from the patients?

Were all these things related? Was someone drugging patients in order to get their money? Had that person turned to murder in recent weeks? If so, why? To get rid of witnesses? Maybe the person was a power-hungry psychotic who was increasing their level of evil. Maybe the deaths had been accidental overdoses, which would suggest someone not that familiar with the medicine. Zinnia's memories of when patients had seemed drugged didn't match with the deaths, but she wasn't always here, and the extortionist could have targeted the same patients more than once.

I sighed and ran a hand over my face. We'd gathered so much circumstantial evidence, but it only led to more questions. And the biggest one remained.

What should I do next?

I dug through my shoulder bag for my notebook so I could write down my thoughts. I also retrieved my phone and checked for missed calls or texts. I wouldn't have heard them in the noisy sunroom.

Mackenzie had texted: *We're in Florence.*

Italy? Unlikely. Wait, Arizona had a town called Florence. I could recall exactly nothing about it, so I switched to an internet search. Florence was about sixty miles from Phoenix. Its main claim to fame seemed to be multiple federal, state, and private prisons. Hopefully Mackenzie wasn't in one.

I texted back: *?*
Greek restaurant good food
Pls explain
Know this guy?

A few seconds later, a picture came through. It was a bit fuzzy from the indoor lighting, but it clearly showed Heather Garcia sitting at a cozy table across from a man.

I texted: *Board member Henry Wilson*
2 far 2 hear but looks romantic

So Heather, director of Sunshine Haven, had a personal relationship with a board member. Specifically, the one she insisted was a great guy and unlikely to be involved in anything nasty. She hadn't seen fit to mention their relationship to me, and they were meeting at a miles-out-of-the-way restaurant. However good the Greek food might be, I found it hard to believe they drove sixty miles for a business lunch.

Heather and Henry. I turned this over in my mind. Heather was a couple of years behind me in school, so she was about forty-seven. Henry looked about seventy and seemed fit, mentally sharp, and attractive. It wasn't an unreasonable romance, though his children might disagree. Mackenzie had done background on Wilson, so I asked: *Is he married?*

Divorced 10 years

I'd gotten the impression Heather wasn't married, but I'd never actually asked her. Since Mackenzie had been researching her as well, I asked: *Heather married?*

Never

Good. The situation was complicated enough without one of them cheating on a spouse. Yet apparently, they wanted to keep their relationship secret, or at least Heather did. Would it be considered a conflict of interest professionally? Probably. Did it hide anything worse?

As usual, I had no idea.

Chapter Sixteen

I NOW UNDERSTOOD why Heather had been so confident Wilson wouldn't have called to threaten me. This also explained why Zinnia had information I hadn't told Wilson. Heather must have given her lover some details of my investigation, and he'd let something slip to his granddaughter.

None of this meant either of them was involved in anything illegal. Still, I'd call Heather on her deceit and see what she had to say.

Mackenzie texted: *Orders?*

I replied: *Gyro, extra tzatziki.*

I couldn't think of any instructions for her, so I added. *Kidding. Enjoy lunch.*

She sent me a thumbs-up icon.

Thoughts of lunch made my stomach rumble, but I wasn't about to leave my post. I sighed and made notes on what I'd learned that morning. Several people came and went, often giving me a curious glance since my chair was in an odd position. The Gregorians escorted their mother to her room and left the building. The son-in-law gave me a frowning nod as he passed.

I looked back over my notes and marked a few highlights. I needed to talk to Heather, both about her actions and about Mendelson. I'd almost forgotten Zinnia's comments about the family of the most recent victim, Brit Egland. Zinnia said Brit's grandson, Ryan, had a stepfather who had been at Sunshine Haven, asked questions about the place, and was creepy. That might be worth exploring.

I'd been ready to absolve family members from blame, since they didn't seem to have a reason to hurt more than one patient, and an employee seemed a more likely culprit when it came to overmedication and extortion. But if I couldn't figure out how all these things were connected, maybe they weren't. Maybe some of it was coincidence, or multiple villains were at work. I'd have to follow every thread until I knew how they fit into the larger tapestry and hope the result didn't look like a Cubist Picasso painting when I finished.

Two attendants headed down the hallway of the Alzheimer's unit, pushing a cart filled with covered dishes.

"Who are they?" I asked Carla.

"Food services, delivering the lunches."

"Do these same two people bring the lunches every Sunday?"

"I think it varies. Some people need more help with their food, or need to be coaxed to eat, so the volunteers help, and the nurse, if she's not busy."

Before Carla finished speaking, an attendant I recognized but couldn't name headed down the hall, along with Zinnia, who waved at me.

Food would be a good way to give someone poison, but having two employees delivering food together made it harder, unless they were both involved. That seemed unlikely, and the number of other employees, volunteers, and family members around heightened the risks, especially on a Sunday. Still, I wandered down the hallway and watched people work. One of the food services employees was a tall, thin, dark-skinned man, possibly Ethiopian. The other was a plump, middle-aged woman from Mexico, judging by her accent. They smiled and chatted with the patients, pretending the bland, soft food was gourmet.

In the first room, a family member took over. Zinnia settled in with the next patient, encouraging her to eat. I made a note of who stayed with which patient, in case someone got ill that night.

I checked in with Mom and Dad. She dozed on the bed while he watched her with tired eyes.

"Everything okay?" I whispered.

He nodded as he got up. We stood in the hallway and kept our voices low.

"The Washingtons are on their way," he said. "I asked them to bring us lunch."

"Wonderful. The employees are delivering meals now. Do we let Mom eat that food?"

We looked at each other for a while.

Dad sighed. "I'd rather not, but how long can we keep this up? And what about the other residents?"

"I know. I don't see how we can tell everyone they shouldn't eat the cafeteria food. I'm hoping our presence will discourage the killer from acting, but will he simply wait until tomorrow? We don't know if the Sunday pattern is an obsession, a matter of convenience, or a coincidence."

"Every day he has to wait is a day where we can learn something," Dad said. "Our best bet is to find out what's happening as soon as possible."

"You're right." I gazed through the doorway at Mom. My chest tightened so much I could hardly breathe. I wasn't ready to lose her. We had to solve this quickly, or get her out of here, which would open up a host of new problems.

I looked at Dad again. "After lunch, I'm going to follow another lead. I'll be more useful doing that."

"Absolutely. Can I do anything to help?"

How could I get Ryan and Lisa Delacruz to talk about the mysterious and unpleasant man in their lives? Lisa claimed no one else lived there, and her anxiety and timidity suggested someone afraid, possibly abused. Ryan had been quiet in a way that could have been interpreted as sullen, depressed, or merely an average teenager. I needed a way to get one of them to open up.

"Do you know where I could borrow a cool sports car?"

AN HOUR LATER, I'd eaten a burrito, Joe had taken over hallway monitoring duty, and Simon had delivered his electric-blue 1967 Camaro convertible. Marty and Simon would follow up on our remaining short list of employee suspects: nursing assistant Ana Marija Jurić and attendant Maximilian Richards. This plan had required giving all the Washingtons more information about the real situation, but that seemed like the best option since we'd gone from a vague possibility of trouble to a solid probability.

I was still half tempted to call the police. However, the CSI programs showing several top detectives and forensic scientists spending all their energy on one case were misleading. Most police departments were understaffed, and most police officers had received less than a year of training before starting their jobs. We still didn't have proof that someone had been murdered. An autopsy might answer that, but the police wouldn't do one simply because we asked. If the bodies had been buried, arranging for exhumation would be complicated and time-consuming. And if they'd been cremated, we were out of luck.

In the short term, at best we might hope the police could spare an officer to watch the hallway. We could do that ourselves, with less disruption to Sunshine Haven. If the police questioned people, it would be upsetting for the surviving family members, stressful for employees, and disastrous for the home's reputation. Reluctantly, I decided to wait one more day and try to persuade Heather to call in the authorities. She could tell her board members what was happening, and it would be better for Sunshine Haven's reputation if someone on staff reported the problem, not an outsider.

Mackenzie followed Heather back to Phoenix. I debated bringing Mackenzie with me to visit the Delacruz house, but a young, beautiful girl might do more harm than good when trying to get Ryan to talk. I wanted him relaxed and chatty, not bug-eyed and tongue-tied. If Heather went home and seemed ready to stay there, Mackenzie could start a deep background check on Norman Mendelson. Maybe I was letting my dislike for him bias me, but I wanted to find him guilty of *something*.

I managed the stick shift and clutch despite the ache in my left leg and pulled up to the Delacruz house about 2 p.m. On a Sunday afternoon, a lot of teens might be out with friends or playing school sports. But based on what Zinnia had said, Ryan was a loner. I parked in front of the house and headed up the walk. Would I be able to talk to Ryan alone? As uncommunicative as a surly teen could be, he'd be more likely to complain about his stepfather. Lisa might prevent Ryan from sharing family secrets.

I knocked on the door and Ryan answered a minute later. He stared at me blankly before recognition dawned in his eyes. "Mom's not here."

Excellent.

"Too bad. I was hoping to catch her." I shifted my body to the side to give him a clear view of the Camaro. "Oh well, it was a nice day for a drive with the top down."

I gestured toward the car.

His gaze slid past me and his eyes widened. "That's yours?" He took two steps out the door.

"Sixty-seven Camaro. Pretty nice, huh?"

He headed for the car as if pulled by an invisible rope, and we spent ten minutes circling it. I knew next to nothing about cars, but Simon had given me a few key phrases. I managed to carry on a conversation with those, murmurs of agreement, and occasional vague responses such as, "What do you think?" We even popped the hood, and Ryan nodded at the engine, though I couldn't tell if he knew any more than I did.

"Feel free to sit in the driver's seat," I said.

His wide-eyed look was half-reluctant, like he thought he shouldn't, but the temptation was too much to resist. He slid into the seat and caressed the steering wheel.

I limped around the car and climbed in on the passenger's side, settling the cane so it stuck up between my knees. Nothing would seem as nonthreatening to a teenage boy as a middle-aged lady with a limp. I tried not to sneeze at the too-strong smell of his manly body spray.

I slipped on sunglasses and leaned back, oozing relaxation and harmlessness. "You have a car?"

"Nah. We only have my mom's piece of sh—junk. But I know how to drive." He sighed. "I'd like to drive a car like this someday." He wasn't asking. He wasn't even hoping. He spoke with the wistfulness of someone who knew dreams didn't come true.

I wanted to hand him the keys.

Simon might not be happy about me letting a teenager drive his prize possession, so I merely said, "I guess it's hard to afford a second car."

"Yeah. I'll probably be *thirty* before I get my own." The despair in his voice suggested thirty might as well be a hundred.

I avoided looking directly at him and kept my voice casual. "Oh, right, your mom mentioned something... I remember. You two lost any inheritance you might have had from your grandmother when she went into Sunshine Haven. Too bad."

He gave a one-shouldered shrug. "It's not like Grandma was rich. And it was her money anyway. But I wish . . ."

"Hmm?"

He sighed again. "She always wanted to visit Europe, where her ancestors were from. We could have gone together. I would've taken care of her, but she waited too long."

"You two were close."

He ran his hands over the steering wheel, up and down, and gazed at the dashboard as if talking to it. "My dad died when I was six. He was an army sharpshooter. Mom kind of fell apart. Grandma picked me up at school every day, did the shopping, cooked meals, read me stories. I don't remember my father very well, but I remember Grandma making everything better."

"You were lucky to have her." A fragile bond stretched between us. I needed to turn the conversation in the right direction without breaking the mood. "I'm sorry she was taken from you so early. It must've been hard visiting her lately, what with the Alzheimer's."

"She talked to me like I was still a little kid. But I didn't mind, really. At least she knew who I was."

"She was lucky to have you as well. Now it's only you and your mother here . . ."

He nodded. If he had a stepfather, either the man wasn't living with them, or Ryan and his mother were hiding it.

"Oh, by the way, I met a friend of yours," I said.

His look suggested I was speaking a foreign language.

"Zinnia," I said. "I'm not sure of her last name, but please tell me you don't have a lot of classmates named Zinnia."

He gave me a ghost of a smile. "No, only one. She's not really my friend, though."

"Maybe not, but I think she'd like to be."

"Really?" The smile was more in evidence, along with pink in his cheeks. "But she's popular."

"She's also nice."

"How do you know her?" His brow wrinkled.

"You might've heard, when I was talking to your mom, I'm working on a story about nursing homes. I met Zinnia at Sunshine Haven. She volunteers there."

"Why were you talking about *me*?"

I had to be careful. "We were discussing some of her favorite patients. She was sad about your grandmother. She wanted to offer you her condolences, but she wasn't sure what to say."

"That's right. I saw her there a few times. I didn't realize she knew Grandma."

"I think when family members are there, the volunteers spend their time with other patients. I gather your stepfather talked to Zinnia."

"He's *not* my stepfather!"

Now we were getting somewhere. "Oh, sorry. Zinnia wasn't sure. She said a man came in with you and your mother, but Zinnia didn't like him much."

"Good." He scowled and his hands tightened on the steering wheel.

"Was he a family member? He must've been pretty close to you to visit your grandmother."

"He *was* my mom's boyfriend. He didn't care about Grandma, only her money."

Better and better. "But once your grandmother was in Sunshine Haven, she didn't have access to most of her money anymore."

"Sure, but *he* didn't know that. He's such a—a—sorry, I can't think of any words that I can use in front of you."

I smiled. "You can use any word in front of me. I don't mind."

"Grandma would."

I was developing a real soft spot for Ryan. Still, I needed to stay on topic. "What was so bad about your mother's boyfriend?"

He looked at me. "A lot of people think kids don't like their parents dating. It's not that. Mom deserves someone great in her life. But Steve is *not* great."

"He didn't treat your mother right?"

Ryan dropped his gaze and turned back toward the steering wheel, shaking his head. "They broke up months ago. He cheated on her, but I don't think Mom would've dumped him even then. Except Mom spent so much time taking care of Grandma, and Steve got tired of it. Then, after Grandma was at Sunshine Haven, Steve came around again. He tried to make up with Mom."

"He wanted her back?"

"That's what he said. He tried to act all nice to Grandma and me too, giving us gifts, but only cheap, stupid stuff. When Grandma died, Steve started talking about the inheritance. Mom said there wasn't any, and he got mad and . . ." Ryan's voice faded to a whisper. "He hit her." His hands choked the steering wheel.

"Oh, I'm so sorry." We sat in silence for a minute before I murmured, "Your mother didn't take Steve back, I gather?"

Ryan let out a long sigh and his shoulders slumped. "I hope she wouldn't have, but Steve stopped bothering her once he found out there was no money." He leaned back in the seat, his eyes half closed. He seemed more relaxed, his body drained of a great tension. I almost felt guilty for luring him into giving up confidences, but it seemed like he'd needed to talk to someone for a long time.

Unfortunately, I needed one more piece of information, and I didn't have a good excuse for asking.

"What's Steve's last name?"

Ryan straightened. "Why? You're not going to write any of this in your story, are you?"

"No, don't worry. Everything you said was off the record." I held his gaze. "Ryan, I'm going to be honest with you. I think something is wrong at Sunshine Haven, or was recently. I want to find out what it is."

He studied me for a minute. "You think my mom's ex-boyfriend might be involved?"

"I don't know, but I'd like to check up on him."

I could practically see the gears turning in Ryan's brain and wondered how much he was putting together.

He nodded. "Steven Hicks. He's a mechanic at a shop in Gilbert. And if he's involved, I hope you catch him and put him away forever."

"If he is involved, I'll make sure he pays. Do you know his home address?"

"Sorry. As long as he's not in our house, I don't care where he lives."

"Thanks, Ryan. You've been a big help. Maybe we can go for a ride sometime, if we get your mother's permission."

He looked hopeful. "She won't mind."

"Maybe not, but you should be cautious about getting in

a car with someone you barely know."

His gaze dropped to my cane and then settled on my forty-nine-year-old face. "What could you do to me?"

"Hey, people can be dangerous even if they don't look it. I might have a gun."

"Do you?" He sounded more curious than afraid.

"No. But you don't have proof of that." I decided not to try to convince him that I might be a martial arts black belt. I knew a woman my age who was, but Ryan might have to see that to believe it, and I was not the person to demonstrate ninja abilities.

He looked at the glove compartment, then my shoulder bag sitting on the floor, places I might have a gun, and shrugged. "I think you're all right, as long as you don't tell anyone what I said. But if you want to wait until Mom is here, okay. She's out shopping so it shouldn't be too long."

I chuckled. "Much as I'd like to take you for a drive now, I need to see what I can find out about Steven Hicks. I promise, I'll come back." I handed him a business card. "Give me a few days to sort out this thing I'm working on, and then have your mother call me. Maybe next weekend we can all go for a drive."

"Okay. If you're going to get Steve in trouble, that comes first."

He got out of the car, and I came around to the driver's side. He looked down at me as I sat. "Good luck."

"Thanks." I needed it.

Chapter Seventeen

A RIZONA HAD A dozen residents named Steven Hicks, so finding his home address would take a little work. The town of Gilbert, part of the larger Phoenix metropolitan area, had several automotive repair shops, but I took a wild guess that Hicks & Sons was the right one. They were open on Sundays, so I headed in that direction.

Hearing about Steven Hicks had given me the tingling sensation I got when I uncovered a key piece of information for a story. Even if I didn't yet know why something was important, that sixth sense told me I'd made a breakthrough.

Not that I'd always been right in the past, but still. If I was getting the feeling, and it turned out to be right, I'd know I hadn't lost all my journalistic talent. I might get back to where I'd been before.

All the factors tumbled together in my mind. I couldn't see how Hicks would benefit from hurting Mrs. Gregorian or Penelope Valentine, but he had hoped to benefit from Brit Egland's death via an inheritance to her daughter. Hicks might have been testing his poison on the other victims, or trying to deflect suspicion by confusing the crime motive through multiple deaths. Or maybe the other two patients hadn't been victims after all. In that case, the coincidence of the three episodes close together might have uncovered a murder that otherwise would have stayed hidden.

If Hicks was the killer, the other patients at Sunshine Haven should now be safe. He wouldn't have any reason to kill again.

Unless he was using additional deaths as a cover-up. Then he might decide to kill one or two more people to further confuse the trail. That wouldn't be smart. He would take a much greater risk by showing up at Sunshine Haven now, when he had no excuse to be there. Besides, multiple bodies piling up would make people suspicious. He might not know we were investigating already, but surely, he'd realize his best bet now was to lay low.

Unfortunately, murderers weren't always logical, and they sometimes got caught because they weren't willing to leave well enough alone. They had an urge to revisit the scene of the crime, throw out more red herrings, even go to the police with made-up evidence. Hicks might also have gotten a taste for murder, for playing God. Serial killers sometimes started by murdering someone for a reason that had some logic: to gain money or to remove a rival. For some people, getting away with that first murder encouraged them to see murder as a problem-solving response. Once they got the bloodlust, a relatively minor annoyance became an excuse to kill.

If Steven Hicks was a killer, we had to prove it and put him in prison. For Brit Egland's sake, and her family's. And for the rest of us. I couldn't be certain my mother and the other patients were safe until we knew what had really happened.

I found the garage and parked across the street. I could bring in the car with some excuse about needing work, but then what? I could stay parked and watch the place, but for how long? The blue Camaro would eventually attract attention. I wasn't sure what Steven Hicks looked like, or if he was working that afternoon.

At least if Hicks had followed me or tried to run me down, he wouldn't associate me with the Camaro. I lingered on that thought. Could Hicks have driven the attack car? That had been shortly after I'd first talked to Heather. I hadn't yet interviewed any of the family members or even the employees. In fact, I'd hardly talked to anyone directly associated with Sunshine Haven except Heather. I still thought the receptionist, June Songpole, might have told someone of my visit, but Norman Mendelson was the obvious choice there. Why would she have told Steven Hicks? Even if he'd somehow charmed her into being an unwitting accomplice, how would she have known my talk with Heather would be of interest to him?

Could I be on the wrong track after all?

I sighed and got out of the car. I was tired of all these questions.

Time to confront Steven Hicks.

I scuttled across the street, glancing back and forth to watch for cars ready to pounce. Once safely on the other side, I retrieved my phone and texted Dad to let him know what I was doing. If I disappeared, at least someone could follow my trail.

I hesitated with the phone in my hand. I often used an app to record interviews so I could double-check quotes, and so I had evidence if anyone tried to deny what they said. Ethically, I had to ask permission to record conversations, but I wasn't acting as a journalist now. Federal law and the state of Arizona allowed private individuals to make recordings as long as one party involved in the conversation consented. That meant I could legally make the recording as long as I was part of the conversation and had my own consent. Getting it admitted in court could be trickier, but not impossible.

I doubted I could get Steve Hicks to openly admit he'd killed his girlfriend's mother, but if he said anything incriminating, I wanted it recorded. I turned away from the automotive shop to hide my actions and started the app. My shirt didn't have any pockets and I was afraid the recording would be too faint if I had the phone in the back pockets of my shorts, so I slipped my phone in my bra. It made an odd bulge over my left breast. Women who carry their phones in their bras all the time must either have smaller phones or larger breasts. I fluffed my shirt out a bit so the bump wasn't obvious.

The shop had a small room with hard plastic chairs along one wall and a counter opposite. It smelled of grease or motor oil or whatever comes from inside car engines. A faint shuffle and clang from the back suggested someone at work.

I rang the bell and waited. Photos on the walls showed men standing proudly beside cars. Several men in blue coveralls appeared in multiple pictures, along with occasional other men in regular clothes and one or two women. I didn't recognize anyone, so I wasn't sure if the mechanics were having their pictures taken with famous customers, favorite customers, or favorite cars.

Several minutes later, a man came in from the garage. He was tall and barrel-chested, late sixties or early seventies, with gray hair and a thick beard that straggled down to his breastbone. His stern face and stiff posture could have illustrated the encyclopedia entry for *patriarch*.

"Help you?" he asked.

"I'm looking for Steven Hicks."

"Found him."

He wasn't at all what I was expecting. "You're the Steve Hicks who dated Lisa Delacruz?"

"You want my son, Stevie."

I glanced at the photos on the wall. The men in overalls might be father and sons. "I suppose I do. Is he here?"

"He doesn't work today."

"Where can I find him?"

He glanced at a clock on the wall. "After four. Probably at the bar."

"Which bar?"

He pulled a rag from his pocket and absently wiped the counter, making it dirtier rather than cleaner. "What do you want with Stevie? Is this about Lisa?"

"Not directly. You know her?"

"Sure, nice little gal. Too good for my son."

Although I tended to agree, it was an odd comment from a father.

"Brought her boy here a couple of times 'cause he's interested in cars. Only wants to drive 'em, though. Don't want to get his hands dirty making them run." He glanced back into the garage, home of polluting chemical products and testosterone. "Too soft. No wonder, raised by a woman with no man around."

Hello, toxic masculinity. "I'd really like to talk to Stevie today. Do you know what bar he might be at?"

He studied me. "You're not his type."

Thank goodness for that. "This is more of a business thing." I decided to throw a pebble in the water and start some ripples. "It's about Sunshine Haven. You know what he's been doing there?"

Steven Senior shrugged, but I wouldn't really expect him to know if his son had been killing patients. Still, if I didn't find Stevie that day, word might get back to him that someone had been asking about his connection to the place. Let him sweat a little, wondering if he was under suspicion.

Mr. Hicks took a breath that filled his chest and blew it out. "Try the place down the street, on the left." He gestured with his head. "If Stevie got himself in trouble again, no point in putting it off."

"Again? Does he get in trouble a lot?"

"Try down the street." He headed back into the garage.

I had a lead, but I still had to find Stevie Junior in a public place. I reviewed the photos on the wall. One showed Steven Senior with a man on either side, all of them in blue coveralls. One of the men might be in his forties and the other a bit younger. It was hard to judge the similarity in their faces because of Steven Senior's beard, but they all had the same barrel chest. I guessed the Stevie I wanted might be the older of the two, but I studied both faces so I'd recognize them.

I headed to my car. I didn't know how far down the

street I had to go, but even a block or two would be tiring, and I needed my energy. The first bar I came to was about four blocks away. I'd been expecting someplace seedy, but this was a sports bar that served food. I drove a couple more blocks to see if I came to any other bars, but the neighborhood had apparently become too trendy for the type of place I'd pictured.

I returned to the sports bar and parked. I'd almost forgotten that my breast was recording everything. I stopped the recording I had going and checked that it had managed to catch my conversation with Steven Senior. My voice was louder than his, but he came through even over the distractions of rustling from my shirt. I started a new recording. If I was lucky, Stevie would be drunk and careless. If I prodded him hard enough, maybe he would say something incriminating.

Inside the doorway, I let my eyes adjust to the dimmer light. Several large-screen TVs hanging high on the walls played different sports events. A waitress dropped off burgers at a nearby table full of young men.

She passed by. "Have a seat anywhere."

I made my way through the room, squeezing between the tables and trying not to catch my cane on a chair leg. Fortunately, the place wasn't crowded, so I didn't have to examine too many customers. A man seated at the bar seemed to have the Hicks build. I took the second stool down from him.

The young bartender said, "Good afternoon. What will you have?"

"Nothing at the moment. Thanks." I turned my body

toward the man next to me. "I'm here to talk to Steve Hicks."

The bartender shrugged and moved off. Steven Hicks Junior—I was sure it was him now—swiveled toward me. "You looking for me?"

"I am. I want to talk about Sunshine Haven."

He snorted. "Sunshine Haven. Stupid name. Trying to pretend it's someplace people *want* to be. Like all these housing developments with names like Shady Oaks, when they cut down all the trees to build it, or Mountain Vista when you can't see past the other houses."

"You were seen at Sunshine Haven the day before Brit Egland died."

His eyes narrowed and he took more time in forming a response. "Sure, I went every week with my girlfriend and her kid."

"You couldn't have gone too many times, since you and Lisa had broken up until a few weeks ago."

He took a swig of beer. I couldn't tell if it was a stalling tactic or if he simply liked to drink.

"What's it to you?" he asked.

"I'm looking into some deaths there."

His lip pulled up in a sneer. "You don't look like a cop."

"I'm not. I'm an investigative reporter. But I'll turn my findings over to the police. Tell me, how many times did you actually go to Sunshine Haven? Three?"

"More than that." He drained his beer and waved to the bartender for another. Hicks watched me from the corner of his eye while the bartender filled a glass and set it in front of him.

The bartender asked me, "You sure you don't want any-thing?"

I shook my head. I didn't want to give Hicks too much time to think.

The bartender moved off. Across the room, the young men cheered at something sports-related.

"The old lady didn't like me much," Hicks said. "When she started losing her marbles, Lisa spent all her time there. I wasn't going to hang around. But I thought, maybe with her gone, me and Lisa could work it out."

"Gone? You mean dead?"

He glared. "'Course not. I meant with her in that dump. They'd take care of her there. What else is the place for? But Lisa still wanted to go all the time."

"And you didn't want to share Lisa?"

"Who are you anyway? Did Lisa send you?"

The person who had called to warn me off had clearly known who I was. The person who tried to run me down surely knew who they were targeting. Hicks seemed sincere in his confusion, and he didn't sound like the man on the phone.

Maybe he was a good actor, but if he didn't already know my name, I wasn't crazy about giving it to him. On the other hand, if he thought Lisa had sent me, he might take revenge on her. I dug in my bag and pulled out a card that showed my connection to the newspaper, with an address that was fortunately over two thousand miles away.

"As I said, I'm an investigative reporter. I'm looking into the situation at Sunshine Haven with the full knowledge and support of the company and the police. Ms. Delacruz is of interest to us only because her mother recently died, and we suspect foul play."

Hicks studied my card. Sweat glistened on his forehead, and it wasn't especially warm in there. "She was old. Old people die."

"She wasn't that old, and she shouldn't have died yet."

Hicks slapped my card facedown on the bar and pressed his hand over it. He sipped his drink, darting glances at me. He seemed nervous, which was suspicious but didn't prove anything. "She wasn't the only old lady to die recently. These things happen."

"That's right. She wasn't. We're looking into two suspicious deaths and one unexplained illness. You know anything about them?"

"Why would I? I didn't have anything to gain." He swung toward me and stared into my eyes. "I didn't have anything to gain from anyone dying. Not even Lisa's mother. All the old lady's money went to that home. Didn't Lisa tell you that?"

My breast buzzed. I flinched and almost slapped it, thinking I had an insect in my bra, before I realized it was merely a text coming in. I ignored it and hoped Hicks hadn't heard it over the background noise of the bar. "I know that, but you didn't. Not until after she died."

"You can't prove anything." Hicks gulped his drink. He slammed the glass down on the bar so hard the last two inches of beer sloshed and spilled over the rim. He twisted away from me to leave his seat and headed for the door. No point in trying to catch up with him. I'd definitely rattled him, though I hadn't recorded anything useful.

The door swung shut behind him. I checked the bar top for my business card, but Hicks must have taken it with him.

As I stood, I glanced at the bartender. "Did he pay for his drinks?"

"No, but he's in here several days a week. I'll get him next time. What did you say to upset him?"

"Only what needed to be said."

I headed out. I should get back to Sunshine Haven, to regroup with the others and see what had been learned in my absence.

I stopped the recording and checked the text that had made my breast buzz in public. It was from Dad, letting me know he'd gotten my message and wondering what my plan was for the rest of the day. I told him I'd be back in about half an hour. Note to self: when using the bra recording system, mute the phone if you don't want your chest making odd noises.

Outside, I scanned the area for Steven Hicks but didn't spot him. I got into Simon's convertible and headed toward Sunshine Haven.

At the first stoplight, a white pickup truck pulled up behind me. The driver revved his engine and leaned on his horn as the light turned green. I barely bothered to swear as I pulled forward. American drivers, no matter how obnoxious, paled in comparison to the craziness I'd seen in the Middle East, where drivers turn a two-lane road into four lanes, or swerve across multiple lanes of traffic to make a turn.

The truck backed off ten feet and then zoomed forward again. It loomed so large in the rearview mirror that I braced for impact. I couldn't see the truck's driver through the glare on his windshield, but one thing was clear.

This wasn't some random driver bullying a stranger. This was an attempt to bully *me*.

Chapter Eighteen

T HE TRUCK DRIVER had plenty of room to pass me, but he stayed right behind, crowding me. Hicks seemed like the logical suspect. I couldn't have upset *that* many different people this week.

I swore louder and longer. This was his petty, immature way of trying to intimidate me. It almost made me miss Mendelson's fussy complaints.

I gritted my teeth and tried to stay calm as the truck backed off and rushed forward, again and again. Each time, the engine revved and his front end loomed large in my rearview mirror, I gripped the steering wheel until my fists ached. Traffic picked up as I crossed town, but Hicks stayed too close for me to safely pull in front of another car and get him off my tail.

I didn't drive often. I wasn't up for action hero evasive maneuvers. I couldn't risk an accident, either for my body or for Simon's car. I could only concentrate on my driving and wish for a police officer.

I didn't know where to find a police station, and I didn't want to pull over and possibly be even more vulnerable to Hicks. If he followed me all the way to Sunshine Haven, what would he do when we got there? I didn't want to hobble across the parking lot, open to vehicular assault.

A strip mall with a grocery store sat next to Sunshine Haven. At the last second, I swung in there. The truck slowed as well and started to turn, but then he swerved back into the lane and sped off. I twisted to see the license plate on the back, but it was already too far away.

In front of the grocery store, I waited for a woman to load her groceries and leave. I had a parking spot close to the main doors, with a constant stream of shoppers walking past. Chances were the grocery store had cameras on the parking lot as well. If Hicks came back, I'd be reasonably safe.

I slumped into my seat with a loud sigh. I was trembling. It hadn't been the most dangerous situation of my life, but I'd set that bar pretty high.

I could call the police. But I couldn't prove Hicks had been driving the truck. I hadn't seen a license plate or his face. I imagined trying to convince the police to check the traffic cameras along our route, in hopes that one had caught Hicks. He hadn't even caused an accident, so the most they could do was ticket him for reckless driving.

I could barely sit up straight. I didn't want to waste time and precious energy trying to explain things to the police when they likely wouldn't do anything.

I pressed my fingertips into my temples. I might be bad at identifying cars, but I could say for sure the vehicle that tried to run me down outside Simon's store was not a truck. Hicks might have multiple cars or have borrowed one from the shop. But he hadn't known I was investigating back then.

Ugh. I debated driving over to Sunshine Haven instead of walking the few hundred yards. But Hicks might still be lurking somewhere. Better to leave Simon's car under constant observation.

I delayed physical activity by calling the Delacruz house. Lisa answered, but I asked for Ryan. Talking to him would require less of an explanation. I warned him to be extra wary about Steve Hicks.

"If he shows up, call the police right away. I tried to leave you and your mother out of it, but it's possible he thinks you tipped me off."

Ryan's voice was low and muffled, as if he was trying to hide his words from his mother. "You think he might want revenge?"

"You know him better than I do, but I wouldn't take any chances."

After a long pause, Ryan said, "You know, I think I'll suggest a picnic in the park. It's a nice evening and it'll cheer up Mom to be out of the house."

"Smart plan." I almost told him he was a good kid, but what teenager could hear that without eye-rolling embarrassment?

I couldn't put it off any longer. I dragged myself out of the car and headed across the parking lot, trying to walk smoothly, but my thigh ached. Everything ached, actually. I still had itchy scabs from my fall on the pavement when I'd dodged the speeding car, plus old bruises from that and fresh bruises from the morning's encounter with the wheelchair and the floor. I'd been home less than a week, and instead of healing, I'd gotten more injuries.

I gritted my teeth and kept moving. Inside the Sunshine Haven lobby, my first stop was for a cup of water so I could take more ibuprofen.

Was this my life now? Constant pain, limited mobility, and not even enough mental stamina to make sense of the story I was tackling? I'd hoped this investigation would help me find my old self. Hah. It was only serving to highlight my limitations: I had a bad leg, a sluggish mind, and a severe case of whining.

I followed the water with coffee, extra vanilla creamer. Coffee might not solve all the world's problems, but it was cheaper and safer than liquor as a reward for getting through a difficult day.

Marty and Simon weren't back yet, but Joe Washington had hallway duty, and I found Dad in Mom's room. I tried to focus on enjoying her company. And staying awake.

Simon and Marty returned about 5 p.m. The moment Simon saw me, he said, "My car isn't out front. How was it? No problems?"

"Not really. Except for that funny sound it made when I tried to shift, but that was probably my fault. And I didn't scratch it *very* badly when I bumped that post."

His eyes widened and he whimpered.

I chuckled. "Relax. I'm kidding. It's a beautiful car, drives like a dream, and against all odds, it's in the same condition as when you gave it to me. I parked in front of the grocery store down the block for its own safety."

"I'd hate you, but I'm too relieved right now. Did the Camaro work? That is, did it do what you were hoping?"

"Perfectly. The way to a teen boy's heart is through a sports car. I'll tell you about it after they serve the patients dinner."

We all wandered the halls, keeping a close eye on everything and everybody. I didn't expect Steven Hicks to show up, but if someone else were poisoning patients, this would be the prime time for them to act.

The same two people who had served lunch also served dinner. A nurse supervised the evening medications. We couldn't tell if she gave patients the right pills, or the right doses, but she didn't react to being observed. We got some puzzled looks, but no one complained about our presence. Family members had a right to make sure their loved ones were getting proper care, and Sunshine Haven was still trying to rebuild trust after their earlier public-relations disaster.

Most of the staff left by 7 p.m. A young Hispanic man took over the reception desk and focused on his nursing homework. The patients who weren't already asleep were watching TV, reading, or knitting in their rooms.

Mackenzie brought two takeout pizzas. Brit Egland's former room was still empty, so we gathered in there to eat dinner and share news. The wind rustled branches against the window. Outside lights made the grassy yard as bright as day. I settled on the uncovered bed, Dad stood in the doorway to keep an eye on the hallway, and the others perched where they could.

"Did anything happen while we were gone?" Marty asked.

Dad glanced back into the room. "Nothing suspicious. If anyone gets sick tonight, we'll have a record of who was in each room."

"Good," Marty said. "Simon and I didn't find anything helpful."

I swallowed a bite of pizza. "What did you do?"

"We followed Maximilian Richards to a Narcotics Anonymous meeting." Marty gestured for Simon to take over.

"I asked if I could sit in and listen," he said. "I'm sure they assumed I needed help and wasn't ready to admit it, but I didn't have to lie."

"Do you think Richards is clean?" I asked.

Simon nodded. "One of the other guys was on probation. He needed to get something signed to prove he'd been there. He was rolling his eyes, snickering, obviously not into it. Max talked about the steps he's been taking to make amends and got choked up at one point. If he was acting, he's an amazing performer."

"No reason for him to fake it," I said. "He didn't know why you were there. If he was only attending because of a court order, he could've coasted through the meeting."

"Right. He's trying to turn his life around. He said Sunshine Haven inspired him, because he sees what other people go through, and he stopped feeling sorry for himself. Now he wants to help people."

"That looks like a dead end, and I'm glad for him," I said. "What about Ana Marija Jurić?"

Marty put down her pizza and patted her mouth with a napkin. "After I dropped off Simon, I tracked down Ana Marija in the grocery store. Thank goodness for social media and people who think the world wants to know about their plans to buy ice cream because Safeway is having a sale. I managed to bump into her there. Literally, I crashed my cart into hers but made it look like an accident. I apologized and we got chatting. I insisted on buying her a cup of coffee at the Starbucks in the store as an apology."

"Nice work."

"I asked where she was from—a natural question because of her accent—and we talked about immigration. She's been meeting with a lawyer and thinks she'll get her work visa extended and eventually become a citizen. We always need more nurses. She's a nursing assistant here, but she was a full-fledged nurse in Bosnia."

"She sounds legit," I said.

"It's been hard, trying to learn English and get through all the red tape, and she's hurt by the anti-immigrant talk. But she lived through much worse, including ethnic cleansing and war, in Bosnia."

"Another suspect off our list. Good." I nudged the pizza box with my cane until I could reach a slice. "We're finally getting rid of some of the clutter. Mackenzie, want to report on Heather?"

Mac, seated cross-legged on the floor, described the romantic lunch. "After that, she did yard work, so I went home and tackled the background check on the guy you asked about." She raised her eyebrows in question.

"Go ahead and report. We don't have any secrets anymore."

"That's a relief. It was getting hard to keep track of who knew what."

"Tell me about it."

"So, Norman Mendelson, the memory care program co-ordinator." Mackenzie studied some notes on her phone. "No criminal background. Not even a speeding ticket. Single, never married. Lived with his mother until a year ago.

She's now in an Alzheimer's unit, though not here."

Marty leaned forward. "Why wouldn't he have his mother here?"

"Sunshine Haven is fancier, and more expensive, I assume. Mendelson's mother has to share a room. I stopped by on my way here." Mackenzie wrinkled her nose. "It's a budget place. I wouldn't want you in there." She straightened and her eyes widened. "Not that I'd be putting you in a home now. Or ever."

Marty chuckled. "It's okay, sweetie. So either he couldn't afford to get his mother in here, or he didn't want to spend the extra money."

Dad leaned against the doorjamb. "Don't judge him based only on that. It was a nightmare figuring out the finances to get Ursula in here. How old is Mendelson?"

Mackenzie glanced at her notes. "Forty-three."

"He'll have his own retirement to worry about." Dad looked at me. "We wouldn't want you girls going bankrupt in order to take care of us."

I put down my empty plate. "All right, we won't assume he's cheap, but I *will* assume he pushed the wheelchair into me this morning." I described the incident for those who hadn't witnessed it. "He's tried to prevent me from talking to patients and their families."

"That still doesn't make him a criminal," Dad said. "Well, the wheelchair thing could be assault. But for the rest, he could be trying to prevent another scandal here."

Joe took over the post at the door and Dad sat on the bed by my feet.

"I don't think he's our killer, but he might be involved in

something else suspicious. Maybe doping patients or extortion." I yawned and stretched. "I'll let Heather decide how to proceed. I have my eye on someone else for the murder."

I told them about my afternoon visits to Ryan and Steve Hicks. When I related how the truck threatened to ram me, Dad gasped and put a hand on my leg.

Simon gasped too. "You're sure he never touched you?"

"Only the bumper. And the rear side panel."

He narrowed his eyes at me, and the others laughed.

"I promise, your baby is fine. Thanks for your concern. Hicks had a motive, at least for the most recent death. He had access. And it probably wouldn't be too hard for Hicks to get poison from around the auto shop. That gives him motive, means, and opportunity. But how do we prove it?"

"Where does that leave us?" Joe asked.

I rubbed my eyes. "Tomorrow I have a physical therapy appointment first thing. Then I'll encourage Heather to call the police. If she's not willing, I may call them myself, but I'd rather have her support. Tonight, we take turns keeping an eye on the Alzheimer's unit. If Hicks is our criminal, he doesn't have a reason to strike again, but until we know for sure . . ."

Joe nodded. "We'll set up a duty schedule."

"Leave it to us," Dad told me. "You get a good night's sleep. You'll need all your energy tomorrow."

"I won't argue. I'm wiped out."

Dad helped me up. "I'll drive you home and come back in a couple of hours."

"I can make it until midnight," Joe said.

Simon and Mackenzie spoke at once, but Dad talked

over them. "Figure it out and call me. I'm taking my daughter home."

Marty patted my arm. "Thanks for telling us everything. We're making progress."

We were. We were getting close. Or at least closer.

But we still had to prove it.

I might have dozed on the way home. When we entered the house, Dad crossed the living room and reached for the cord to pull the drapes closed. "Need anything? A cup of tea?"

I stood at the other side of the large window, leaning on my cane more than I was supposed to. "Just bed."

If only I could find enough energy to make it up the stairs.

Pop! Thud!

Gunshots split the night, cracking our window and slamming into the wall.

Chapter Nineteen

"KATE! ARE YOU okay?"

The world slowly came back into focus. I was lying on our living room floor, my fingers gripping the carpet. Dad crossed the room to me, wriggling on his belly. He collapsed next to me, clutching my arm so hard it hurt. Outside, a car engine revved and tires squealed on the pavement, the sound almost hidden by Dad's raspy breathing.

I swallowed a few times. "I'm all right. You?"

I rolled onto my side and scanned Dad's face and body. I didn't see any blood.

"I'm okay. What was that? Was it . . . a gunshot?"

I twisted to look at the window. Fragmented glass sparkled like a spider web around two holes piercing the window.

The night had settled into silence. I didn't trust silence. "We need to get out of this room. Stay low."

We crawled into a back room and called the police.

When officers arrived, they took pictures and discussed trajectory and bullet type. I told them I suspected Steven Hicks, because I had interviewed him, and he seemed to think I was causing trouble. I described how someone in a truck had harassed me, and they said they'd check if he had one, but I couldn't give a description beyond "big white truck." Fortunately, when they heard I was a journalist, the officers assumed the interview was for an article and didn't ask for details. Not that I was as concerned about secrecy anymore, but after the initial adrenaline wore off, I was so tired I could barely speak.

When the police left, Dad and I hugged each other for a long time before we stumbled to our beds.

Painkillers and exhaustion knocked me out. I slept until my alarm went off in the morning. After ibuprofen and twenty minutes in a hot shower, I felt almost human. I had pangs of guilt over using that much water in a desert, but I couldn't resist the luxury. How often had I ducked under a lukewarm trickle for five minutes and been satisfied? Living in the US definitely had advantages.

Apparently "not getting shot at" wasn't one of them, but still.

By the time I was dressed, my various pains had faded enough that I could hobble downstairs, only swearing silently instead of out loud. The aroma of coffee and spices drew me to the kitchen, where Dad heated up the leftover cinnamon rolls.

I put my hand on his shoulder. He covered my hand with his own and squeezed. We held on for half a minute before he loosened his grip and I dropped into a chair.

"What did I miss?" I asked.

"The police seem to think Mr. Hicks—or whoever shot through the window—tried to scare us rather than kill us." He shrugged. "I guess because the bullets went right between the two of us and were pretty high. I'd say they're taking it seriously, but they doubt anyone will go to jail for it."

I eased into a chair. "I noticed the blinds are still closed."

Dad handed me a mug of coffee. "They'll stay that way until this is over. No use taking any more chances. I'll put a sheet of cardboard over the glass after breakfast. It won't offer much security, but I don't want a bird bumping into the glass when it's already weakened."

"I hope things weren't this exciting at Sunshine Haven last night."

"I talked to Joe a few minutes ago. Nothing to report."

I sipped the coffee and imagined the elixir rushing through my veins, awakening every cell of my body. Unfortunately, I was one of those people with biology that never reacted to caffeine, but I was hoping for the placebo effect. "You didn't go back?"

His eyebrows rose. "And leave my baby here alone? No way. After what happened, the others agreed to cover the night shift. When Mackenzie relieved Joe this morning, they checked each room. Everyone is fine."

I sighed and a little of the stress left my aching body. "We made it through the danger zone. Either Steven Hicks is the killer, and he's done because Brit Egland was his target, or if it was someone else, our presence must have discouraged them from their Sunday night pattern."

Or we were missing some other person or factor, but I didn't want to think about that. My stomach growled enthusiastically, and I started on a cinnamon roll.

"We still have to prove it was this Hicks guy and get him put away. We can't watch the place forever."

I nodded and finished chewing my bite. "I asked Heather

to clear her schedule today after 9 a.m., when I get out of PT. One way or another, we'll get the police involved today."

Dad had to put up the cardboard and do some chores he'd been putting off, such as paying bills. I drove to Sunshine Haven and parked by the physical therapy office a few minutes before it opened. The boxy, pale-blue car I'd seen near Kellie Armstrong's house pulled into the lot after me. I dawdled until I could see the driver: the young man who'd been working in the PT clinic during my first visit.

Might as well clear up that mystery.

I waved to him as he approached the building. "Nice car."

He looked at me warily. "Thanks."

"It's fairly noticeable. In fact, I noticed it outside Kellie Armstrong's house a few days ago. But you didn't stick around to say hello."

He hurried closer. "She told me you're working on an article about Sunshine Haven."

"Did you tell everyone else about it?"

"What? No! I don't want . . ." He checked our surroundings again.

Someone was going into Sunshine Haven, but they were too far away to overhear.

"I need to keep it quiet about Kellie and me. Please."

"You don't want people to learn about your affair? Would it cost you your job?"

He ran a hand through his hair. "No, not that. I never treated Kellie, only her mother. That's how we met. The rules say you can't date a patient, but they don't say anything about a patient's daughter."

"So why is it a secret?"

He frowned. "Off the record?"

I nodded. "I don't write for gossip columns."

"Kellie is still married. They're separated but not divorced."

"I thought her husband still lived in that house."

"He does. They moved to separate bedrooms five years ago. Said his snoring was keeping Kellie awake. They wanted to stay together until the kids were all out of the house."

"That's a long time to pretend to be a happy couple."

"Yeah." He scanned the empty parking lot. "It's been hard on Kellie. Her kids are all grown now, but then her mother moved into the home, and that was tough for everybody, so they didn't want to add to the stress by announcing a divorce. Now that her mom has passed on, they'll give it a couple of months and then make it official."

I studied the young man. He was about thirty, lean and muscular, with healthy good looks if you liked the jock type. Regardless of the age difference, he and Kellie would make a pretty couple. "So Penelope Valentine's death was to your advantage."

"What? No. She was a nice old lady. I liked treating her."

"But if she hadn't died, you'd have to wait longer to be with Kellie."

He tipped his head and squinted as if I'd turned purple and spouted gibberish. "I don't know what you're getting at. We weren't planning to wait until her mother died, only until everyone was used to her being in the home. Kellie didn't want to tell her mom about the divorce, but Mrs.

Valentine wouldn't have remembered it anyway, what with her Alzheimer's. Kellie was only worried about the kids."

He might be fooling himself. If things had been dragging out, Kellie might find another excuse not to initiate the divorce. But it didn't seem likely that this young man had killed his girlfriend's mother. He certainly wouldn't have any reason to kill Brit Egland.

"All right, I'll keep quiet about it."

"Thanks. I need to get to work." He headed to the door.

Someone behind me called, "Kate, good morning."

I glanced back at Berta Lopez as she hurried toward us. She squeezed a key fob and the sleek sports car behind her gave a beep and flash of lights as it locked. The male PT—I still didn't know his name—lingered long enough to hold the door for us, so I didn't comment on Berta's fancy car. I'd need to find a fresh opening line to probe the issue of why she had so much extra money to spend. Maybe I'd wait until after our therapy session, so she couldn't take revenge by torturing me with "deep tissue massage" or something.

Inside, the man took off toward the back room. Berta waited while I checked in at the reception desk and then escorted me to one of the small rooms. We went over my health history, focusing on the damage from the explosion. I mentioned "a recent fall" to explain the additional bruises and scrapes. Berta was cheerful and professional as we discussed my concerns and goals. For an hour, I concentrated on my body.

Berta checked my range of motion—poor—and leg strength—worse.

"You're doing pretty well for an injury this recent," she

said.

I grunted. Why couldn't I heal faster? Why couldn't I be back to normal? One measly bomb explosion and I was out for months.

Berta did some amazing pressure point releases that worked out my muscle knots. As I reclined on a padded table toward the end of our session, Berta led me through some "assisted stretches," which meant I relaxed while she moved my limbs. We'd mostly talked about what she was doing and my pain level, but we could chat casually through this. I asked how long she'd been a physical therapist—five years—and then she asked about the places I'd lived overseas.

When she finished, I sat up on the padded table. I had a whole new set of aches, but they were the elusive "good pain" that came from the right amount of exercise fatigue, stretching, and bodywork.

"I love to travel," Berta said. "Last year, I went to Australia and it was amazing. I'm thinking about Machu Picchu next year. I wish I had someone to go with, though."

I silently thanked her for the lead-in.

"Those are expensive trips," I said. "I don't imagine many people your age would be able to afford them."

"Yeah, none of my friends can. They're satisfied with California or Mexico. I'll probably do a tour of Machu Picchu. Most people on those tours are a lot older, but at least I'll have company and someone else to take care of the details."

"I'm surprised you can afford that kind of travel. I didn't think physical therapists made all that much."

"We sure don't. I'd have to save up for years to pay for it

out of my own salary." She washed her hands at a small sink. "My mom died in the hospital a few years back. The doctor . . . it was malpractice. We got a big settlement."

"Wow. I'm sorry about your mother. I don't imagine the settlement made up for losing her."

She dried her hands and dabbed at an eye with the towel. "Not even close. In a way, I hate the money. It's a constant reminder of her. I want to spend it and be rid of it, but I don't want to waste it, you know?"

"Ah. The vacations are expensive but not a waste."

"Right. Mom always wanted to travel. I imagine she's with me and talk to her about what we see." She gave me a crooked grin. "Not out loud, to myself. Don't want people knowing how crazy I am."

"No crazier than the rest of us. I hope your mother can hear you and enjoys traveling with you."

"I know she does."

One more minor mystery solved with a tragic but plausible answer. And I'd found an excellent physical therapist. I walked the short distance to Sunshine Haven without obvious limping. She gave me hope that someday I might walk comfortably without the cane. Maybe I'd even be able to return to normal—or at least my own personal brand of crazy.

I felt mellow as I entered Sunshine Haven. Maybe too mellow for the tasks ahead. Well, that feeling probably wouldn't last.

I stopped at the coffee station. As long as I didn't fill the cup too full, I could carry it without sloshing. I kept my eyes on the mug and my attention on walking smoothly as I crossed to the reception desk where June Songpole, the young weekday receptionist, sat. Since pressuring her had only made her anxious, I took advantage of my relaxed mood and smiled. "Good morning, June."

"Ms. Garcia is ready for you."

"Thank you, but could you do something for me first?"

"Uh, sure."

I took a sip of coffee. "I'd appreciate it if you would please tell me whether you informed Norman Mendelson of my first visit to Heather last week."

Her eyes widened and she swallowed. "I didn't mean any harm! He likes to know what's happening." She dropped her gaze and her chin jutted out slightly. "I didn't think it was a secret."

"I understand. You were trying to help."

She glanced at me, away, and back again. "I knew you were a journalist. Your dad mentioned it once when I asked him why he looked worried. It was when you'd been hurt."

"People confide in you because you're sympathetic. And you thought I might be trying to hurt Sunshine Haven with a negative story?"

"Not exactly," she mumbled.

"What then?"

June sighed. "Mr. Mendelson has been really upset lately. His mother is in a care facility, but not as nice as this one because he couldn't afford it. I know people think he's, well, uptight, but I think he's mostly sad."

"I'm not sure I follow. What does this have to do with me?"

She gazed up at me. "Promise you won't tell Ms. Garcia?"

"If it has to do with anything illegal, or against the interests of this place, I'll have to tell. I won't share gossip or feelings."

She glanced at the open door behind her and then leaned forward and whispered, "Mr. Mendelson doesn't like Ms. Garcia. He thinks she cares too much about money and not enough about the patients. She's the one who made the final decision about his mother. He thought they should make an exception because he's worked here so long."

"I can see why he might think so."

She nodded. "His mother's really sick now, and it's breaking his heart. I thought he might be pleased that someone was investigating Sunshine Haven."

I took another sip of coffee while I processed that. "You thought he might get revenge if I found out something bad about this place."

"I guess I wasn't thinking clearly. It's not like I actually want you to find anything bad and shut the place down. I'd lose my job. Anyway, Mr. Mendelson didn't take it like I thought he would. It only upset him more." She gave me a big-eyed, innocent look, like a puppy that knew it had been bad but hoped to be forgiven due to cuteness. "I'm sorry?" She made it sound more like a question than a statement.

"All right. Thank you for telling me. I don't think we'll need to talk about this again."

"Thanks." She beamed. "Are you ready to see Ms. Garcia now? Would you like me to carry your coffee?"

"That would be nice. Thank you."

So Norman Mendelson knew, or thought he knew, that I

was investigating something at Sunshine Haven almost from the start. Even before the car that caused me to fall in the street. Ironically, if June hadn't gossiped to the man who hated gossip, we all might have had an easier few days.

I sat across from Heather, who told June to close the door on her way out. Heather and I looked at each other. Her hands clenched on her desk.

"What kind of car does Norman Mendelson drive?" I asked.

She blinked a couple of times. "Um, I don't know. Something kind of bland and practical, like him. A silver compact of some type."

That could be the car that tried to run me down. An innocent person wouldn't be so upset about the thought of me investigating Sunshine Haven that he'd try to hurt me. Mendelson had to be hiding something or protecting someone.

"Does it matter?" she asked.

"Not really. Not at the moment. We'll get back to him. First, let's talk about you and Henry Wilson."

Chapter Twenty

H EATHER'S LIPS TWISTED in an attempt at a smile. "I should have known you'd find out."

"Why didn't you tell me?"

She twined her fingers together. "Because it's not relevant. But I can't expect you to take my word on that."

I waited.

"I'd better start from the beginning. You'd learn it anyway." She sounded more resigned than resentful. "I came to Sunshine Haven almost four years ago as the memory care program coordinator. That's the job Norman Mendelson has now. I focused on my own job, the patients, and their families. But after a while, I noticed problems."

She pressed her hands on the desk, spreading her fingers wide. "Most of the employees were decent people, trying to do a good job, but they were understaffed and overworked. A few bad employees ruined the atmosphere for everyone else. One lazy person doesn't do their job and the others take up the slack for a while, but eventually they burn out. They wonder why they're doing more work for no more money, and why the bad employee isn't disciplined or fired. Everything gets worse. Accidents start to happen."

"I know what you mean. One manager who's incompetent, or who manages based on favoritism and grudges, can spoil a whole department."

"Right." Heather pushed her hair back from her face. "In a place like this, patients get neglected when employees don't do their job, and accidents can be deadly. I was making promises to patients' families, promises in line with our official policies, but they weren't being kept."

"Such as?"

"Well, we claimed we had a nurse on duty at all times. In reality, we only had a registered nurse come in thirty hours a week, which wasn't nearly enough. My boss said a nursing assistant counted, and while we technically didn't promise an RN, when people hear 'nurse,' that's what they assume." She sighed. "I went through the official chain of command and got ignored, so I sent reports to the company that owns this place. I guess they simply sent them back to the director, because all that happened was I got in trouble. I was put on probation and threatened with dismissal."

I tensed, my hand gripping the head of the cane so hard my fingers hurt. Her story was too familiar, and one that never stopped making me angry. I took a slow breath and commanded my muscles to relax. My thoughts could be angry, but I didn't want to undo all the relaxation work Berta had done.

Heather licked her lips and studied me. She must have decided I wasn't angry with her.

"I couldn't let it go, not when patients were being mistreated." Her eyes begged me to understand. "I was gathering evidence, preparing to go to the state licensing agencies, even the news if I needed to."

"Good for you."

"The director figured out what I was doing, or he'd already planned to get rid of me. He fired me, blamed me for every shortcoming, and hinted strongly that I'd been personally abusing patients."

"He blamed you to protect himself."

She nodded. "I was the sacrificial lamb."

"And yet . . ." I gestured toward her desk and office.

"I have Henry to thank for this. He was on the board then, although it wasn't too active. They met the minimum number of required times and basically took reports from the director, accepting whatever he said. When I got fired, I was . . . paralyzed. In shock. I thought my career was over. I could have wound up in jail." Her face softened, and she seemed to be looking at something in her memory. "Henry asked for my side of the story. He believed me, at least enough to find the truth. He insisted on an outside audit. In the end, they cleared me and fired the other director."

"And promoted you."

"I still feel like I have to prove myself, but Henry gave me a chance. Can you see why I love him?"

"I can see why you owe him. That's not quite the same thing." I'd had my butt saved more than once by a bodyguard or soldier assigned to protect me while I worked on a story. The rush of gratitude could be powerful, especially if mixed with mutual attraction and the high of surviving a near-death experience. It had led to fooling around more often than I cared to admit, but I'd never pretended it was love.

"I do owe him," Heather said. "But I don't love him because he saved my career. I love him because he's the type of person who would do that. He's a good man."

"Yet you're hiding the relationship. What would the company say if they knew about the two of you?"

She glanced away. "As soon as his term on the board is up, he'll step down. It's only a couple more months. Until then, we want to keep our relationship quiet. You know how people are. Some of them would think we must have been dating *before* he helped me. It would bring everything into question."

I finished my coffee and put the cup on her desk. "All right, I understand your explanation. I wish you'd told me earlier, but I see why you didn't. I'm not concerned about your private life. But it's pretty hard to keep secrets. You'd be better off either coming clean or putting the romance on hold until it's safe."

"It didn't take you long to find out." Heather's brows drew together. "Is that the only reason you wanted to meet with me? When you told me to cancel my appointments today, I figured you had something major to report."

"Right. Now that we've cleared the air, we can get down to serious business."

The previous evening, I'd thought a lot about what I should share. I could skip the dead ends, such as the employees whose suspicious activities turned out to be innocent. Steven Hicks and Norman Mendelson were the important points. I started with Steven Hicks, my pick for the killer, since that was the problem requiring immediate outside help.

When I'd finished, Heather slumped back in her seat. "So I was right. Damn it."

"It's not definite, but it's possible you've had at least one murder here. I don't know how we'll prove anything, but it's time to call in the police."

"If we can't prove anything, what will they do?"

"Take over the investigation. They can do things I can't."

"Like what?"

I shrugged. "Exhume bodies to check for poison? Interview Hicks in the police station instead of a bar? It's either drop this and hope no one ever finds out, and Hicks is done now that his ex-girlfriend's mother is dead, or call the police." I wasn't willing to drop it and forget it, but I wanted to know if she was.

She groaned. "We have to find out for sure. I'll need to notify the board of directors. I really *should* do that first, but it might take all day to reach everyone, and if they want to meet in person before approving anything . . . I think this is one time it's better to ask for forgiveness than permission. You'll help me explain things to the police?"

"Absolutely."

She reached for the phone. "I guess we'd better get started."

Heather was on the phone for about ten minutes, getting passed around to two or three different people. Finally, she hung up. "They'll send a detective over. It'll be at least half an hour, maybe an hour. I'll start calling the board."

I hadn't yet told Heather about Mendelson possibly giving patients the wrong amounts of drugs and/or extorting money from patients, but she seemed to have as much as she could handle at the moment.

I got to my feet. "I'll visit my mother. If I'm not back when they come, send someone for me."

Heather nodded. "Do we have to tell the police about Mrs. Gregorian and Mrs. Valentine? In retrospect, those may have been natural, and only Mrs. Egland's death . . . questionable."

"Maybe, but you wouldn't want the police to uncover something suspicious later and then wonder why you hadn't said anything."

I could practically see her internal battle, wanting to do what was right, but also wanting to do damage control, to protect Sunshine Haven's reputation—and her own.

"I suppose you're right. Besides, it'll be hard to explain why we started looking at Brit Egland's death in the first place without mentioning the other problems."

"You've gotten through worse before. Trust that you can get through this." I glanced back from the door.

Heather sagged forward with her head in her hands. Being proved right isn't always satisfying. Sometimes it stinks.

I found Mom and Dad in the sunroom.

When I joined them, Dad asked, "You here for a while?"

"Sure. I've got at least half an hour."

He kissed Mom's cheek and got up. "I need to stretch my legs."

Mom asked about my cane again. I said I'd had a minor injury but would be fine soon. We chatted, but I felt like we were having two parallel conversations, and I couldn't figure out what hers was about. Maybe it was my fault. It wasn't easy to focus on Mom's words when I had so much on my mind, especially with the rumble of another conversation nearby.

I fished around for a topic of interest. Alzheimer's patients often did better when discussing the past. "Hey, Mom, tell me about when you and Dad fell in love."

Her expression softened as she reminisced. After half a minute, I pulled out my phone and started recording. Stories like this would be great to share with Jen's kids, to let them know who their grandmother used to be. And one day, when I could no longer hear Mom's voice in real life, I'd have it here.

Mom shared stories for about fifteen minutes. Then she searched for something in her purse, but she wouldn't explain what she wanted. My patience ran thin.

"Keep your temper. It's not her fault." Jen stood over us.

She was right, but her comment didn't help my mood. I grabbed my cane and shoved myself to my feet. "I need to get going anyway."

Her eyebrows rose. "Busy schedule?"

"Actually, yes. I have to help Heather with something." I wouldn't explain about the police, not then and there.

Jen gestured toward the door. "Fine. Hang out with your friend. I'll help Mom."

I tried not to grind my teeth. "Do you know Mendelson?"

Her brows drew together. "The composer?"

"Ha, no. The guy who works here."

"Oh, right. Dad and I met with him about Mom's care. Several times."

"What did you think of him?"

She shrugged. "Not someone I'd hang out with socially,

but he was knowledgeable and clear about what the place could offer. He seemed to care about patients with Alzheimer's. Why?"

"Doesn't matter."

Dad controlled the joint bank account now, so Jen wouldn't know of any problems. I brushed past her, trying not to limp, although the positive effects of the morning's PT had faded. I swung through the doorway without glancing back. Why did Jen push my buttons so much? She thought she was in charge of everything, that she was the only one who cared about and took care of Mom. She didn't even suspect the problems at Sunshine Haven.

I stopped in the middle of the hallway. She didn't know anything because I hadn't told her anything. My initial reasoning had been sound—the fewer people who knew, the better, and Jen would have wanted to take control, do things her way, call in the police right away . . .

Or would she? She knew better than I how hard it had been to find this place for Mom. Jen was annoying, but she was also smart and practical. I'd eventually trusted Mackenzie, Joe and Marty, and Simon with the truth. But not my own sister. It hadn't even occurred to me to include Jen in our surveillance the night before.

I sighed and kept walking. Jen and I had been close, once, a long time ago. How had we gotten so far apart, and would we ever be able to bridge that gap? I didn't even know *why* she was so cranky with me.

Of course, I hadn't actually asked her.

And I wasn't about to do it then and there, in Mom's presence, and with a police detective coming any minute.

My sister could wait until I'd dealt with murder.

I found Heather pacing the lobby, straightening chairs and restocking the sugar packets at the coffee station.

"Hard to sit still," I said.

She nodded. "I wish they'd show up. I want to get this over with."

I didn't point out that it probably wouldn't be "over with" for some time. Weeks, maybe months, or even years, if the police ever found enough to arrest Hicks and go to trial. Telling Heather about Mendelson would be a distraction but not one that would make her feel better.

"When we're done with the police, I'll take you to lunch," I said.

"Let's hope we're done by lunchtime."

The main doors opened. Heather stiffened and swung toward them. A thirtyish Hispanic woman entered the room. Heather's shoulders dropped and she turned back to me. The woman crossed to the reception desk and spoke to June, who pointed in our direction.

"I think your detective is here," I said.

The woman wore dark slacks and a white shirt. "Ms. Garcia? I'm Detective Yaquelin Padilla."

Heather managed a sickly smile. "Let's go into my office."

Once there, with the door closed, Heather introduced me and let me take the lead in explaining the situation. I spoke for a long time, even focusing only on Hicks.

Detective Padilla took notes and asked questions. Finally, she said, "Let me make sure I have this straight. You suspect that this patient, Brit Egland, may have been murdered—

perhaps poisoned—although the doctor who signed the death certificate didn't suspect anything, and no autopsy was done. The suspect, Steven Hicks, had a motive because he might have thought his girlfriend would inherit. In the end, that's all you have."

Heather and I looked at each other.

I said, "There's my shattered window and the bullet in my wall, but I can't prove that was Hicks."

Padilla's eyebrows went up. "You piss off a lot of people?"

"Lately, it seems that way. I don't think my sister would use a gun, though."

Mendelson, maybe, but mentioning him would only confuse the situation. Explaining my reasoning to the detective made our case seem a lot weaker than it had sounded in my mind, or when I'd described it to Heather, who was already suspicious. That was the problem with being accurate and honest. Exaggeration was often so much more effective.

I said, "Look. I know we don't have enough to go to court, but surely, you can do something."

Padilla stood. "It's enough to make me want to question this guy. Who knows, he may panic and admit everything." She grinned. "If we're really lucky, maybe he'll get physical and give us an excuse to arrest him and search him."

I slumped back in my chair with a sigh. She hadn't dismissed our concerns after all. "I realize that's a long shot. Can we do anything else?"

"We can try for an autopsy, if the body is still available."

"I know what funeral home she went to. I can check,"

Heather said. "I haven't heard of any burial yet, but she might've been cremated."

"Then we're out of luck unless it's a type of poison that can be detected in the cremains, and they haven't scattered the ashes," Padilla said. "It's nearly impossible to convict someone of murder if you can't prove a murder happened. Find out if they still have the body. Get the family's permission for the autopsy. Makes things easier."

"What about Penelope Valentine and Mrs. Gregorian?" I asked. "Hicks might have been practicing on them."

"I know Mrs. Valentine was buried locally," Heather said. "I doubt her family would want her exhumed without a pretty solid reason, though."

"Most families don't," Padilla said. "Hard to make it happen when we don't have a real good case against this guy. I don't want to tell a judge we want to dig up this woman's body, upset her family, without evidence."

"Mrs. Gregorian is still alive," I said. "Maybe the poison left some residue in her tissues or something."

Padilla frowned. "It's been what, three weeks? Lotta stuff will be gone by now but not everything. It would help if we knew what kind of poison we were talking about. Most tests will only find what you're looking for. You can't simply run a test for *everything*. It's odd, though. Poison is usually a woman's crime. Your Hicks sounds like a macho guy, the kind that would use a gun or knife, or his fists."

"Not if he wanted to keep it secret," Heather said.

"Smothering then. It leaves signs a doctor might notice, but not everyone realizes that."

"This might give us a clue to the poison," I said. "I'll bet

Hicks didn't do a lot of research. More likely he used something he had on hand."

"You said he works at an auto shop?" Padilla grinned. "Probably lots of deadly chemicals there."

I shivered. The idea of somebody dosing elderly women with brake fluid or motor oil or whatever was sickening. We had to stop this guy.

Heather stood and offered her hand to Yaquelin Padilla. "Thank you for believing us."

"Can't see why you'd make up a story like this. It's only going to cause problems for you. I'll warn you, though, if we don't find something fast, this won't make our priority list. Too much else to do." She strode out of the room.

Heather collapsed in her chair. "She's so right about causing problems."

I leaned over the desk to get Heather's attention. "Listen to me. We're doing the right thing. That's what's important."

Her laugh edged toward hysteria. "Yeah, that worked out so well for me last time."

"It did. Remember that part. Doing the right thing got you this job and Henry Wilson."

"You're right. Of course, you're right. And it wouldn't matter. We can't let this guy get away with murder." She stretched and groaned. "I think you promised me lunch. I'm ready for some stress eating, and it's going to be a busy afternoon."

She only knew the half of it. Maybe I'd wait until after lunch to tell her my suspicions about Norman Mendelson. If Heather tried to stress eat her way through everything, we'd have another dead body on our hands.

Chapter Twenty-One

WE WENT TO a nearby restaurant and got a table in a back corner, away from the loud group of young women by the windows. The scent of french fries wafted from the kitchen. My mouth watered.

After we ordered, I said, "Detective Padilla seems competent."

"Mm. But not what I expected. I've been a feminist for three decades now, and yet when I hear 'police detective' I picture a man."

"Tall, muscular, square-jawed, and ruggedly handsome?"

Heather chuckled. "Or, knowing my luck, potbellied, reeking of cigarette smoke, and with a seventies porn mustache. Either way, definitely a stereotype. Shows what I know. This whole experience is going to be one of those annoying personal growth things for me, isn't it?"

"You and me both."

"That's comforting, I guess, but you've seemed completely in charge."

I made a face. "You didn't see me with my sister this morning."

"Ah. Family is different."

The server dropped off our soup and sandwiches, and we

enjoyed our lunch while carefully avoiding any topic involving Sunshine Haven.

When we'd finished, Heather said, "I'm tempted by a piece of pie, but I think I'm too full to eat it."

"Get it to go. You might need more comfort food this afternoon."

She stared at me. "Because of what the police might find out? Or is there . . . don't tell me there's something else."

"I'm afraid you've still got a rat in your woodpile."

She groaned and gestured to the waiter. "One piece of chocolate cream pie to go, please." She looked back at me. "Just when I was feeling better."

"This one isn't as bad, at least, I don't think so. Let's get out of here before we discuss it."

Back in her office with the door closed, I explained my concerns about Norman Mendelson.

By the time I finished, Heather had her fingertips pressed into her temples.

"It's too much to take in." She frowned. "Do you think Steven Hicks and Norman Mendelson were working together?"

"I doubt it. Mendelson may be guilty of something else, though. He doesn't want me to talk to other patients or their families."

"He's pretty uptight, but that is extreme."

"I think he called me pretending to be Henry Wilson and he pushed the wheelchair into me. Hicks drives a big white truck, but the car that almost ran me down could be Mendelson's. He's hiding something."

"I don't understand all this," Heather said. "He's not my

favorite person, but I would've said he was a good employee. Shoot, his mother is an Alzheimer's patient. How could he feel anything but sympathy for the patients here?"

"I get the impression, from things I've heard, that Mendelson might resent you for not letting his mother in here."

Her eyes widened. "He's still upset about that? It wasn't my decision. I followed company policy."

"People can take disappointment personally. Maybe he feels he's devoted himself to this place and should get a discount for his mother's care."

"It wasn't only the money. Alzheimer's patients vary in how they behave and what they need. We pride ourselves in having a home-like environment, where the patients are allowed to leave their rooms at will. That means we can't take violent patients or those who harass people. Sometimes patients change after they get here, and we take steps to protect them and others. But we won't accept a patient who is already dangerous. Mrs. Mendelson got agitated and verbally abusive. She tried to slap people. We don't have the security to handle someone like that, and we could be liable if one patient bullies or injures another."

"I'm not blaming you, but that doesn't mean Mendelson isn't."

"Here I thought I was doing such a good job. You must think I'm an idiot."

I thought she was making it too much about her, rather than Sunshine Haven and the patients.

"You're doing a good enough job that you suspected something was wrong and followed through," I said.

She sighed. "I'll hold on to that. Do I have to tell the

police about Norman?"

"Not yet, but you should probe further. If Mendelson has been misusing his position to manipulate patients and extort money, you need to stop him, but how is up to you."

If she could handle it quietly, it would be better for Sunshine Haven's reputation and probably easier on the patients—and the police wouldn't think we were paranoid, pointing accusing fingers at everyone.

Heather slumped back in her chair with a moan. "I can put him on probation while I check into things. It would be nice if we could deal with this Hicks guy first . . . but there's no use in putting anything off. I'll talk to him right now." She looked at the piece of pie sitting on her desk in its clear plastic container. "That'll be my reward."

"I'd better go."

She straightened. "I wish you wouldn't."

"I must admit, I'd like to hear what he has to say, but I'm not sure it's appropriate for me to be here during a conversation between a boss and employee."

She stood and paced the small office. "You're right, of course. I have to do this on my own." She opened the door. "June, could you please ask Mr. Mendelson to come to my office?"

I said, "Don't name Zinnia. Or me, if you can avoid it."

"I'll tell him I have concerns and ask for his side of the story. Then I'll put him on leave until I can check into things."

I crossed the lobby, got another cup of coffee, and settled down in a corner. Mendelson might suspect I was responsible for his downfall, but I didn't have to rub his face in it.

He had enough of a grudge against me already.

Mendelson didn't glance in my direction when he went into the office, his movements stiff and jerky as if he already knew something was wrong. I did some of the stretches Berta had shown me, the ones that could be done in a chair without looking like I was having a fit and needed an ambulance.

Ten minutes later, Mendelson stumbled out of Heather's office and rushed for the front doors. In seconds, he was gone.

Heather stood in her doorway and stared after him. I grabbed my cane and limped toward her. June Songpole looked up from the reception desk, her eyes accusing.

Heather glanced down at June. "Mr. Mendelson is on leave until further notice. If he enters the building, report it to me. Don't give me that look. I did what I had to do."

"But his mother!"

Heather rubbed her forehead. "What about his mother?"

"She's really sick, not expected to live out the week. He said he might have to take some time off."

Heather sighed. "I'm sorry about his mother, but the timing can't be helped. At least he has his time off." She waved me into her office.

Once we were private, she said, "At first, he denied everything, claimed he didn't know what I was talking about. When I pushed him about patients getting the wrong doses of drugs, he insisted he only does what's best for people. They shouldn't ever be in pain, he said. Which may be true, but it's not his call."

"So he messed with drug doses?"

"He didn't admit anything, but he kept insisting he does what's best, he does what he has to do, he only wants to help people. The way he said it made me think that his view of what's best is not always what he is *supposed* to do, by law and by our policy." Heather shook her head. "I don't know. I told him to take the rest of the week off, paid leave. I'll get an inventory of the drugs and check with the nurses to see if anything's missing."

"Okay. Talk to the Gregorian family about Mrs. Gregorian's finances. See if there's anything suspicious there." I stifled a yawn. "I'm going home. It's been a long day. Call me if you need anything or learn anything."

I left her sitting at her desk, staring at the piece of pie.

I tracked down Dad in Mom's room. Jen had gone, fortunately. The TV was on, but Mom's eyelids kept drooping, while Dad gazed at her rather than the screen. He looked almost as tired as I felt.

"Ready to go home for a while?" I asked.

He sighed. "I guess we can't stay here forever." He rose and kissed Mom before following me out.

I felt like I was leaving part of myself in the room with Mom, but as Dad said, we couldn't mount a twenty-four-hour guard indefinitely. We'd gotten through the suspicious Sunday evening through Monday morning period, and the police would hopefully keep Hicks busy for a while. It was time to step back.

But it wasn't easy.

At home, Dad wanted to lie down. A tempting thought, and I eyed the stairs. Did my bed warrant the trip up and down? I compromised by stretching out on the couch.

Five minutes later, the doorbell rang. I groaned, pushed Harlequin off my legs, and dragged myself to my feet. As I passed the stairs I called up, "I've got it."

I peeked through the small window inset in the door before opening it to Detective Padilla.

"Come in." I waved her toward the living room.

We sat, and she studied me. Harlequin brushed against her legs and Padilla reached down to stroke the cat's back. If she was waiting for me to spill my secrets to fill the silence, I knew that trick.

Finally I asked, "Did you learn anything?"

"I heard about you when I was serving in Afghanistan. We never met, but you did some good stories. Respectful."

"Thanks, but that wasn't exactly what I meant. Did you learn anything about this case?"

Padilla stared at the ceiling for ten seconds. "You're a journalist. You're not employed by Sunshine Haven."

Did she come here to tell me things I already knew? "My mother lives there. I care about what happens."

"That's my point. You might be biased, but it's a different bias from people who work there. What do you really think?"

"I'm not sure I understand the question."

"I talked to this guy Hicks. He denied any involvement, which only means he's not stupid enough to confess. But he claims he suspected something wrong, and the employees are to blame. He said he asked a few questions, and the next thing he knew, his girlfriend's mother died and he didn't have any excuse to be there anymore."

Drat. I hadn't really expected him to crumble in the face

of the police and admit everything, but I also hadn't expected him to flip the story around. "Do you believe him?"

She leaned forward to scratch Harlequin under the chin. "I try to keep an open mind."

"By his own claim, he only visited once a week, for a few weeks. He doesn't strike me as the kind of man who is conscientious and sympathetic enough to notice any problems beyond his own. Why should he be the one person who suspected a problem?"

Harlequin decided he'd had enough attention. He swatted at Padilla's hand, and when she jerked away in time, he stalked off with his tail held high.

She sat back and brushed cat hair off her hands. "Yeah. When I tried to pin him down on who he thought might be involved, he couldn't name or even really describe any of the staff. Then he started throwing a few accusations your way."

I frowned. "He complained about me questioning him? Or he thought I was the one who sent you after him?"

"He suggested you might be trying to get a good story by *making* a good story."

My mouth dropped open. "He's blaming me for the patient deaths?"

"Pretty much."

"Good luck with that. I've been in town less than a week. I never went to Sunshine Haven until after Brit Egland's death, and I was in another country, in a rehabilitation facility where the staff saw me every day, for weeks before that. It's easy enough to check."

Padilla grinned. "Apparently, he didn't know that. I may have an open mind, but it's not open enough to trust him over you in these circumstances. I asked a car to keep an eye on him for a day or two. We can't allocate the resources beyond that, without more evidence."

"So that's it? It ends there?"

"Like I said, we need more evidence. I talked to the girl-friend, Lisa Delacruz. She said her mother has already been cremated, so that's a dead end. Sorry, no pun intended. Ms. Delacruz wouldn't say much, but she might have been nervous about talking to the police where she works. I'll stop by her house tonight. Maybe I can draw her out more."

"Her son, Ryan, might be more forthcoming. He's a quiet kid, but he did not like Steve Hicks."

My phone buzzed. Padilla said, "I'll take that as my cue to leave. Let me know if you find out anything else. I can let myself out."

I waved to Padilla as I grabbed my phone, which announced a call from Zinnia. "Kate here. What's up?"

"He was here! He shouldn't be here, right?"

"Who? What are you talking about? Where are you?"

She dragged in a breath. "I'm at Sunshine Haven. Ryan's stepfather or whatever—he was here! I saw him leaving, he was wearing overalls and carrying a toolbox, like he was on a job, but he's never done work here and he shouldn't be here now that Mrs. Egland died, so why was he here?"

My vision blurred and my limbs went cold and tingly, but I surged to my feet. Hicks was at Sunshine Haven. That couldn't be good. We had to stop him.

But he was leaving.

He'd finished whatever he'd come to do.

I stepped away from the couch, banged my shin on the

end table, and half fell, grabbing the table with one hand and the sofa with the other. My phone shot from my hand and across the floor.

I twisted to grab my cane and dragged it along as I crawled toward the phone. When I had it firmly in my hand, I pushed to my feet and ran for the door. Pain shot up my leg with each hard step, but it paled beside the anxiety that twisted my guts and sent my heart hammering.

Why would Hicks go to Sunshine Haven?

Did he think he could somehow cover his tracks? Did he want revenge?

What had he done?

Chapter Twenty-Two

I SHOVED OPEN the door and careened down the walk, wildly waving. A dark sedan pulled away from the curb. I stumbled into the gate and fumbled with the latch, calling out to Detective Padilla.

The car stopped, she leaned to peer back at me, and then she stretched across the front seat to push open the passenger door.

I threw myself into the seat and slammed the door behind me. "We need to get to Sunshine Haven. Now!"

Her eyebrows rose. Steering with one hand, she pushed the button to lower her window with the other, then reached down and grabbed a portable light. She slapped it onto the roof of the car and set it flashing.

My phone squawked. "Kate? Are you there?"

"I'm here."

"Should I follow him? He's in the grocery store parking lot, getting into his truck—"

"Zinnia, listen. Forget him. I need you to go back inside and find out where he was."

"Okay." After a moment, she said, "How do I do that?"

"Ask June if she saw him. The receptionist. Hurry."

"All right, hang on."

Padilla slowed at a red light. Two cars crossed in front of us, but the next driver saw the flashing light and stopped so we could dart through the intersection. We swung around the corner so hard I fell against the side door.

Padilla kept her eyes on the road. "Care to explain?"

"He's there. Hicks. He was. He just left." I sounded as rattled as Zinnia had at first. I sucked in a breath and slowed down. "Steven Hicks left Sunshine Haven a minute ago."

She frowned. "He went inside? My guy should have stopped him!"

"I guess that didn't happen."

Zinnia was back on the phone. I put it on speaker so Padilla could hear. "June didn't see him. He went out the emergency exit, so maybe he came in that way. It should have been locked so no one could come in from outside, but it should have set off an alarm when he left, and it didn't."

"You're sure it was him?" Padilla asked.

"I only got a glimpse, but I think so. No, I'm sure."

"You said he was wearing overalls and carrying a toolbox." Was it merely a disguise or had it hidden something?

"June said nobody was scheduled to do work today." Zinnia's voice rose. "What do I do now?"

I said, "Find out exactly where he went. Which room or rooms? The emergency exit, which one was it?"

"In the Alzheimer's unit."

"Start there. Ask the patients, or anyone else who's there, family members or staff, if they saw a man in overalls." Would patients with memory problems have already forgotten? Would they understand what they had seen? "Ask June to help you. No, have her call an ambulance first."

Maybe I was overreacting. Maybe it was all a mistake. But maybe we'd need that ambulance. I was sure now that Hicks was a killer. Had he killed again? Instead of stopping him, had we set off his murderous rage?

Who would he choose as a victim? Did he know my mother was there?

He had my card, with my name. Mom's name was on her door.

"We'll be there in a few minutes," I said.

"Okay." Zinnia ended the call.

We were halfway there. At the rate Padilla was driving, we'd arrive in another five minutes.

"Seat belt," Padilla said.

"What? Oh, right." My cane was tangled between my legs and digging into my foot. I sorted myself out and fastened the seat belt. While most of my focus was on the problem ahead of us, I had a nagging sense that I'd forgotten something behind me.

The phone rang again. I answered it and said hello before my mind registered that this time the screen had identified the caller as Dad.

"Kate, what's going on? I heard yelling. The front door was open."

That's what I had forgotten.

"Dad, sorry." What should I tell him? Sending him into a panic, having him race after us and maybe get into an accident, wouldn't help. I tried to keep my voice calm. "I wanted to catch the police detective before she left. Something came up, and we're heading back to Sunshine Haven.

Would you mind heading over there as soon as you can? I'll need a ride home."

After five seconds of considering silence, Dad said, "I'm on my way."

We were only a couple of blocks from Sunshine Haven. Bands of tension squeezed the air from my body, leaving me light-headed. How could I plan the next step when I couldn't even breathe?

We pulled into the parking lot. Ambulance sirens wailed in the distance.

Padilla swung up to the entrance. "I'll let you out at the door and call for backup."

I fumbled with my door handle. My hand felt clumsy, as if it wasn't properly attached to my body. Finally, I shoved open the door and launched myself out.

I lurched toward the automatic doors and squeezed through as soon as they opened far enough to admit me. My phone rang and I lifted it to my ear.

"Kate?" Zinnia's voice seemed to echo.

I glanced up as she burst into the lobby from the far end. Her voice carried across the lobby as it came through the phone. "Kate, he was in your mother's room!"

The phone fell from my numb hand. I clung to the cane as my legs turned to water. When my vision cleared enough to see Zinnia's pale, worried face, I dodged past her toward the hallway to the Alzheimer's unit. I wobbled rounding the corner and smacked my shoulder against the far wall before finding my balance enough to stumble down the hallway.

At Mom's room, I grabbed the doorframe and jerked to a stop.

Mom sat in her chair, her knitting lying in her lap. She glanced at me, as did the woman in scrubs kneeling beside her.

"Mom! Are you all right?"

She gave me a puzzled look. "Of course I am. I don't understand all the fuss."

The other woman stood and turned to me. "What's going on? June called for an ambulance but couldn't explain why, and then that girl raced out of here like her hair was on fire, but Mrs. Tessler seems fine."

"You're a nurse?"

She nodded. I stepped toward Mom and bent over a little. I wanted to get closer to eye level, but I if I crouched I might not be able to get back up again.

"Mom, a man was in this room a few minutes ago. What did he do?"

She frowned. "He was very pushy. He kept telling me to take some medicine."

The sirens were loud now.

I turned to the nurse and mouthed the word, "Poison." I whispered, "Should we make her throw up?"

"Not if the ambulance is here. Some substances do damage coming up as well as going down. They might want to pump her stomach instead."

I winced and turned back to my mother.

"Stop whispering," she said. "It's rude."

"Sorry, Mom. What happened with the man?"

"He kept saying my daughter wanted me to take the medicine. 'Tell them your daughter gave it to you,' he said. He didn't look like a nurse." She glanced at the other woman's scrubs, lavender with teddy bears on them. "It's hard to tell sometimes. No one wears uniforms anymore."

"In here." Zinnia's voice came from the hallway.

A moment later, two EMTs pushed into the room. "What's the problem?"

"My mother was—someone gave her something—the wrong medicine." I didn't want to worry Mom with the word *poison*, but I turned my back on her and whispered it.

One of the EMTs, a muscular young man, asked, "Do we know what she took?"

The other attendant, a woman, squeezed between us and knelt beside Mom, starting an examination.

"Mom, what did the stuff look like?"

"A funny green color. It was sweet, but I didn't like it." She giggled. "I held it in my mouth and when he went away I spit it out."

"Mom! I love you!"

"I love you too, sweetie."

"Did you swallow any of it?"

"Maybe." She made a face. "I can still taste it."

My mother had been poisoned. But she hadn't taken all of it. She might have gotten some, though. My emotions zigzagged.

The woman EMT handed Mom a glass half-full of water from the nightstand. "Rinse and spit it back out." She glanced at me. "She seems stable, but we'll take her in. It would help to know what the substance was."

"Mom, where did you spit it out?"

"The wastebasket."

I grabbed the trash and peered in. Green liquid soaked

some tissues at the bottom of the can, the smell cloyingly sweet. I twisted toward the man and lowered my voice. "The guy who gave it to her works in an auto shop, so it might be something to do with cars."

He looked into the trashcan and sniffed at it. "Antifreeze. We'll take this to be sure, but it sure looks and smells like that."

I could barely force my next words out. "Can you save her?"

He nodded. "Leave it to us."

The woman helped Mom to her feet. "Let's get you on the stretcher."

"Really now, I can walk. I'm old, but not that old."

"You wouldn't want me to get in trouble for not doing my job, would you?"

"Of course not, but I'm not an invalid."

I squeezed out the door behind them. "Mom, please do what they say. Trust me."

As the two ambulance attendants eased her onto the stretcher, Mom smiled at me. "I trust you, sweetie. But you don't need to fuss. That's my job."

I clung to the doorframe, willing the adrenaline-rush numbness to leave. Experience told me I'd be shaky for a while yet.

The staff nurse stood with her hand over her mouth. From behind it, she whispered, "I can't believe this happened."

Zinnia was pressed against the wall of the hallway, letting the EMTs pass. When she turned to me, her eyes were damp with tears. She handed me my phone.

I slipped it in my pocket. "Thanks. You did good." I glanced from her to the staff nurse. "You two make sure he didn't visit anyone else, all right? I doubt it, but let's be sure."

I headed after the EMTs. As I followed them out the main entrance, I came face-to-face with Dad. He went gray when he saw who was on the stretcher.

"Dad, it's all right. We got to her in time. She'll be fine." Maybe I shouldn't have made that promise, but I couldn't bear the look on his face.

He gripped my arm as he swayed. After a couple of gasping breaths, he said, "I'm going with her." He shoved the car keys into my hand.

I'd be more help staying at Sunshine Haven, but tears blurred my vision as the doors closed behind him. I leaned against the building while the flashing lights sped away and the sirens faded into the background noise. I tipped my head back to gaze at the clear blue sky. A perfect day. I shivered. The sun slowly warmed my chilled skin but couldn't reach my numb heart.

I was done. No more thinking I could do the job of the police. No more putting my family in danger for my own ego. Maybe I *had* lost my journalistic instincts. Maybe I wouldn't be able to get back to the work I loved. Better to accept that and move on than to kill my own mother trying to prove something.

Detective Padilla joined me, and Heather approached, looking pale and shocked. "What happened?"

I swallowed the lump in my throat. "He gave her antifreeze. My mother."

Padilla smiled. "I love stupid criminals. He might as well have checked himself into prison." At my look, she said, "I'm sorry, I know it was your mother. But you got her help quickly. They'll take care of her before the poison does much damage."

I would've preferred the word *any* to *much.* "Are you familiar with antifreeze poisoning?"

She nodded. "It's one of the most common poisons, since it's easy to buy antifreeze without arousing suspicion. Antifreeze is sweet, so it's not that noticeable in food. It takes time to work, but at first the victim may only seem drunk."

She waved toward the entrance and the three of us headed inside.

I tried to put my thoughts into logical order. I had to make sure Padilla knew everything, so the police could do their job, and I could get to the hospital with my parents. "I suppose if he gave antifreeze to Brit Egland, any drunken behavior might have been blamed on the Alzheimer's."

"Tests would show the presence of the ethylene glycol, but someone would have to think to test for it. Didn't you say one woman got sick but recovered after her dialysis? Dialysis is one of the treatments used in severe cases of ethylene glycol poisoning."

I collapsed into a chair in the lobby. "So maybe Hicks was testing his poison on other patients. He wanted to get the dose right, or make sure it worked or something."

"Horrible," Heather said.

"But reasonable from his point of view," Padilla said. "If anyone had been suspicious about the first illness or death, they wouldn't have suspected him, because he wouldn't benefit."

I rubbed my face and ran my hands through my hair. "It didn't work the first time, so he tried again, maybe giving the next victim more. Once he'd successfully killed Penelope Valentine without arousing suspicion . . ."

"He thought he was home free to kill his girlfriend's mother so she would inherit," Padilla said. "Then he'd either live off her money or find a way to steal it from her."

"Maybe marry her and then kill her too." I shivered to think of what might have happened to Lisa and Ryan.

"Why on earth did he think hurting your mother would help him?" Heather asked.

"He told Mom to tell everyone her daughter gave her the medicine." I turned to Padilla. "He suggested I'd been harming patients in order to get a good story. He must have thought that killing my mother would make me look guilty. If she mumbled something about me and the medicine before she died, I might have been blamed."

Padilla frowned. "It's twisted logic, but he's a twisted man. I suppose it goes back to the idea that if multiple people died, it's harder to find the motive."

I shook my head. "Did he really think anyone would fall for that? He should have kept quiet and hoped we couldn't get enough evidence for what he's already done."

"Fortunately, most criminals aren't that smart. They're convinced they're clever and the police are dumb, and they don't realize they're leaving a trail of evidence right to their door. Sometimes literally. Last week, a meth addict broke into a house, and we followed the trail of dropped stolen goods five blocks to his house."

I pressed a hand into my stomach, nausea churning. "So Hicks was foiled by his own arrogance?" What would have happened to Mom if Zinnia hadn't seen him and thought to call me? "Where was the cop who was supposed to be watching him?"

"Hicks ran a red light and caused a traffic accident. The police car following him stayed to help the victims. They called it in, but by that time, Hicks was out of sight."

"Was anyone hurt?"

"No fatalities," Padilla said. "But Hicks is keeping the ambulance drivers busy today."

I huddled in my chair, weak and trembling after the long minutes of panic. "At least we have more evidence against him now. Poor Zinnia, though. I hope she won't be in danger, since she's the only real witness besides my mother. Even if Mom remembered everything long enough for Hicks to go to trial, a good defense lawyer would be able to cast doubt on her testimony."

"No," Heather said.

When we both turned to stare at her, she gave a grim smile.

"There's a camera in the corner of the lobby, behind the front desk." She pointed to it. "It used to cover the lobby, but last week, when I started to get worried about what was happening in the Alzheimer's unit, I turned it to focus down that hallway. Everything that happened today is recorded."

Padilla laughed. "Perfect! Hicks might've known where the camera was originally. He thought he could avoid being seen by parking next door and breaking in through the emergency exit. They're dusting for prints now, but even if he wore gloves, we've got tons of evidence against him. Chances are the prosecutor will try for a plea bargain, attempted murder of your mother in exchange for not trying to prosecute the other deaths, which would be hard to prove."

I sighed. "He's going down."

Padilla nodded. "At least for a few years. But we have to catch him first."

Chapter Twenty-Three

I FOUND MY parents at the hospital. Mom dozed in a private room. Dad sat beside the bed, his hand on hers. When I paused in the doorway, my nose twitching at the smell of disinfectant, he rose and waved me toward the chair. I took his place as he rounded the bed to stand on Mom's other side, touching her shoulder. For a minute, we were silent. Voices murmured in the hallway and someone's shoes squeaked as they passed, but the machine by Mom's bed made only a faint hum, its lights steady.

"She's going to be fine," Dad said softly.

The nurse I'd asked for directions had told me the same. Though maybe "fine" was pushing it. At least she'd return to her new normal, needing nursing care as her mind faded. At the moment, that seemed better than the alternative we'd dodged.

I looked at Dad. "I'm sorry."

He shook his head. "Not your fault."

I opened my mouth to protest, but he put a finger to his lips and jerked his head toward the door. I followed him down the hall to an alcove with comfortable chairs. We slumped into the chairs with identical groans of exhaustion.

Dad said, "I got some of the story from the lady medic,

but why don't you tell me the whole thing?"

I started with Padilla's visit to the house. When I'd finished explaining everything, I said, "If I hadn't pushed
Hicks, let him know he was under suspicion—"

"You know better. Don't blame yourself for his actions."

I wanted to protest, but I bit back the words. It was a
lesson I'd had to learn as a reporter. In theory, you should
always speak the truth. But innocent people could be hurt by
the truth. In a war zone, reporting the military's action, or
not passing along an informant's lead, could mean death and
destruction. That made it hard to stay neutral. I'd learned to
do the best I could with the information I had, ask for a
second opinion when necessary, and stop beating myself up
over the results.

Practice hadn't made it easier, though. And my mother
had never been caught in the middle of a story before. Logic
worked better when you only had to apply it to strangers, or
to the military personnel and other reporters who accepted
the danger.

"If your mother had known the price, she still would
have paid it."

I tipped my head back to rest on the arch of the chair
back, but the glare of the overhead lights stung my eyes. I
blinked and rubbed them. "We got off easy. It could've been
a lot worse."

"Even so."

She'd suffer no long-term effects. Meanwhile, we had
enough evidence to put Hicks away, which might save future
lives, including those of Lisa and Ryan Delacruz. Mom
might not understand all the repercussions, but the woman

she'd once been would have been proud to play a part in all this.

"I would rather have paid the price myself," I said.

"You still could. Hicks might try to take revenge on you next."

"Maybe, but the police are hunting him now. If he thinks he got away with everything, he'll have no reason to hide."

How far away had he been when the ambulance pulled up with its sirens screaming? Close enough to realize his actions had been observed? If he suspected he'd been caught, surely he'd flee town, or at least lie low and try to bluff his way out of this, as he had previously. He hadn't tried to poison Mom simply for revenge. He'd wanted to throw blame on me. It would be stupid to risk getting caught in order to punish me.

On the other hand, Hicks hadn't proven himself to be one of the great minds of our times.

"I'll be careful. You too."

"I'll spend the night here." He peered down the hall toward Mom's room. "Your mother saw him, and I won't take the chance that he decides to get rid of a witness. That couch thing folds out into a bed, so I'll be comfortable enough. You go home. You look exhausted."

My heart wanted to stay with Mom, but my body complained that I'd never sleep without the good painkillers. My brain weighed in, noting that someone had to feed the cat. Anyway, if I stayed, Dad would insist I take the foldout bed, which would leave him sitting up all night. "All right."

I edged forward in the chair. The seat was too low, so I'd

need strength to push myself up. Did I have any strength left?

"I guess we should call Jen and tell her everything," I said.

"I did. She's on her way."

That got me out of my seat in a hurry. "Right. Call me if anything changes or if you need anything."

His eyes twinkled up at me. "We'll be fine. Get some rest."

"You too."

He stood and we embraced. I peeked in at Mom before fleeing the building. My sister would be furious that I'd put Mom in danger, that I hadn't told Jen everything sooner, that I'd failed in my duties as a daughter. I wasn't up for that argument, even if I deserved it.

By the time I got near the house, I was so shaky I probably shouldn't have been driving. I stopped at the end of the street and scanned the area. I didn't see a big white truck like the one Hicks had been driving, or anything else suspicious. I pulled up to the house and studied it. Everything looked normal. Well, not the cardboard taped over the front window, but its abnormality made sense.

I fished my phone out of my bag and held it in my hand, ready to make an emergency call. I got out and slowly approached the house, eyeing the bushes on either side of the front door. The evening sun cast long shadows and a breeze sent the leaves whispering.

I pushed aside my paranoia and unlocked the door. I glanced all around as I slipped inside. I tried to ease the door shut softly, but it was a little warped, so it wouldn't close all the way unless I slammed it. I threw my shoulder against it, wincing at the *bang*, and locked it behind me.

I flipped on the living room lights. The closed drapes looked ominous, since I knew they covered the gunshot holes in the window. Great, I had a locked door and holes in the house covered only by a thin sheet of cardboard. Not that the holes made the window that much less secure, since it wouldn't take much to smash the glass, but I *felt* more vulnerable with the reminder of last night's fright. Too bad I hadn't been telling Jen everything as it happened. She'd have that glass replaced already.

The list of "too bad I hadn't . . ." went on and on. I should have called the police sooner. Been quicker, stronger, more alert. Known what would happen.

Idiot. By this logic, I should go back in time and avoid getting hurt. While I was revising reality, I could stop Alzheimer's. Bring world peace. Get rid of jerks who cut in line or manspread on buses. Fix all the problems I'd spent my life reporting.

And then I'd revised myself right out of a job.

Despite my exhaustion, I walked through the first floor to check for intruders. What would I do if I found one? Who knows, but at least I wouldn't worry about monsters in the closets.

I paused at the base of the stairs. Once I got to the second floor, I wouldn't want to come down again. I hadn't heard a sound, and Hicks didn't strike me as the kind of guy who would patiently wait in an upstairs bedroom if he wanted to attack.

Something moved at the top of the stairs. I flinched,

jerking my hand upward. My phone flew into the air, bounced off my forehead, and hit the steps.

Harlequin bounded down with a meow of greeting. More evidence that no one else was here, I hoped. I took a few deep breaths to ease my nerves.

The phone rang and I almost jumped out of my skin.

"You want to get that?" I asked Harlequin.

He sat right next to the phone, stared at me, and licked a paw.

"Fine." I picked up the phone and answered. Mackenzie and Simon wanted to know what had been happening. I flopped on the couch and updated them as Harlequin purred next to me, and my heart rate slowly came down.

"What do we do next?" Mackenzie asked.

"Nothing. You are officially off duty."

She paused for a long time before finally saying okay. "If you ever need help again . . ."

"Thanks." I still owed her some mentoring. I'd find a nice, safe task for that. Later. At the moment, it took all my energy to say good night.

I stuck the phone in my pocket, fed Harlequin, and heated up some leftover lasagna for my dinner. Once my belly was full, I dragged myself up the stairs. My bed whispered seductively despite the early hour. After checking the upstairs for intruders and finding none, I took a hot shower and put on comfy shorts and a T-shirt. I sat in bed with pillows propped behind my back. I'd sleep better if I stretched and massaged my leg first, so that was what I'd do. In a minute. Or ten.

A sound came from downstairs. The front door opening?

I froze, straining to hear. The sound must have come from outside.

It was the cat. Or the water heater.

It was my imagination.

Bang! The front door closed, an unmistakable sound.

It had to be Dad. Hicks wouldn't slam the door.

But why would Dad have changed his mind about spending the night with Mom at the hospital?

I grabbed my phone from the bedside stand and eased off the bed. My mind whirled as my heart pounded. Investigate? Close and barricade my bedroom door until the person identified themselves? Call Padilla, or 911? I hovered in the doorway, peering down the hall toward the stairs. Hicks might search the downstairs first. Dad would call out to me, wouldn't he? Maybe not if he thought I might be sleeping. But he would have seen the upstairs light on.

So would Hicks.

The stairs creaked. With one hand, I dialed 9-1, while the other hand grabbed the door to slam it closed. I hesitated with my thumb over the last number. Part of me still couldn't believe Hicks would really come here.

My heart pounded. A shadow moved at the top of the stairs.

Jen rounded the corner. We stared at each other.

I was still tempted to slam the door, but 911 would not appreciate a call. I canceled it and staggered back to bed.

Jen stopped in the doorway. "Can I come in?"

I scooted over a bit and patted the edge of my bed. She perched on it looking . . . nervous? Sad?

"I've been to see Mom."

"I'm sorry I didn't tell you what was happening earlier."

"Why didn't you?"

I sighed. "I had reasons that seemed to make sense at the time."

"It's hard to believe all this."

I tensed, but she seemed to be making a statement, not accusing me of lying. "Did Dad tell you everything?"

One corner of her mouth twisted up. "Everything? Who knows? He told me a lot."

"Do you have questions?"

"Did someone actually shoot at you?"

"The official theory is that he shot high up to scare us."

She shuddered. "Still, I can't even imagine. It must have been terrifying."

I shrugged. "It's not the first time I've dealt with gunfire."

Jen's eyes were huge. "Don't you get nightmares?"

"Back at the beginning, sure. Not so much anymore. I've been doing this for a long time. I've developed coping mechanisms. To some extent, you get used to the adrenaline and even crave it. That's pretty common among war correspondents."

I grinned, trying to lighten the mood. "In fact, I should be thanking Hicks for easing my transition into civilian life. I don't know how I'd adapt if I didn't have that occasional jolt of fear."

Jen's jaw worked, but no words came out. She shook her head.

I finally asked, "Didn't you come here to yell at me?"

"Actually, I came here to thank you."

I gaped at her.

She laughed. "You should see your face."

I had to laugh too. It felt good.

When I could breathe again, I said, "I'm not fishing for compliments, but why do you want to thank me? I thought you'd be mad."

"I'm not happy. Still, you were protecting Mom. I shouldn't have been so hard on you."

Of course. Now that I felt terrible about everything I'd done, Jen was ready to forgive and move on. I couldn't think of anything to say.

Jen looked toward the bag she'd set on the floor. "I brought a bottle of wine. I thought maybe we could share it."

"I can't. I developed an allergy to beer and wine after getting sick in Tibet."

Her eyebrows went up. "Really?"

"It's whiskey or nothing." I snuggled back against my pillow. "You go ahead. I'm on painkillers anyway."

Jen opened the bottle and poured herself a glass. I inhaled the rich, fruity scent and pretended that was as satisfying as drinking a glass.

The silence turned a little awkward. Jen frowned over the collection on my bedside stand and picked up the prayer rope. It looked something like a rosary with its knotted loop ending in a cross.

"Why do you have this?"

"It was a gift."

She tipped her head slightly to one side.

"A woman in a refugee camp gave it to me after I interviewed her for a story. She wanted to thank me for the work I was doing, for letting the world know. They'd felt so ignored. Her family had owned a shop in Syria. Militants threatened to kill them if they didn't convert. Then the bombs hit. They fled. They were living in a tent with their four kids, barely enough to eat, their nice middle-class life literally up in smoke. She said I was one of the few people who seemed to care. To listen." I gazed at the prayer rope. "I didn't want to take it."

Jen's eyebrows went up. I decided she was interested, not critical or shocked.

"They had so little. If she carried this all that way, it had to be important to her. How could I take one of the few treasures she had left?"

"But you had to."

I nodded. "It would have been insulting to refuse. So I keep it to remember. I gave a camp coordinator extra food for the family. I didn't want to embarrass them by delivering it myself, but I watched to make sure it got to them."

Jen ran the prayer rope through her fingers, coiled it, and gently set it back on the leather bag. She studied the other items, touching a few delicately, before turning back to me. "You don't have anything from here. Didn't you want something to remember us by?"

"I had photos on my computer." But not back in the beginning, in the days before laptops. I'd walked away, run really, with hardly a thought of what lay behind. But I hadn't been fleeing home. I'd simply been looking for something else, something more. I looked around my old room, so familiar that I could take it for granted, and more comfortable than I'd wanted to admit. I considered the white jade phoenix pendant. Maybe home wasn't a prison built by my injury, a trap to escape as soon as possible. Maybe this was my phoenix's nest, where I could be reborn.

"You know what? I didn't have to bring anything with me. Because I knew it would still be right here." I met Jen's gaze. "You'd still be here. I could wander, because I could always go home again."

She smiled, the first full smile I'd seen since I got home. Her gaze dropped to my legs—the fresh scar, still puckered and purple, several older scars from more minor injuries, and a scattering of bruises from my various recent falls. Her eyes widened. "You look like you've been in a war."

"Well, I have."

Her face twisted as if trying to make sense of something she was seeing for the first time. "I guess so." She peered at the newest scar. "Does it hurt?"

Since she was being nice, I resisted the urge to say, "No, I limp and use the cane for fun." Instead, I said, "It's getting better. The muscles tend to knot up, but massage helps, and this cream relieves pain."

She picked up the tube of cream and studied it. "Right, Gary got some of this after he hurt his back." She gestured toward my leg. "May I?"

I'll give myself credit for not hesitating too long before I nodded. Jen's hands were gentle and competent, and after a minute, I leaned back with a moan.

Jen smiled. "I don't know how many times I've done this kind of thing after one of the kids had a sports injury."

"You have magic hands."

Her smile grew. She worked on me for ten or fifteen minutes. She avoided massaging the area right over the scar, but at the end, she laid her hand gently on it. The warmth seeped into the muscle.

She sat back with a sigh and met my gaze. "I was so jealous of you. You had this exciting life, independence, freedom, doing whatever you wanted. But it wasn't that simple, was it?"

"It has been exciting. But I guess *excitement* isn't always *pleasant*. Anyway, I always thought you had exactly what you wanted—husband, children, home, and community."

"I know, but . . ." Her face crumpled.

"Jen! Is it really so bad?"

"No, of course not, but . . ."

"What? Tell me."

"I got old!"

I smothered a laugh. "Yeah, me too. Turns out that's what happens if you don't die."

She managed a weak chuckle. "I got everything I wanted, but . . ." She shrugged. "Maybe things don't always live up to expectations? I don't mean that I regret anything. I love Gary and the kids. But sometimes . . ." Her eyes swam with tears and her shoulders heaved as she tried to hold back sobbing.

"Oh, Jen." I leaned forward to embrace her.

She let me hold her for half a minute before she pulled away and rose, keeping her back to me as she fished a tissue out of her bag and dabbed at her eyes. Like me, she saw her suffering as weakness, and she wasn't willing to let people see her weakness. But we'd finally connected, and I wasn't willing to let her pretend nothing was wrong.

"Jen, please tell me what's the matter."

She took another minute to compose herself before perching on the edge of the bed. "It's nothing, really. Only sometimes . . . sometimes I don't know how I got here. What to do with myself. The kids are growing up and don't need me much anymore. That's good. I know it is. In a few years, they'll be in college, starting their own lives. I want them to be independent, but—"

"You want to be needed too."

She nodded. "And Gary and I . . . the love is still there. It is. But it's different. We've been parents together for so long. I can't remember the last time we've been truly romantic."

I wasn't about to ask if she was referring to their sex life. "With the kids growing up, maybe you can find that romance again." I topped off her wine and handed it to her.

She wrapped both hands around the glass and stared into the ruby liquid. "I'm not the woman he married. I've changed so much. I'm not even sure who I am anymore."

I was out of my depth, and I wasn't much of a counselor, but as a reporter, I knew how to listen and ask relevant questions. "What do you mean?"

She brushed her hair back from her face. "My identity has been 'mother' for so long. What else is there?"

"You do a lot of other things. The PTA, um . . ."

"Everything is related to being a mother. School fundraisers, coaching sports, helping with band camp. Once the kids are done with all of that, what will I have?" She looked at me as if I might truly find the answer for her.

"I'm the last person who should be giving advice on marriage and family, but maybe it's time for you to find yourself again. Take some classes. Try some new hobbies. I don't know. Think about the things you used to do, or want to do, and see what appeals to you. Stop focusing on others so much and focus on you."

"What if I don't like what I find?" Her voice dropped. "What if Gary doesn't?"

"You will, because you're not just finding yourself, you're becoming the person you want to be. I think Gary will like you too, and love you. I think a lot of people will like you. Even if Gary doesn't, you'll move on, and that will be okay. You're strong enough to handle whatever happens."

She pressed her lips together. I don't think she was breathing. Finally, she nodded.

"Thanks," she whispered. "I'm glad to have my sister back."

"Me too." And I meant it.

Chapter Twenty-Four

S ENSIBLE WOMEN WOULD have gone to Jen's house for the night. On the off chance that Hicks was looking for me, he wouldn't know to look there. Neither of us suggested moving. Jen raided the ice cream stash in the freezer—my parents always had eight to ten pints on hand—and we binged while catching up. I told her about my encounter with Mayor Paradise. She said he'd married a classmate of ours but had divorced a couple of years ago. Not that I was interested, of course.

Dad came home in the morning, looking sleepy and rumpled. "They took your mother for some final tests. Assuming those go well, they'll release her to Sunshine Haven in an hour or two. I wanted to grab a shower first."

"I'll make breakfast," Jen said. "We can all go together to move Mom."

Dad looked from her to me, raised his eyebrows, and smiled before heading upstairs.

As we ate Jen's omelets, Dad asked about my plans for the day.

"I'm not sure. This investigation has taken so much of my time. I don't know what to do with myself now. Somewhere, I have a list of all the other stuff I need to take care of."

In a way, I would miss tackling the problems at Sunshine Haven. Not that I wanted the danger, but the challenge had given me purpose. Even though my leg was improving, I was still a long way from being able to head back to reporting on international conflicts. Maybe I'd never get there.

The thought wasn't as painful as it had been a few weeks before. Did I even want to return overseas? If I only saw my parents once or twice a year, how many visits would I get with Mom before she didn't recognize me, and I didn't understand her? How much longer did Dad have? Ten years? That wasn't a lot of visits, and even if he had no major health problems now, things could change suddenly. Then I had Jen again, and the niece and nephew and brother-in-law I hadn't even seen yet.

Maybe it was time to come home for good.

My mind flinched at that thought. What would I do with myself? Who would I be? I didn't have so many years left myself. I'd always assumed I had plenty of time to do more, be more. But my brush with death trumpeted the truth: one never knew how much time remained. What had my parents wanted to do but had never gotten around to? Had they assumed they had years left?

What did I want to do with the time allotted to me? Or the age-old question, what did I want to be when I grew up?

I put those thoughts away for later. I'd had enough soul-searching for one week.

We were leisurely getting ourselves ready to go when my phone rang. I didn't recognize the number but answered.

"Jenny?" a woman's voice asked.

"No, it's Kate. Mom?"

"Oh, hello, Kate. He said talk to my daughter. I got confused."

"Who said? Mom, what's going on?"

A man's voice came over the phone. "It's time you listen to me."

My vision blurred and my legs sagged. Hands grabbed me and lowered me to the couch. As my vision cleared, I saw Jen and my father staring down at me.

The voice came through the phone. "You ruin lives, and you have no idea what you're doing."

The voice wasn't Hicks.

I started breathing again. "Norman Mendelson?"

"That's right. You think you know me. You don't know anything."

"What are you doing with my mother?"

His laugh sounded hysterical. "Don't worry. We're still at the hospital. It's nice up here. We have a great view."

"Where are you exactly?" I had to force the words out. "What do you want?"

"I want you to listen. You never listen!"

"I'll listen. What do you want me to know?"

"Not like this. Come here, to the roof. Alone. No police, no one else, or I'll—I'll push your mother over the edge. The hospital won't be able to save her then."

I tried to keep my voice calm, gentle, when inside I was screaming.

"I'll do what you say. I'll be there in fifteen minutes." That sounded like forever, but it would take at least that long. "Please don't—"

"Alone. Hurry. We're waiting." He hung up.

Dad and Jen had slumped down on either side of me. I didn't know if they'd heard Mendelson's words, but my part of the conversation must have terrified them.

"I shouldn't have left her," Dad said. "Not even for a minute. But the nurse—they took her to another room—they said—"

"It's not your fault." I hoped he remembered everything else he had told me about blaming oneself. At the moment, I couldn't.

Jen jumped up. "The hospital was supposed to be watching her!"

"They were warned about Hicks, not Mendelson. They knew someone from Sunshine Haven was coming to get her. They wouldn't know he was on leave. He probably still has his ID." I wasn't sure I could stand, let alone walk, but I said, "Let's go. We have to get to the hospital."

Jen grabbed the cane I'd let fall and helped me rise. She led the way to the door. "I'll drive."

We didn't speak again until we were all in her car. I explained what Mendelson had said.

"Do we call the police?" Jen asked.

My head pounded. "He said not to."

"In those police shows, it's always bad when the families of kidnap victims don't call the police."

I had experience judging dangerous situations, dangerous people. But I wasn't always right. Poor judgment had gotten me injured. Poor judgment could kill my mother. I dragged in breaths. I had to calm down and think clearly. I had to make the right call.

A few hours earlier, I'd wanted to leave everything to the police. But could we afford to do that now?

"I don't think Mendelson is a killer. I don't think he wants to be. He said he wants me to listen. If we make him panic, he might go further than he intends."

"He sounds crazy," Dad said. "I can't bear the thought of you and your mother on the roof with him."

Mendelson wasn't a big guy, but Mom and I wouldn't win any fitness awards at the moment. I'd taken some self-defense training. Would the techniques work with my injured leg? I could still drop to the ground and kick at his knees with my good leg. That wouldn't help if he dragged Mom to the edge of the roof.

I couldn't let it turn physical. I'd listen, as he wanted. Maybe that would be enough for him. If not . . .

"I'll call Detective Padilla. I won't let her send in squad cars with screaming sirens. Give me a chance to talk to Mendelson first. A door must open onto the roof. You two and Padilla can be waiting on the other side of the door. If things start to go badly . . ."

"How will we know if it's going badly?" Jen asked.

"Before I go out, I'll call you and put my phone . . ." I needed to start wearing shirts with pockets. "In my bra. You should hear the conversation if I point the microphone outward."

Neither of them looked happy, but they nodded, so I called Padilla and filled her in. By the time I'd finished, and Padilla was done swearing at herself, the hospital staff, Mendelson, and me for not telling her about Mendelson earlier, we were at the hospital. I lowered my window and craned my neck. The building was at least six stories high, the roof too high to see clearly. All I did was make myself sick picturing my mother up there, too close to the edge.

Jen pulled up to the hospital's main entrance.

"We're going in," I told Padilla. "Join us when you can." I ended the call.

While I wrestled my body and my cane out of the car, Jen dashed to the valet parking kiosk and tossed the guy her keys. She spun back and reached the doors before I did. The valet chased after her and shoved a ticket in her hands.

Dad stayed by my side, one hand ready to support me if I faltered. Jen rushed to the information desk and rejoined us before we'd crossed the lobby.

"Those elevators." She pointed. "They go to the top floor. She didn't know about roof access, but hopefully, we can get up from there."

She darted ahead again to push the elevator button and hold the door open, her foot tapping as we tried to catch up.

When a man stepped in front of us, Jen snapped at him. "This elevator isn't stopping until we get to the top floor. Take another one."

He edged sideways with a wary look.

The elevator seemed to take forever. What if Mendelson got tired of waiting? What if he thought I wasn't coming, and decided to punish Mom?

Don't check the time.

It wouldn't do any good. I should have called him back, kept him on the phone, distracted him. But I'd been busy calling Padilla and making plans. Had I made the best decision? What should I have done differently, better?

Finally, the elevator doors opened. I stepped out and looked around. Where was the roof access? Once again, Jen bounded ahead, disappearing around a corner.

Seconds later, she waved us forward. "This way!"

My leg ached, but it was nothing compared to the pain squeezing my chest. My mind whirled with blame for all the mistakes I'd made, terror for Mom, fear that I wouldn't be able to save her. I tried to shove all those thoughts down deep. I didn't have time for them.

Focus on now. Do what needs to be done.

A sign said Roof Access next to stairs going up. I leaned against the wall, trying to steady my breathing, and pulled out my phone with a trembling hand. Jen grabbed her phone and nodded. I turned on a recording app, so we'd have evidence of anything Mendelson said, then put the call through to Jen. I tucked my phone in my bra, under my shirt, but with the microphone sticking out and pointing forward.

Jen backed away a few paces.

"Test it." She punched a button on her phone.

When I spoke, my voice came through on speaker.

Jen nodded. "Loud and clear."

Dad and I exchanged a last look of anxiety and hope.

"You can do this," he whispered.

He had to be right. I would accept no other option.

I pushed open the door and headed up the steps to save my mother.

Chapter Twenty-Five

HOW COULD A single flight of stairs take so long? With each step, each tap of my cane, my breath heaved and my heart pounded louder in my ears. Dad and Jen crept up the stairs behind me, their impatience pushing me. The stale smell of cigarettes grew stronger. Hospital employees must use the roof for smoke breaks, out of sight of the patients they chastised to quit.

The door had a piece of wood propping it open, more evidence of employee break use. I paused on the small landing.

You can do this. You've faced worse than Mendelson. Don't think of Mom.

I breathed deeply and pushed open the door.

Sunlight blinded me. I braced the half-open door with my shoulder and shaded my eyes with my hand.

Jen's voice came from behind me, and from my chest. "Do you see her?"

"Shh!" I'd forgotten to mute my phone. Too late now to go fumbling under my shirt.

I scanned the roof. A thigh-high wall went all the way around it. Thirty feet away from me, two people huddled together at the edge.

My heart stuttered. Mom and Mendelson. I wanted to race to them, but besides my inability to race anywhere, a sudden move might spur Mendelson into a nasty reaction. They sat on the wall, side by side, hunched forward a little. He had his arm around Mom.

Wait, *she* had her arm around *him*.

Both heads lifted to look at me, and then they turned back to each other.

I whispered, "They're here. She looks okay."

The door swung shut behind me as I slowly crossed the roof.

As I neared them, Mom smiled.

"Good morning, sweetie. It's nice to see you." Her gaze dropped to my cane and her eyes widened. "Have you hurt yourself?" She patted Mendelson on the back. "Pull a chair over for my daughter. Can't you see she's injured?"

Mendelson ducked his head as he rose and walked toward a cluster of chairs farther along the roof. He held nothing in his hands, and I hadn't noticed a bulge that could be a weapon hiding in his clothing.

I took the last two steps to Mom and reached for her hand. "Come on!"

She frowned. "We're not finished here."

I glanced at Mendelson, who had his back to us as he dragged over a chair.

I tried to pull Mom to her feet. "We need to get away from the edge!"

With my weak leg and one hand on my cane, I wobbled. My gaze slid past the low wall to the street below. Tiny cars darted around like toys on a model track. I jerked back, clutched my cane for balance, and gulped air.

"I didn't know you were afraid of heights." Mom looked troubled. "Did I? Did I know that?"

"I'm not." Not usually. Only when my mother's safety was involved.

"Please," I whispered, "we have to get you out of here, away from him."

"I'm surprised at you. Didn't you volunteer with the suicide hotline?"

"No." I almost snapped that I was concerned with murder, not suicide, but if Mom wasn't frightened, I didn't want to upset her.

"Oh, that must have been your sister. In any case, we don't leave someone in trouble."

Before I could think of an answer, Mendelson rejoined us, and Mom directed him to place the chair facing her. He did so and then sat beside her again. I watched with my mouth opening and closing but no words coming out. I'd played many variations of the scene in my mind, but not this one.

Mom shook her head. "You'd better sit, you look worn out."

I sank into the chair and stared at them. The November sun shone down on us, but a breeze blew mild air. My body couldn't decide if it was too hot or too cold.

"Are you all right?" I asked.

"Yes, of course. I don't understand all the fuss. Hospitals and tests and whatnot." She patted Mendelson's arm. "Norman is going to take me home, but he wanted to chat first. He's had a hard time of things lately."

I eyed him. "I heard your mother wasn't doing well."

His shoulders heaved and he blinked rapidly. "She passed away last night."

"I'm sorry to hear that." I'd feel even more compassion back inside, maybe with Mendelson in handcuffs or a straitjacket.

He sighed. "Everyone says they're sorry. They don't really mean it. I know Mother wasn't easy. Who knows it better? She could be difficult, but she could also be sweet. And I took care of her. But now . . ."

"You don't know what to do with yourself." In a way, I could relate. Darn it, I didn't want to understand him.

He nodded. "She needed me. I tried to do what was best for her. Now she's gone and I have nothing."

Mom patted his arm and looked at me. "He wanted you to understand. You should write a story about the difficulties of finding good nursing care. Someday, you may need to do that for your father and me."

"Maybe I will write about it." I glared at Mendelson. "But threatening my mother is no way to get my sympathy."

His eyes widened. "I would never hurt your mother. I would never hurt anyone, and certainly, not the patients in my care."

"You said you would."

"I didn't mean it!"

Well then, clearly it was on me for believing he might say what he meant.

I rubbed my forehead. "You wouldn't hurt them, but you'd steal from them?"

He avoided my gaze. "They had it so easy. Big families,

plenty of money, lots of people to help. I only wanted enough to take Mother out once in a while, to give her a few little luxuries."

"Not everyone at Sunshine Haven comes from a rich family. I met Brit Egland's daughter, Lisa Delacruz. She and her son don't have much."

"I only took from the ones who could afford it. A few hundred dollars, now and then, for my mother. It made me so angry, seeing how she suffered. And Sunshine Haven wouldn't help."

"That doesn't excuse your actions." He was no Robin Hood in my book.

"I know. I came up here, thinking I would tell you my story and then end it all." He twisted to peer down toward the ground and jerked back with a shudder. Mom took his hand and his shoulders relaxed. "But your mother helped me. She listened. I feel better."

"Everything will work out," Mom said. "You'll see."

I wasn't sure about that. "What about the drugs?"

Mendelson's brows drew together. "What drugs?"

"You gave patients the wrong doses."

"I don't have access to the prescription medicine." He shifted uncomfortably. "I may have given patients painkillers when they were in a lot of pain, or sleep aids when they couldn't sleep. But only over-the-counter stuff. I hate to see them in pain."

He might have been lying. We'd never prove it. Zinnia might have been mistaken, or the symptoms she'd seen could have been the combo of prescription medicine and over-the-counter drugs, or Hicks experimenting with poisons.

"You shouldn't give patients anything without the nurse's knowledge," I said. "There could be interactions."

"It's better than letting them suffer." He sighed. "It doesn't matter now. I won't work there anymore."

"Did you call me pretending to be Henry Wilson? And did you try to run me down in the street?"

He cringed and glanced at Mom.

"What's that?" she asked. "What are you talking about? Norman, what did you do?"

"I wasn't trying to hit her. I only wanted to scare her, get her to stop asking questions."

"Oh, you'll never do that." She gestured to my cane. "Is that how you got hurt?"

"No, that was—" It was too much to explain. "Never mind. Norman, did you pretend to be Wilson?"

He nodded. "I wanted you to stop."

"My actions at that point had nothing to do with you. What about the shots through my window?"

"I don't give shots. Wait, your window—you mean gunshots? No! I don't like guns."

I gave him my most intimidating scowl, but he didn't buckle. The gunshots must have been Hicks. "You been in a white truck lately?"

He shook his head, looking confused. At least we'd cleared up a lot of points: fake Henry Wilson and car that almost knocked me down, Mendelson. White truck and shots through the window, Hicks.

"Anything else we should know?"

He thought for a minute. "I guess not."

I gave Mendelson another stern look. "All right. I won't

promise you'll get off scot-free. But I know Sunshine Haven wants to avoid more controversy. If you let my mother go down safely now . . ." I wasn't sure what I had the right to offer, or what I was willing to offer.

Mendelson stood. "It's all right. I'm willing to pay for my crimes." He smiled at Mom. "Ursula, may I assist you back inside?"

"I'll do it." I tried to jump to my feet, but my feet tangled with my cane, and by the time I straightened myself out, Mom had taken Mendelson's arm. I edged close and watched carefully as he led her away from the wall. He was on her right side, which put me on her left. The doctors insisted that with a left leg injury, the cane went in the right hand. I made an exception so I had a free hand close to Mom in case he turned maniacal. So what if I lurched across the rooftop like an orangutan learning to walk?

We neared the door. I imagined Dad and Jen spilling out as the door opened. Things might still go badly if Mendelson got startled and upset—or if Mom did.

I raised my voice to make sure it would carry through the phone. "Once we get back downstairs, my father and sister will be waiting near the elevators."

"Oh, isn't that nice," Mom said. "I haven't seen them in ages."

I spoke over the scuffling sound that came from my shirt. "They'll take Mom back to Sunshine Haven, and you and I can figure out what to do next . . . Norman." Using his first name felt odd, but I wanted to maintain the friendly connection he felt with my mother.

I went down the stairs first, stretching my arms to hold

the railings on each side, even if that meant one hand had to awkwardly hold both the railing and my cane. Mendelson seemed calm and agreeable now, but what if he pushed Mom down the stairs? This way, I'd block her fall with my body.

We made it to the next level. Jen and Dad waited in the hallway a few paces down. I stepped aside to let Mom and Mendelson pass, so I could get behind them. We had them surrounded.

Mom brightened. "Isaac! Have you met my friend Norman?"

"We've met." He eased between Mom and Mendelson and ushered Mom toward the elevator.

Jen blocked Mendelson from following.

Detective Padilla stepped around the corner from the elevators. "I'll take over now."

I squeezed past as she addressed Mendelson. Mom and Dad embraced next to the elevators. If Mom didn't quite understand why Dad was so affectionate, she certainly didn't mind.

I told Jen, "Get them out of here and back to Sunshine Haven. Otherwise, we could be stuck here all day. I'll deal with things here."

She nodded, gave me a quick hug with hands that trembled, and nudged our parents into an elevator the moment it arrived. I slumped against the wall and waited while Padilla cuffed Mendelson and led him over to wait for another elevator.

I asked Padilla, "You get Hicks yet?"

She grimaced. "He's in the wind. Didn't go home, dumped his cell so we can't track it. Left his truck behind, but he might have borrowed something from the shop. His dad and brother aren't talking."

Damn. One criminal down but not the worst one. We got in the elevator. Mendelson stood with his head bowed, a plain, ordinary man, flawed and crushed by circumstances. With Mom safely away, I had room to pity him.

I'd have said anything to get them off the roof safely, including promising to do a story on whatever he wanted. Now that the daughter in me could breathe easily, the reporter came to life. His experience, and his reaction to it, was extreme. Yet taking care of aging relatives was a big challenge, and only likely to get worse as the population aged.

The average newspaper wouldn't give much coverage to tedious policy issues. Even in war zone coverage, my editors always wanted the "flash-bang" excitement, not the gritty details of how and why these problems seemed so hard to solve. But the story of Sunshine Haven had extortion, kidnapping, and murder by poison. Maybe I could find a home for a long magazine piece, with plenty of time to get into the issues, and enough action to keep the readers' interest.

Some stories were perennial, always green because the problem never went away. I had minimal savings and no children to take care of me, so in another twenty-five years or so, I'd be seeing this problem from the other end. It would be nice to imagine we'd have solutions by then, but I knew better than to think I might write the story that suddenly made politicians and bureaucrats take notice. Talking about problems wasn't enough. Still, it was a start. At least we could make sure people paid attention and *tried* to come up with answers.

I was already writing the story in my mind as I rode down the elevator with the detective and Norman Mendelson.

My phone slipped down in my bra, so I turned my back on Padilla and Mendelson, fished it out, and stopped the recording. I could offer it to Padilla. The courts would have to decide if it could be admitted as evidence, but it was legal by what I knew of state law. However, I doubted Mom would want us to pursue the kidnapping charge. I had mixed feelings. Mendelson needed counseling, and I wanted him punished, but prison? That wouldn't help him or us. He could still be a productive member of society, even without his job at Sunshine Haven.

Mom had charmed Mendelson, relieving some of his grief and anger, or he might have done something worse. Mendelson was the kind of person Mom could charm. Hicks wasn't. He was the real villain, and this would have gone much worse if he'd been involved.

Hicks was still out there. The police were looking, but they had too much to do. If Hicks kept a low profile, or if he'd already fled the state, they might not find him until he committed another crime, and only then if someone could catch him. That might take years. What damage could he do in the meantime?

His plan to kill my mother and implicate me had failed. He hadn't shown himself sensible enough to give up and get out while the getting was good. Would he come after us again? Would he target Lisa and Ryan?

It was time to stop waiting for him to act.

We needed to set a trap.

Chapter Twenty-Six

FIRST, WE NEEDED to finish with Mendelson. I called Heather, interrupting a meeting with the board. At least she wouldn't have to contact them yet again with more bad news. The company had a lawyer on retainer, and they sent him to handle Mendelson. Representing the guy who stole from their patients sounds funny, but Sunshine Haven was in damage-control mode. They'd try to get Mendelson through the system quietly, maybe have him plea-bargain instead of going to trial. The company would have to pay back the patients who had lost money, but that beat another scandal.

After checking with Dad and Jen, I did my own damage control, telling Padilla we'd overreacted. Mendelson had invited Mom to the roof, and she had gone willingly, so it could hardly be called kidnapping. Sure, when he'd asked me to join them, I'd interpreted his language as threatening. But we didn't lock up everyone who said, "I'm so angry I could kill so-and-so."

Padilla didn't buy it, but she agreed she had better things to do—like find Hicks. She took Mendelson to the police station, where he'd likely get booked on a lesser charge.

I mentally filed him under No Longer My Problem.

I didn't tell Padilla about trying to trap Hicks, since she'd simply tell me to leave it to the police. She'd be right, but I wanted him locked up ASAP, so I could stop worrying that he'd jump out of nowhere and attack me, or go after Mom again.

My plan didn't go beyond "trap Hicks," so I called a meeting for later in the day. I invited Joe and Marty Washington, Simon and Mackenzie, Jen, and my father. After some consideration, I also called Ryan Delacruz. He must feel angry and helpless after what Hicks had done to his mother and grandmother. Allowing him to help plan our revenge—even if we kept him out of the action—might offer some sense of control. I even arranged for Simon to pick up Ryan in the convertible, so the boy would get his ride.

Dad and Jen took Mom out for the day. They asked me to join them, but I didn't want to abandon Heather with this mess. I found her at Sunshine Haven, where Carla said she was "in a meeting" with Henry Wilson. The other board members had left.

When I entered the office, Henry rose and offered his hand. "Nice to see you again." He quirked a smile that almost convinced me he meant it.

"Someday, maybe we'll meet in better circumstances."

"I look forward to it."

The office had two guest chairs, but Henry rounded the desk and stood next to Heather, his hand on her shoulder. Heather tensed as if bracing for me to drop yet another bomb.

I got right to the point. "Do you have a plan for dealing with the media?"

"Other than ignoring them? Or saying no comment?"

"I wouldn't advise that. You might downplay what Mendelson did, but the police are looking for Hicks. Whether they charge him for the attempted murder of my mother, or the murder of Brit Egland, or both, it's going to make the news. It's too good a story to ignore."

Heather sighed. "I missed a call from a reporter this morning, while I was in our meeting. I suppose it's too much to hope they'll simply go away."

"Not going to happen. If you try to stonewall, they'll go around you and dig up as much dirt as they can. If you lie, they'll find out and it'll be worse in the long run. If you cooperate and give them a dramatic story, they may not dig much deeper. Better to be a valued source than an enemy withholding information."

Heather's eyebrows went up. "I suppose you'd know."

Henry nodded. "In my experience with the press, 'ignore it and it will go away' doesn't work."

"I don't know what to say to them," Heather wailed.

"Give me an hour and I can have an article ready to go." I rubbed my thigh to relieve the ache. "It would help if we could find a friendly editor or two. People who would be glad to get the inside story from a reporter who was on the scene."

"That sounds ideal," Henry said. "You're known as a hometown gal, even if you haven't worked here in years. They'd be glad to have your story. Would you really tell it to our benefit?"

"I can make Heather into the hero."

She snorted. Henry patted her shoulder.

"No, really," I said. "You suspected a problem and you did something about it. Nine out of ten people in your situation would ignore everything, hoping it would go away. I don't have to lie to make you look good."

Her mouth wasn't quite ready to smile, but it was getting closer. "If you can do that, I'll owe you . . . even more than I owe you already. More than I can ever repay, I'm sure."

I shrugged. "I'm a journalist. This is what I do. You help take care of people like my mother. Keep doing that."

"I wish I'd had you on my PR team," Henry said. "I've been interviewed a few times. I might be able to track down a reporter's name, but I don't know anyone in charge."

"Me either," Heather said.

I fished in my bag and pulled out a business card. "Mayor Todd Paradise. Or, as I once knew him, junior class president. He must know the press pretty well. Is he still honest and enthusiastic?"

"From everything I've heard, yes," Heather said. "But why would he help us?"

"Because this is his community and if it looks good, he looks good." Or maybe, if he was the man I remembered, simply because he was nice. It was worth a shot. I ignored the little voice calling this a good excuse to show him the real me, in charge and having broken a major story rather than limping and covered in gravel. "I'll ask if he can put me in touch with the right people in the media."

"Do you want to use my office?" Heather asked. "My computer? What can we do?"

I grinned. "Pick up lunch. Then Henry can help you rehearse your talking points in case you have to face the media directly, while I work on the article."

If everything went well, I could take care of this in an afternoon, and then be ready to tackle Hicks.

They left me alone in the office. I appreciated the solitude for a minute before calling Mayor Paradise. I got a receptionist, who put me through quickly.

"Kate! I'm so glad you called. I didn't really expect—that is—" He chuckled. "Sorry, you caught me off guard. I wanted to apologize for calling you Kitty the other day. I know you don't go by that name anymore. Old habits, you know."

"As long as you don't meow or call me Pussy, we're good." I winced. Maybe I shouldn't remind people of the embarrassing past.

"I never did that, did I?"

I thought back. "No, I don't believe you did. Anyway, the reason I'm calling is I need a favor."

"Okay. What's up?"

I briefly explained the situation. Todd gave me the names of editors at both the local paper and the TV news station.

"I can call them first if you'd like," he said, "but I think they'll be delighted to hear from you. They should recognize your name."

"Thanks. I owe you one." Or Heather did.

"Pay me back by having dinner with me some evening soon and telling me all about this."

Dinner with Todd Paradise. Every girl's dream, years ago. But we were in a different place now. Was this a schmoozing dinner? He was a politician. Did he want a friendly reporter in his pocket?

"I'm sorry," he said. "I didn't mean that as some kind of quid pro quo. No pressure, and I know you must be busy. Of course, I'll help regardless." He gave an awkward laugh. "I just wanted to catch up with someone I may or may not have had a crush on in high school."

My face heated. My whole body heated. Maybe I was starting hot flashes. "In that case, you're on. This weekend?"

We arranged dinner for Saturday and got off the phone. For a minute, I sat and thought about the possibilities. Look at me, going on a date with the high school hunk.

I chuckled. No, going on a date with a nearly fifty-year-old divorced man with kids. Either way, it would be fun to get to know Todd better. I'd leave it at that.

I turned my attention to more phone calls—first to my boss to let her know what I was doing and make sure she wouldn't consider it a conflict of interest. With her approval, and the promise of a smaller story for the wire service, I called the local editors to set up my delivery of "the inside story" of a local crime.

Several hours later, I checked the time. Right on schedule. My stories had been delivered, and Heather was at a salon getting her hair and makeup done in preparation for a TV interview that evening. I called Padilla to confirm that Hicks had not yet been caught, and then I headed home to plan a sting operation to get Steven Hicks off the streets for good.

I got back to the house with time to do my PT exercises. Dad and Jen returned. Joe and Marty arrived a few minutes later, and then Mackenzie. While we waited for Simon to pick up Ryan, we discussed the morning's adventures.

My phone rang. I glanced at the screen and answered. "Hey, Simon. What's up?"

"Ryan isn't here."

I checked the time. "He was supposed to be ready ten minutes ago."

"I know. His mom says he's not here and he's not coming. She sounded upset, maybe angry."

"About our meeting?"

"I don't think so. We talked for about thirty seconds and she checked her phone twice. Wait. She's leaving the house, carrying a canvas grocery bag. It looks full. She's getting in her car. Didn't even glance in my direction. She's in a big hurry."

"Follow her." My instincts said this was important.

"Okay." He hung up.

I explained our conversation to the others.

"You sound worried," Marty said. "A flaky teenager and a frantic mother don't seem that unusual."

"I am worried." The wheels in my mind spun, trying to figure out why. "Hicks is still out there. If he's on the run, he might need money or other help. From what I've seen of his father, Dad isn't going to be much help. But Hicks might turn to his ex-girlfriend."

"After what he did to her mother?" Marty asked. "She wouldn't help him."

I shrugged. "She might not know about that yet. It's hard to say what a frightened woman will do. She might assume the police won't hold him, and he'll take revenge if she turns him in. She might help Hicks leave town to get him out of her life. If Hicks wanted to make certain she'd help . . ."

Mackenzie's eyes widened. "He might take her son."

"Right. And Ryan is a teenager, but he doesn't strike me as that flaky. He was enthusiastic about this meeting—or at least about riding in the Camaro. I'd like to know where he is."

I called his number. It rang twice and went to voicemail.

"My kids have apps on their phones so I can check where they are," Jen said. "We'd need access, if he even has that."

Mackenzie grabbed her laptop. "We might not need the app if we have his phone number and e-mail." She frowned over her laptop, fingers flying as she mumbled, "It depends on the type of phone he has, and how it syncs . . ."

She said some other stuff I didn't understand, but I gathered one could track someone else's phone, if you had certain information and they hadn't turned on specific security locks.

Time seemed to drag, but it had to be less than ten minutes later when she sat up straighter.

"He's at the racetrack."

Dad looked as confused as I felt. "Horses?"

"No, cars."

"He loves cars," I said. "But why would he be there now? For that matter, how did he get there? His mother has their car. I don't think he has a lot of friends." I called Simon. "You still following Lisa?"

"Yeah, it hasn't been easy because she's speeding and pushing the yellow lights. I don't think she's noticed I'm behind her. She's in a bank now."

"A bank? Doing what?"

"I didn't go in, since she'd recognize me, but I checked her car. That bag she was carrying looks like groceries."

"What kind of groceries?"

"You know, a loaf of bread, a bag of chips. I couldn't see everything. She's coming out of the bank. She was inside less than five minutes."

"How does she look?"

"Um, she's hugging her purse to her chest. Now she's in her car. Keep following her?"

"Yes." She was carrying groceries away from her house, and she'd stopped at a bank, perhaps to get money. Food and money for someone on the run? This wasn't looking good. "Which direction are you headed?"

I put him on speakerphone and set the phone on the coffee table. He told us where they were.

Mackenzie brought up a map and checked Lisa Delacruz's path on it. "She's headed the right direction for the racetrack."

"I don't like this." My senses blared alerts like a warship hit by torpedoes. "I think Ryan's in trouble."

Chapter Twenty-Seven

"WHAT DO WE do?" Dad asked.

"We get over there."

Everyone rose and scrambled to gather their things.

"We can all fit in the van," Joe said.

"Don't lose Lisa. We'll meet you at the racetrack." I hung up on Simon. I was still working on gut instinct. When a story heated up, you rarely had time to make detailed plans.

We piled into the van, and Marty got the racetrack on their GPS while Joe headed out of our neighborhood. Mackenzie, seated next to me in the middle row, had her laptop propped on her lap.

Jen leaned forward from the back seat. "Can you get internet on that while we drive?"

"Just need to connect to a hotspot," Mackenzie murmured.

"I'll call Padilla," I said.

Her cell went straight to voicemail. How could I explain everything in a message? "We might know where Hicks is, or where he's going. Call me back."

Maybe she was already on his trail. But we couldn't count on that.

What other officers had I met in the last couple of days? Who would already know the situation? I came up with a couple of names, but I didn't have a direct line to them, and I didn't trust them the way I trusted Padilla.

At the moment, Hicks thought he had the upper hand. He expected Lisa to show up alone, fearful and harmless, ready to trade food and money for her son.

"We're better off letting Hicks make the exchange, Ryan for whatever Lisa has. If he *doesn't* release Ryan, then we move on to Plan B."

"What's Plan B?" Dad asked.

"I have no idea. I'm still figuring out Plan A."

"How likely is it that Hicks will release the boy?" Jen's voice sounded calm and steady, but her eyes looked larger than normal, her skin paler. She had children close to Ryan's age. "Why would Hicks let go of his leverage?"

"Good question." Unfortunately. "On the one hand, it doesn't make sense for Hicks to keep a hostage once he has what he wants. Ryan would be a liability. He could try to escape or attract attention."

"Assuming he's still alive," Joe murmured.

"Killing him would cause even more trouble." I hoped I was right. "Hicks wouldn't have any hold over Lisa, and he'd face another murder charge."

"But if Hicks releases Ryan right away, what's to stop Lisa and Ryan from calling the police?" Jen asked.

I groaned. "I don't know. Maybe he'll drive away before he lets Ryan go. He might say he'll release Ryan at the Mexican border or something."

Or he might drive some distance and kill Ryan. He

might take Lisa with him as well. She'd go to stay near Ryan. He might kill both of them to get rid of witnesses or to punish the people he blamed for his current situation.

Considering every "what if" led only to panic. I drew a deep, meditative breath and tried to release the anxiety the way I usually tried to release pain from my body. It worked about as well.

But people were counting on me for a plan.

"Our goal is to get Ryan away from Hicks at the racetrack. If Hicks doesn't have Ryan there, or if we can't separate them, then we follow Hicks and keep eyes on him at all times. Hicks will recognize Lisa's car and Simon's Camaro but not this van. If we follow without him noticing, we might still have a chance to quietly rescue Ryan, or get the police after them."

And we'd make sure Hicks never got to a place where he could kill the boy unobserved.

"That makes sense," Dad said. "We can have the police set up roadblocks."

I pictured our group as chess pieces, getting ready to cross the board. Too bad I didn't know where the opposing side's pieces were.

"Simon is following Lisa. Dad and Jen, you find them. Lisa has seen Simon, but neither Hicks nor Lisa has seen either of you. If Lisa meets Hicks and then they split up again, stick with him. If we have a chance to talk with Lisa and confirm what's happening, great. But we *can't* lose sight of Hicks."

Dad and Jen looked at each other and nodded. I leaned forward. "Joe and Marty, stay in the van. If Hicks leaves by car, go after him, even if the rest of us aren't back yet. If Hicks is alone, we'll call the police. If we think he still has Ryan . . . We'll see."

Marty twisted toward me. "You can count on us, honey."

I turned to Mackenzie. "You're still tracking Ryan's phone?"

"It hasn't moved from the racetrack parking lot."

"Then you and I go after him. He may or may not be with Hicks." Ryan had to be restrained, either physically or by threat. I didn't say that he might be injured or dead already. Or that his phone might not be with him. If Ryan was conscious and had his phone, he'd call for help. Maybe Hicks had kidnapped Ryan, dropped his phone at the racetrack to lay a false trail, and gone elsewhere. In that case, our only option was to stick with Lisa. But it was worth finding that phone and hoping Ryan was nearby.

"After Jen and my dad relieve Simon, my dad can join us."

Then Mackenzie would have a partner if I couldn't keep up. I massaged my thigh, trying to get the muscles loose and ready. Good thing I'd remembered to take the latest dose of ibuprofen, and adrenaline forced the pain into the background.

Had I covered all the bases? I tried to picture the scene we might find. "Is anything happening at the raceway right now? Will it be empty or busy?"

Either option could work for Hicks. An abandoned track offered privacy for an exchange, but a crowd made it easier to hide and harder for police to get aggressive. For us, the crowd would be better.

Mackenzie checked the track's calendar on her computer. "Moderately busy, I'd say. It's not a pro race or anything, but tonight anyone can bring a car, truck, or motorcycle and use the track."

Jen's eyes widened. "That sounds dangerous."

Mackenzie scrolled down her screen. "Only one person goes on the track at a time, so you compare your time to others instead of racing them directly. Free parking, gates are open now, racing starts in about half an hour. Um . . . judging by the reviews, it doesn't get too crowded and is good 'family fun,' but we certainly won't be alone."

"It'll be full of other innocent people, even children," Jen said.

"But on the bright side, we can blend in with the crowd," I said. "We have two goals tonight. Get Ryan away from Hicks safely, and keep bystanders and ourselves safe. Capturing Hicks is a distant third, and something we can leave to the police. If there's security at the track, we might clue them in. No need to go into the complicated details, just tell them a guy kidnapped his ex-girlfriend's son to threaten her. Seeing security around shouldn't worry Hicks the way a police uniform might. And their first goal should also be to keep the track patrons safe."

I closed my eyes and played the possible scenarios over in my mind, but we couldn't plan for every contingency. Too many detailed instructions might confuse the others. Better to trust them to use their own good sense.

We'd done all I could think of to prepare.

The drive seemed to take forever, and yet before I was ready Marty said, "We should reach the track in ten minutes."

"Everyone knows the plan?" I asked. "Everyone has a phone on and charged and ready?"

Mine was down to thirty percent power, but that would last several hours. If we weren't done long before that, we had other problems.

My phone rang.

"We're here," Simon said. "Lisa parked and got out. She's standing by her car, on her phone, looking around. I managed to park behind an SUV so she can't see me."

"Okay. We're not far behind you. Stick with her."

I explained the rest of our plan.

We pulled up to the racetrack and Joe slowed to study the signs.

I told Simon, "We're turning onto the dirt road that leads alongside the racetrack."

"Good. Lisa has joined the crowd. She might be heading toward the concession stand. Can't tell yet."

I looked out the window. "Concession stand, anyone see it?"

Jen pointed. "There."

Joe stopped the car as close as he could.

"Okay, Jen and Dad, you two find Simon. He should be nearby. Mackenzie, where's Ryan's phone?"

Dad and Jen scrambled out.

Mackenzie said, "The phone has started moving. It was in the parking lot, but now it's heading this way."

I blew out a breath. "If Ryan is walking around free, we're wrong about all this. It may be Hicks with Ryan's phone."

"So what do we do?" Joe asked.

The phone hadn't moved until Lisa arrived. Hicks would want to stay near Ryan until then, wouldn't he?

"Mackenzie, how close can you identify the spot in the parking lot where the phone was a minute ago? We should go there."

"I can't pick out a specific car, but it was in that back corner."

Joe pulled up to the right area.

I opened the door. "Mac and I will get out here. Joe, head back toward the entrance so we don't miss Hicks if he tries to leave."

As the van drove away, Mackenzie and I stood on the packed dirt, studying the three dozen cars in that section of the parking lot. Some of them might be employee vehicles. A couple had serious damage, maybe race day failures waiting to be towed away for scrap. I didn't see the truck Hicks had driven before, but he might have another vehicle from the garage.

My phone rang.

"Lisa met some guy behind the concession stand," Jen said. "I assume it's Hicks. She gave him the bag of groceries, but she won't let go of her purse. They're arguing. No sign of a teenage boy. Well, none having anything to do with these two."

"Good. I hope she can delay him a few minutes. You know what to do."

I hung up and studied the cars. "Ryan could be in one of these. Maybe unconscious or tied up. Maybe in the trunk."

"I can look in the seats and knock on the trunks," Mackenzie said, "but if he's unconscious how will we find him?"

"Start looking. If you don't find him, maybe by then I'll have an answer."

She darted to the closest car, thumped on the trunk, called out, "Ryan!" and ducked to look in the windows.

I hobbled to the next row of cars. By the time I got there, Mackenzie was on her third car. She had speed, but I had . . . absolutely nothing. No ideas, no answers. What if Ryan was unconscious in a trunk? What clue might tell us which car Hicks had driven? Other than him coming back and getting into it again, that is.

I rapped on the trunk and listened. No response. No one in the seats.

My phone rang again. "Hicks is heading toward the parking lot with Lisa," Jen said.

I turned to scan the direction of the track. No one coming yet. But time was running out.

"What was that?" Jen asked.

I must've whimpered. "Stick with him." If we had to confront Hicks, we'd need all the help we could get. Or would it be better to hide and watch what he did next?

I checked the next car.

Nothing.

And the next. Empty. Mackenzie had finished her row and skipped over mine to start on the next. *Knock knock knock*. Duck, peer. Next car.

I rapped on a side panel. She hammered on a trunk.

Someone else knocked?

"Be quiet a second."

We both froze, tense and listening.

I scanned the direction of the track. Still nothing.

Wait.

Two people emerged from the denser area of cars. They'd reach us in a minute, two at most.

Thunk thunk thunk.

The knocking came from closer to us, barely audible over all the background noise from the track. The muffled thuds didn't sound like our sharp rapping on metal. They sounded more like . . . someone kicking the car from *inside*.

I shuffled forward, turning my head to try to locate the source of the sound. A flutter of movement caught my eye. Something small, flickering at the back of a beat-up brown sedan. Sun glinting off the taillight?

No. A hand. Sticking through a hole where the taillight had been.

"I think we found him." I pointed and limped toward the sedan.

Mackenzie rushed ahead. Once she spotted what I'd seen, she crouched behind the trunk. The hand disappeared, and the thumping—probably Ryan kicking the trunk from inside—stopped.

"Ryan? Hang on. We're going to get you out," Mackenzie said through the hole. She stood and tried to open the trunk.

It didn't budge. *How* were we going to get him out? We had no tools.

"See if a door's unlocked," I said. "Pop the trunk from inside."

She checked all the doors. "Nope."

"Break a window."

Mackenzie dashed to the edge of the parking lot and grabbed a rock as big as two fists. She paused by the driver's door.

"Careful. Don't cut your hands."

She stepped back about three feet and threw the rock. It hit with a sharp *tink* and bounced back. Mac leaped out of the way and grabbed the rock from the ground before it stopped rolling. She hoisted the rock and stayed close for the next hit, though she turned her face away.

Tink. Tink. The window held.

Two people crossed the open dirt area. One large and broad through the chest, one shorter and plump. Had they noticed us yet?

My head went fuzzy and my vision blurred. *Breathe.*

I had to protect Mackenzie until she freed Ryan. I needed to hold off Hicks, with words, if possible, or physically, if necessary. I shifted into a "ready stance," feet apart, weight on the balls of my feet.

My left leg trembled, throwing more of my weight onto the cane. I wobbled.

Finally I found some kind of balance. How was I supposed to make use of the adrenaline, the fight or flight response, when I could neither fight nor flee?

Behind me, Mackenzie growled. Several thuds came in rapid succession. The sound of breaking glass did not follow.

At long last, a thud turned into a brief tinkle of falling glass.

Mackenzie dropped her rock. She braced one hand on the car roof and used her foot to push the remaining glass fragments into the car. Once, I could have managed that move, but not today. Good thing I had her along.

She swung open the door and ducked inside the car.

The people drew close enough to definitely identify Steve Hicks and Lisa. Had he spotted us yet? What would he do?

A clunk sounded behind me as the trunk popped open. I got one glimpse of Ryan, sitting up with a gag in his mouth, before Mackenzie blocked my view.

"Let me get this off you," she said.

"Hurry." I swung in the other direction.

Hicks raced toward me.

Chapter Twenty-Eight

L ISA SCREECHED AND started running. She must have spotted Ryan.

Hicks glanced at Lisa and back toward our group. His hostages were escaping, his leverage vanishing. He shifted direction so his path collided with Lisa's.

He swung her around. She yelled and kicked, but Hicks pushed her to her knees and fisted a hand in her hair.

He reached under his jacket and pulled out a gun.

Time seemed to slow as everyone froze. Even from thirty feet away, Hicks's glare promised violence.

"Nobody move! Lisa is going to drive me out of here. Ryan, you come too."

Ryan stepped forward as if jerked on a string, but Lisa wailed, "No, don't!"

Mackenzie hauled him back. "You won't help anything by giving him a second hostage."

We backed away as Hicks dragged Lisa to her feet and toward his sedan. He shoved her into the driver's seat. He waved his gun at us and we all ducked behind various vehicles. Despite what TV and movies show, the average car would *not* reliably stop most bullets. But maybe it would interfere with his aim, and at least it made us *feel* safer.

Unfortunately, if we were out of Hicks's sight, he was out of our sight. I risked a peek over the hood of the car as Hicks got in the back seat behind Lisa.

The sedan backed out and jerked away. Hicks yelled at Lisa, but she probably couldn't hear him over her own sobs. They wove through the parking lot.

"We have to do something." Ryan strained against Mackenzie's grip. "We need to follow them."

Mackenzie looked to me for direction.

I didn't know what to do. We'd rescued one hostage but lost another. Hicks knew we were after him. Had we made things worse?

The electric-blue Camaro swung up in front of us. "Need a lift?" Simon asked.

Mackenzie, Ryan, and I piled in.

Ryan pointed. "Follow them!"

I didn't have a better idea, so I didn't argue.

Ahead of us, Joe's van lurched forward in the middle of the dirt road, blocking the track's exit. The sedan swung away from the van in a wide arc, barely missing several cars, and bumped down a slope onto the track. Lisa's shrieks and Hicks's bellows carried to us a hundred feet away.

The van followed the sedan. We followed the van, even though Simon winced as the bottom of his car scraped dirt before the back wheels hit the slope.

Lisa led the way around the oval racetrack, fortunately only going about thirty-five miles per hour. A bright yellow VW Bug zipped around the track ahead of us. The driver veered off at the main entrance, leaving the track to us.

As we passed the starting line, a couple of officials ran

out and waved their arms wildly. We kept circling.

"What are they doing?" Mackenzie asked.

"Lisa is probably in too much of a panic to think straight." I could relate.

Ryan leaned forward as if he could make the Camaro go fast enough to rescue his mother.

"This is ridiculous," Simon muttered.

The engine roared as he shot forward, passing the van and the sedan so closely I thought we would scrape their sides. We rounded the narrow end of the track, where it curved more sharply, and the speed of the turn pushed our bodies to the right. I slid against the door and fumbled for a grip on the seat.

"Hold on!" Simon hit the brakes and swung the car across the track a hundred feet in front of the sedan.

Now, Lisa had a choice of stopping, hitting us, running into the fence in front of the viewing stands, or swinging into the dirt center of the track.

The sedan kept coming at us.

Not the choice I would make.

"Everybody out," I yelled.

They scrambled out and ran for the side of the track. I followed as quickly as I could. Simon shot an anguished look back at his pretty car and mumbled something that might have been a prayer.

Surely, Lisa would hit the brakes.

Ten feet from the Camaro, the sedan jerked to a stop with a squeal. Hicks yelled at Lisa and she screamed back. He jumped out of the back seat and reached for the driver's door, but she slammed the lock and covered her face with her hands.

Hicks swung around, waving his gun. His gaze landed on me. He lowered his head and barreled at me like a charging bull.

Twenty feet. I couldn't run. I'd never win a fight. Was I about to become his new hostage?

Ten feet. I braced all my weight on my good leg and leaned forward.

Five feet. I swung my cane up toward him.

The cane caught him right in the stomach. He hit it with such force that it ripped out of my grip.

I pivoted as he flew toward me. He stumbled past, barely brushing my flailing arms, and crashed to the ground. His gun slid across the pavement.

I was going down. I couldn't recover from that with only one good leg.

Arms caught my elbows, hoisting me back to my feet. The world spun for a moment and then settled as I glanced over my shoulder into Ryan's pale face.

We turned to Hicks. He groaned and pushed himself up on his arms. Mackenzie dove for the gun.

Ryan and I exchanged a look and worked as one. We took two steps to Hicks, Ryan's hand still supporting my elbow. I collapsed onto Hicks's back, straddling his hips. I grabbed an arm and twisted it up behind his back. Ryan piled onto Hicks's legs behind me. Hicks twisted and jerked, but he couldn't dislodge the two of us.

A swarm of people surrounded us. It took me a minute to sort out all the faces and voices. Mackenzie stood grinning a few feet away. Dad and Jen drew close, along with a man I didn't recognize. Burly and potbellied, with a thick, drooping mustache, he wore a black shirt with the word SECURITY across the front.

He spoke into a radio and then knelt beside me. "I can take it from here, ma'am."

I eased off Hicks to sit beside him as the security guard slid into my place. When we were sure Hicks couldn't escape the two-hundred-pound weight, Ryan got up and helped me rise. Simon handed me my cane and then moved to his car, patting the hood with a sigh of relief.

Lisa grabbed Ryan and held him tight, sobbing. He glanced at me over the top of her head and shrugged, but he patted her back and let her hang on. After a moment, he closed his eyes and his shoulders relaxed.

Another guard ran up and Mackenzie offered him the gun, butt first. He stepped away from our group and checked whether the gun was loaded. Police sirens wailed in the distance.

I leaned back against the sedan's hood as Hicks bellowed threats. At that moment, I didn't mind my uncomfortable seat and aching leg one bit.

My phone rang and Padilla's name lit up.

The second I answered, she asked, "You got a line on Hicks?"

I laughed. "You could say that."

WHAT DO YOU do when you've solved not one but two mysteries in your first week back at home? Have a party, of course.

By Saturday, my bruises were fading and two more PT visits had me walking less like Dr. Frankenstein's hunchbacked lab assistant. Berta had warned me to keep my expectations optimistic but realistic. I might never walk without a limp. I might have lingering pain forever, especially after intensive activity. But she believed I could improve to the point where the pain didn't interfere with most activities and I no longer needed the cane. For the time being, getting to that point was a satisfying goal.

I invited many of the people involved in our crazy week to the party. Dad and Jen set up tables in the backyard. Joe baked three different kinds of cupcakes. Marty brought an industrial-sized blender and made margaritas, virgin for the kids and decidedly not for those who wanted alcohol. Jen's husband ran the grill while their kids got to know Ryan and Zinnia. Joe and Marty challenged Simon and Mackenzie to a game of beanbag bocce ball, which seemed to involve as much laughing and kissing as throwing balls.

Dad brought a round of drinks to the table where I sat between Jen and Mayor Todd Paradise. Todd and I had postponed our date for the party. It was easier to get to know each other in the group setting anyway. Everyone told him the story of what had happened, so I didn't have to feel like I was bragging. We could connect on a more personal level later.

After delivering the margaritas, Dad rested his hand on my shoulder. We'd had a lot of long talks, and I felt closer to him than ever before. He headed back to join Mom on lounge chairs in the shade. From here, Mom looked the same as always. Maybe in a lot of important ways, she was the same. Lisa Delacruz had been talking to her for some time, and even with Mom's shaky memory, she had that way of listening and letting people know they'd been heard.

Jen lifted her margarita glass in a toast. "To my sister, the accidental detective!"

Sitting across from us, Henry Wilson and Heather joined the toast.

"I can't believe everything you've been through," Todd said.

Heather shook her head. "I can't believe I still have a job."

"Any update on Mendelson?" I asked.

"Not really. They're still working out the plea bargain. Good thing you gave the news a more dramatic case to talk about, one that can't be blamed quite so much on Sunshine Haven. We've had a few people put up a fuss after hearing about the murders, but with the killer in jail and a waiting list at most care facilities, no one has actually removed a patient."

"Excellent," I said. "I talked to Detective Padilla earlier today. She might swing by when she gets off duty. She says the DA is refusing any plea bargain from Hicks. They have him for murder and kidnapping, plus some other random charges like child endangerment for transporting Ryan in the trunk of the car. Hicks will be inside for a long time."

"Good riddance." Jen grinned at me. "You had quite a first week back. What are you going to do for an encore?"

I laughed. "I don't know. It's taken me the rest of this week to catch up on my sleep."

They chuckled and continued the conversation while I drifted into my own thoughts. I'd been assuming that if I wasn't a journalist, I wasn't anything. By sharing important news stories, I did something good for the world. I had value. But maybe my value didn't lie only in the stories I told.

Of course, I still believed in the power of the news, and I hoped to do some good by writing stories about the challenges of caring for the sick and elderly. Still, I had to admit, I really enjoyed the specific and immediate reward of solving an individual crime and seeing the criminal brought to justice. Sometimes journalism felt like pointing out a problem but not doing anything about it.

I wore the hamsa charm on a chain around my neck. It felt like the combination of hand and eye were a good metaphor for the way we'd had to both see a problem and take action to solve it. On the same chain, the jade phoenix pendant lay warm against my skin. I was being reborn after my brush with death. But maybe I didn't have to be reborn as the same person I'd been before. I'd advised Jen to figure out who she wanted to be now. Maybe I wasn't too old to learn new tricks either?

Todd leaned closer. "I'm glad you're back." His low voice sent an echoing rumble through my body.

"Me too."

"You may be exactly what I need right now."

I surreptitiously inhaled his scent, which reminded me of spiced rum and wood smoke. "Oh?"

He glanced around before whispering, "I have a little problem, and I need someone to look into it. Someone I can trust to be discreet."

"I see." Maybe he was joking or making an excuse to see me, but the tingle in my journalism senses—or maybe they were detective senses now—argued otherwise. Another case to investigate, and a chance to see Todd more? Count me in.

I nodded once. "Discreet investigations are my specialty, apparently."

"This could take some time." His gaze caressed me. "Think you might stay here a while?"

I tried to look thoughtful and serious, but my smile wanted to break through. "You know what? I think I might."

The End

Want more? Make sure to pre-order
Something Deadly on Desert Drive!

Join Tule Publishing's newsletter for more great reads and weekly deals!

If you enjoyed *Something Shady at Sunshine Haven,* you'll love the next book in….

The Accidental Detective series

Book 1: *Something Shady at Sunshine Haven*

Book 2: *Something Deadly on Desert Drive*
Coming in June 2022!

Available now at your favorite online retailer!

About the Author

Kris Bock writes novels of mystery, suspense, and romance. She has lived in ten states and one foreign country but is now firmly planted in the Southwest, where many of her books are set. Her romantic suspense novels include stories of treasure hunting, archaeology, and intrigue. Readers have called these novels "Smart romance with an Indiana Jones feel." Learn more at www.krisbock.com or visit her Amazon page.

Kris's Furrever Friends Sweet Romance series features the employees and customers at a cat café. Watch as they fall in love with each other and shelter cats. Get a free 10,000-word story set in the world of the Furrever Friends cat café when you sign up for the Kris Bock newsletter.

Kris writes for children under the names Chris Eboch and M. M. Eboch. She has published over 60 books for young people, including ghostwriting for some famous mystery series. Her novels for ages nine and up include *Bandits Peak*, a survival thriller; *The Eyes of Pharaoh*, a mystery that brings ancient Egypt to life; and *The Well of Sacrifice*, an action-packed drama set in ninth-century Mayan Guatemala, used in many schools.

Kris lives in New Mexico, where she enjoys hiking, watching the sunset from her patio, and hanging out with her husband and their ferrets.

Thank you for reading

Something Shady at Sunshine Haven

If you enjoyed this book, you can find more from all our great authors at TulePublishing.com, or from your favorite online retailer.

TULE
PUBLISHING

CPSIA information can be obtained
at www.ICGtesting.com
Printed in the USA
LVHW041629310322
714843LV00010B/915

9 781954 894495